Finding Becky

MARTHA ROGERS

ReALMs
A STRANG COMPANY

Most STRANG COMMUNICATIONS BOOK GROUP products are available at special quantity discounts for bulk purchase for sales promotions, premiums, fund-raising, and educational needs. For details, write Strang Communications Book Group, 600 Rinehart Road, Lake Mary, Florida 32746 or telephone (407) 333-0600.

FINDING BECKY by Martha Rogers
Published by Realms
A Strang Company
600 Rinehart Road
Lake Mary, Florida 32746
www.strangbookgroup.com

All Scripture quotations are from the King James Version of the Bible.

This is a work of fiction. The characters in this book are fictitious unless they are historical figures explicitly named. Otherwise, any resemblance to actual people, whether living or dead, is coincidental.

Cover design by Nathan Morgan
Design Director: Bill Johnson

Library of Congress Cataloging-in-Publication Data:

Rogers, Martha.

Finding Becky / Martha Rogers. -- 1st ed.
    p. cm.
ISBN 978-1-61638-024-3
1. Young women--Fiction. 2. Ranch life--Oklahoma--Fiction. I. Title.
PS3618.O4655F56 2010
813'.6--dc22

2010024996

First Edition

10 11 12 13 14 — 9 8 7 6 5 4 3 2 1
Printed in the United States of America

Acknowledgments

Thank you to the 19th Century Historical Loop for all their help in getting my facts straight in historical details.

A big thank-you goes to my editor, Lori Vanden Bosch, who made the manuscript come alive with her suggestions and help.

Thank you to my family for all their love and support.

Ask, and it shall be given you; seek, and ye shall find; knock, and it shall be opened unto you.

—MATTHEW 7:7

Chapter 1

Oklahoma Territory, June 9, 1905

*R*ebecca Haynes slammed her book shut. If those children didn't quiet down soon, she would scream. A mother ought to be able to control her own young ones, but the haggard, worn look of the woman across the aisle told Rebecca that the problem was more than unruly children. She was just the type of woman Rebecca hoped to liberate in her efforts with the women's suffrage movement.

The landscape outside the train window sped by, drawing Rebecca closer to home with each clack of the wheels. To this point the journey had been quite pleasant, but when the mother with her brood of three had joined the travelers, all peace disappeared. Not that she blamed the mother, but the commotion was bothersome.

Rebecca turned her attention to the youngsters. They had quieted down some, but the two older ones still roamed the aisles while the baby whimpered in her mother's arms. She loved children, but she preferred the well-mannered, quiet ones like the cousins she'd met during her stay in Boston.

A deep sigh escaped. How she would miss the friends she'd

made while in college at Wellesley. Her aunt Clara had made sure she would have the best education possible, and Rebecca had loved every minute of it, but it was now time to go home and see what a difference she could make in the world.

She mused at the similarity of her situation with that of Lucy Starnes, one of her cousins from Boston now living in Barton Creek. Just as Lucy had come to live in Oklahoma Territory to live with her aunt and uncle, Rebecca had traveled to Boston to live with an aunt and uncle there. The difference being that Lucy's parents had died, forcing her to move out West to live with family. Rebecca had gone back East to further her education and get to know her father's family.

Now she was headed home to Barton Creek, where she hoped to begin the steps toward a career in journalism. Mr. Lansdowne, her new boss, had balked at first at the idea of having a female reporter working for him, but then he'd relented and hired her. Her father was bound to have had some influence there, but that didn't matter. She had the job, and if she did it right, she'd be ready for a larger city paper when the opportunity arose.

A hand tugged at her skirt. A blond-haired little boy gripped the fabric with grubby fingers. She glanced over at the weariness in the face of the mother and realized the load carried by the young woman was taking its toll. Instead of scolding the child, Rebecca's heart softened, and she took matters into her own hands. She grasped the boy's hand in hers and removed it from her skirt, thankful for the gloves she wore. His bright blue eyes opened wide in surprise. "And what is your name, young master?"

At first he said nothing. He tilted his head as though deciding if it would be all right to answer. A grin revealed a space in his bottom row of teeth. "I'm Billy, and I'm six."

"Hello, Billy. That's a fine name."

A little girl wedged her way next to Rebecca. "My name is Sally, and I'm six years old too. What's your name?"

A smile filled Rebecca's heart, her previous vexation gone. The two were twins. No wonder the mother had her hands full. Her heart filled with sympathy. "My name is Rebecca."

The twins looked at each other, then back to Rebecca. As one voice they said, "We like that name. Can you tell us a story?"

"Children, please don't bother the young lady." The mother cast an apologetic frown toward Rebecca.

"That's all right. I'll tell them a story." Doing so would give their mother a much-needed break to take care of the baby.

The mother rewarded her with a relieved smile. Rebecca reached down and lifted Sally to her lap while Billy climbed up beside her. Since she planned to be a writer, Rebecca decided to make up her own story for the two. As she wove the tale of two children on a great adventure across the plains in a covered wagon, Sally's and Billy's heads began to nod.

The young woman across the aisle laid her now sleeping baby on the seat and came to Rebecca's side. "I'll take them now."

Though almost reluctant to let her go, Rebecca handed Sally to the mother, then picked up Billy. She followed the two back to their seats. The mother laid Sally on the seat facing her own, then picked up the baby. "You can put Billy by his sister."

"Do you mind if I sit here and hold him? You must have your hands full with the three of them."

A tentative smile formed. "That would be nice."

Rebecca settled herself and shifted Billy so that his weight was more evenly distributed. Just as she craved to speak with another woman, the young mother might enjoy the same. "My name is Rebecca Haynes, and I'm going to Barton Creek."

The weariness left the woman's eyes, replaced with a sparkle of excitement. "I'm Ruth Dorsett, and I'm headed for Barton Creek myself."

Rebecca searched her memory for a recollection of a Dorsett family in Barton Creek. Of course, in the four years she'd been gone, many new families had moved to the town. "I grew up there. Are you visiting, or do you live there now?"

A sadness veiled Ruth's face. "My husband passed on a few months ago, so we're going there to live with my parents."

A lump formed in Rebecca's throat. "I'm so sorry about your husband. Who are your parents? Perhaps I know them."

"Their name is Weems. Ma owns a dressmaking shop, and Pa works in the telegraph office."

"Oh, I do know them. I remember when Mrs. Weems opened her business. We were so glad to have someone who could keep us up-to-date on the latest fashions. She does wonderful work."

"Thank you. They heard about the opportunities in Oklahoma Territory and moved there when Pa learned they would open a new telegraph office in Barton Creek."

"Business is doing quite well for your mother. Will you be helping her?"

"Most definitely. Ma taught me to sew at an early age, and I've been doing it for my family. I was learning to be a nurse when I met my husband, a doctor, and quit to marry him. I helped with his practice until our babies came along, and then gave assistance whenever I could. Henry was killed in an accident with his buggy going out to deliver a baby on a stormy night. After he passed on, I didn't know where to turn. I didn't have the time or money to finish my nurse's training. The people in Glasson, Kansas, were so helpful, but they weren't family. After a few months, Ma insisted that I come live with her. She's delighted to have her grandchildren so close."

What a small world. Rebecca marveled at the coincidence. The people in Barton Creek were going to love Ruth and these adorable children who had captured Rebecca's own heart with their big blue eyes and captivating smiles. Now that Aunt Clara lived in town as Doc Carter's wife, she would certainly spoil them if Mrs. Weems didn't, and Ruth couldn't be much older than Lucy. They would be great friends, and Doc Carter could probably use her nursing skills.

The young woman's desire to work with her mother in business and her nurse's training impressed Rebecca. If more women would be willing to take charge and seek careers besides baking, cooking, and taking care of children and husbands, more would be willing to join the movement to secure voting privileges for women. Perhaps she could convince Ruth to join the fight. Women had as much right to have a say in who ran the government as any man.

"The twins told me they are six, but how old is the baby?"

Ruth eyed the sleeping child. "Emma is fifteen months old and just started walking without falling every few steps."

"They're all beautiful children." Talking with Ruth reminded her of the story she wanted to write for the editor of the *Barton Creek Chronicle*. If she were going to be a success at the newspaper, she must show her capabilities right away. "Ruth, if you will excuse me, I have some work I must do before our destination. We'll talk again later, and I'm happy to already find a new friend in Barton Creek."

"So am I. It'll be nice to have someone I can visit with and talk to on occasion."

Rebecca placed the still sleeping Billy beside Sally. "I look forward to it." Someday in the distant future she might have such a family, but at the moment her mission was to become the best reporter in Oklahoma Territory and then on to bigger and better opportunities in a larger city.

A grin spread across her face. No matter that she'd won the traditional Hoop Race at Wellesley. After her dunk in the fountain, she'd declared she would break the tradition and not be the first in the class to marry. Hoots and hollers from her fellow classmates told her they didn't believe that. Let them laugh. She'd prove there was more to life for a woman than being a wife and mother. Although nothing was wrong with that, she simply wanted to see what the world had to offer before settling down, if she ever did.

Geoff Kensington studied the attractive young woman in the seat across from him. She had amazed him several times during this trip. First she'd been reading a book by Sarah Orne Jewett, then she befriended the children who had made enough noise to be heard across the prairie, and then she sat and spoke with their mother. Remarkable! None of the young women he'd known in Chicago would have had anything to with the children, much less their mother. Now the young lady furrowed her brow and stared at a tablet while she tapped a pencil against her cheek.

The stylish cut of her light brown gored skirt and braid-trimmed jacket was of a fashion he'd seen worn by women in the upper classes in Chicago, and it fit her form quite nicely. Her straw hat trimmed in matching ribbon and braid sat at a rakish angle on her upswept hair. He stroked his chin, trying to decide on the color of her hair. Finally he decided that it reminded him of the fine cherry furniture in his mother's dining room.

In the conversation with the young mother, he had overheard her name, Rebecca Haynes. What a stroke of luck. She had to be kin to one of the men he hoped to meet on this trip. Ben Haynes, Sam Morris, and Jake Starnes were three of the most successful ranchers in the state, and he needed their support for the project he'd been assigned. Perhaps Miss Haynes was Ben's daughter.

Geoff pulled out his pocket watch and checked the time. He had two hours to charm the lovely Miss Haynes before their arrival in Barton Creek. If his good fortune held out, the children would sleep until then, and he could have an uninterrupted conversation with her.

He stood and bowed. "Pardon me, Miss Haynes. Allow me to introduce myself. I am Geoffrey Kensington, spelled with a *G*, and I overheard you tell Mrs. Dorsett that you are going to Barton Creek. That is my destination also."

Miss Haynes's cheeks blushed pink. "Yes, Barton Creek is my home." She smiled and indicated the seat next to her. "Please, Mr. Kensington, would you join me?"

"Thank you, I'd be honored. I do have many questions about the town."

She laughed. "Ask away, but I haven't been home for four years. I've been at college. Wellesley to be exact."

So, Miss Haynes was not only pretty but well educated too. What a stroke of good fortune to have chosen the same train for the final leg of his journey. "That is a fine school for young women. What are your plans now?"

Her smile only served to accent her beauty. "I'm going to be a reporter for the *Barton Creek Chronicle*. It's a weekly newspaper now, but Mr. Lansdowne hopes to publish it more often in the coming year."

"How interesting. I've heard that more women are going into the field of journalism these days. Are you a supporter of the suffrage movement?"

Her eyes, more green than brown, opened wide with excitement. "Oh, yes, I am. I've read everything I can about Susan Anthony, Elizabeth Cady Stanton, and Carrie Chapman Catt. Did you know

Mrs. Catt has been in Oklahoma, and that women here almost had voting rights granted to them in 1899? And she worked for a newspaper for awhile too. She's wonderful."

"Those are all fascinating women." The animation now in her expressive hands and eyes beguiled him and reminded him of his sister, who was near Rebecca's age. Even if he didn't support the movement, he could appreciate her enthusiasm. It might even be a help to him in the business he had in Barton Creek. "Are you related to Ben Haynes, the cattle rancher?"

"I am his daughter. His aunt Clara is the one who insisted that I go back East to go to college. Both of my parents are originally from Boston."

"I've never had the pleasure of visiting that city. I've spent most of my time in Chicago and St. Louis. But at the moment I'm more interested in Barton Creek." And the attractive young woman seated with him.

"Then I shall be happy to share my town with you."

Her voice had a musical quality that enchanted Geoff. This assignment would be the best one yet in his career. "I have business with your father regarding a cattle purchase. Perchance you will be able to introduce me to him when we arrive."

"Oh, yes, I'd be delighted to do just that. Father has some of the best cattle to be found in the Territory."

"Then I shall look forward to our meeting." He grinned and sat back to enjoy her description of the people in Barton Creek.

Rob Frankston paced the platform at the train station. He flipped open his watch and read the numbers. Two minutes since he last looked. The train was supposed to be on time, but he could neither see nor hear any indication of it coming on the tracks.

The Haynes clan and several friends milled about as a group near the depot, as anxious to see Becky as he was. Of course their reasons were far different from his. He'd waited four years for Becky to return to Barton Creek. He'd loved her since they were thirteen, but she never gave any indication of her feelings one way or the other in those last years of school. Her correspondence with him while he attended the University of Oklahoma indicated nothing more than friendship, and even those letters declined the past year.

When she had up and proclaimed her plans to go off to college in the East, he had to bite back his own disappointment. Aunt Clara spotted his hurt. She took him aside one day and, without naming Becky, told him that if he loved someone more than life itself and let her go her own way, true love would bring her back. He prayed that would be true with Becky's return to Barton Creek.

The newspaper had announced her arrival with bold headlines in the weekly edition. Rob read of her accomplishments and shook his head. Becky had certainly grown up and made her contribution to activities at the college. After reading the account, even his mother had been impressed, and that was no easy task.

He raked a hand through his dark hair and resumed his pacing.

Matt Haynes, Becky's brother, made his way toward Rob. The tall, lanky cowboy had captured his sister Caroline's heart, but he seemed in no hurry to court her.

Matt stretched out his hand in greeting. "I see you've decided to join us in welcoming Becky. She'll be glad to see you."

"I hope so, but she hasn't written to me much this past year, so perhaps she's forgotten her friends here."

Matt laughed and clapped him on the shoulder. "Don't worry. She was probably busy with all those things the paper said she did at Wellesley. You know our Becky. When she's involved in something, she gives it all she's got."

Yes, he did know, and that was one of the things Rob loved about her. Back in their school days here, she had always been a leader and one to speak her mind and do things her own way. She could ride and herd cattle as well as any man on the ranch, but then could appear as a beautiful young lady on Sundays at church.

"She is really someone special." He sighed. "I hope your father thinks I'm good enough for her."

With hands on his hips, Matt chuckled. "You won't have any problem there. You're gaining a fine reputation in the law firm."

Rob couldn't be so sure about that. What with all the run-ins his mother had with Becky's mother, the Haynes family might not be so interested in letting him become a member, good reputation or not. As the mayor's wife, his mother may think it her duty to set high social standards and be particular about the people with whom her children associated, but he didn't intend to let her run his life.

In the distance a train whistle sounded, and Matt nodded toward his family. "Come on over and join us. Be a part of our welcoming party."

Rob grinned. "Think I'd like that." He followed Matt back to the group. In the next half hour he'd know whether he still had a chance with Becky. If not, then he'd spend day and night winning her love no matter what anyone may say or do.

Chapter 2

*R*ebecca's heart pounded in her chest. In a few minutes she'd see her family again. She'd missed them all, especially her visits with her cousin Lucy and her baby. She hadn't seen them since last summer when she spent a month at home just after Amanda had been born. Mother and Father would welcome her with open arms, but they might not take too kindly to the plans she'd made for herself.

When the platform came into view and she saw her waiting relatives, she shook her head. Calling them Mother and Father as she had planned to do now sounded much too formal for the man and woman waving at her. They were still Ma and Pa—no getting around it. And that comforted her and assured her she was home at last. She raised the window and leaned out to return their waves and greetings.

The whistle shrieked once again in the warm summer air. The train jolted to a stop, and Rebecca jumped up and turned to the aisle. In doing so she ran into Mr. Kensington, her face hit his chest, and her hat threatened to fall from its now precarious perch.

He reached out to steady her. "I can see you are as excited about being home as your family is that you've come."

Her cheeks burned, and she caught her hat before it became even more dislodged. "I'm sorry. I should have looked before I leapt from my seat."

His dark blue eyes sparkled with amusement as his hand cradled her elbow. "Then let me be of assistance." He guided her into the aisle and then followed her to the exit.

Rebecca's cheeks still burned from the contact. The fabric of his coat had been smooth and silky, and the scent he wore reminded her of the spices her mother used in cooking. His hand had left a heated imprint on her arm, and it was a most pleasant heat. Though he wasn't that tall, she still had to tilt her head to look up at him.

When she stepped down to the platform, her father enveloped her in a hug. "Ah, it's good to have our Becky home."

Ma, Aunt Clara, Matt, and Lucy crowded around. Comments flowed like the creek when full after a rain. "You look wonderful." "I love your hat." "It's good to have you home." She drank in the love in the words and bottled them up in her mind to be tasted again later when her family might not have such good feelings toward her.

She cleared her throat. "It's wonderful to be home, and I'm so happy to see all of you. One thing, I'd prefer to be called Rebecca now instead of Becky. Rebecca Haynes is much more suitable for a reporter."

Matt laughed. "Oh, so now you're getting uppity on us. Does that mean you're not going to be riding out on the range with me and Pa?"

"Of course not. Riding is one thing I will always want to do. Besides, I'm not being uppity. The name simply sounds more professional." From the looks on their faces, that announcement created no problem. One hurdle over, but the next one might not be so easy.

A cough sounded behind her, and she stretched her hand toward Mr. Kensington. "Excuse me, I've been remiss." She pulled him forward. "I'd like for you to meet Geoff Kensington. We met on the train. He's come from Chicago to do business with us in Barton Creek."

Pa and Ma turned their attention to the young man, and Rebecca stepped back. She turned to see Mr. and Mrs. Weems with Ruth and the children. Both Billy and Sally waved at Rebecca from their grandparents' arms. She waved back and blew them a kiss.

Lucy leaned close, baby Amanda in her arms. "Who might those two little ones be? They seem to know you quite well."

"That's Ruth Dorsett, the Weemses' daughter. She's a widow and come to live with them. She's not much older than you are, and I hope you'll make friends with her." If anyone could make Ruth feel welcome in Barton Creek, it would be Lucy Starnes, the most generous and loving woman she knew except for perhaps her own mother.

"Becky." She turned to find Bobby Frankston smiling at her. Her heart did a little flip at the sight of his dimpled cheek and dark chocolate brown eyes. "Bobby, how nice of you to come to meet me."

He removed his hat and stepped forward. "I've missed you and didn't want to wait until later to see you again."

Geoff cleared his throat, and Rebecca's hand went to her mouth. "Oh, dear, I've forgotten my manners again. Bobby, this is Geoff Kensington from Chicago. We met on the train earlier today. He's going to be visiting in Barton Creek on business for a few weeks. Geoff, this is Bobby Frankston, an old friend."

Bobby's eyes narrowed as he stretched forth his hand in greeting. "I go by Rob now. Welcome to our town."

As the two shook hands, Rebecca sensed them sizing each other up. Heat rose in her face. She'd known Rob practically all her life and had only just met Geoff, but something passed between them that gave her a shiver of delight. The next few weeks may prove to be much more exciting than she first thought. Rob was comfortable to be around, but Geoff could prove to be the most interesting thing to happen to her since she left college.

Geoff eyed the man before him. He had an interest in Miss Haynes, no doubt about it. But then, competition always whetted Geoff's appetite. From the looks of his clothes, Rob Frankston was no rancher. Then he remembered Frankston was the name of the town's mayor. This was one friendship he needed to cultivate, but it wouldn't keep him from pursuing Miss Haynes. She stepped away for a moment to speak to a woman she addressed as Lucy.

Rob asked, "What business brings you to Barton Creek, Mr. Kensington?"

To tell the full truth immediately would undermine his main purpose and put Mr. Haynes on alert. "I'm here to check out cattle to purchase for Bryan Meat Packing in Chicago." He hoped the cover chosen by Barstow would suffice to keep the cattlemen interested until he found the facts he wanted.

"Then you've come to the right place. The Haynes, Starnes, and Morris ranches have some of the best beef cattle in the state. Jake Starnes also has some fine-looking horses if you're interested in that part of ranching."

Geoff grinned. "No, cattle are what my company needs at the moment."

Mr. Haynes stepped up. "Did I hear you say you're here looking to buy cattle?"

"Yes, sir, you did." Geoff had planned to wait a few days before approaching the ranchers, but when the opportunity presented itself, he wasn't one to let it pass.

"Now that's something I don't mind discussing. Come on out to our place with us. We're planning a big welcome home for Becky, and we'd be pleased to have you as our guest."

"I would like that, Mr. Haynes."

Miss Haynes returned to join them. "Pa, have Hank take my things to Mrs. Claymore's boarding house. I'll be staying in town."

Mr. Haynes's eyebrows shot up, and Mrs. Haynes hurried to join him. "What did I hear you say, Becky Haynes?"

"It's Rebecca now, Ma. Since I'm going to be working here in town, I wrote and asked Mrs. Claymore if she had room to board me. She said yes."

The raised eyebrows and closed-mouth expression on Mrs. Haynes's face clearly spoke her displeasure. It would be interesting to see how this situation played out. He had already detected a stubborn streak in Miss Haynes, and her back stiffened now.

"Rebecca Susan Haynes, you will do no such thing. Tell her, Ben. She has to come home with us."

Ben Haynes shook his head. "Now, Mellie, Rebecca is an adult and capable of making her own decisions. I don't like this one, but it does make more sense with her working for the newspaper."

Relief flooded Rebecca's face, and she kissed her father's cheek. "Thank you, Pa. I'll come out to the ranch until Sunday. Then I'll come back here and get ready to begin my new position on Monday."

Mr. Haynes either had the good sense to know when not to argue with his daughter, or he doted on her so much he was willing to let her do anything she wanted. Either way, it would work to Geoff's advantage as he pursued the true purpose of his trip.

Mrs. Haynes blew out her breath in a puff. "Come along, then. Everyone from all over the area will be coming later this evening for the party. We must get back and finish preparations."

Rebecca turned to Geoff. "Did I hear you say you will be joining us?"

"Yes, and I'm honored to be asked, but first I will check into the hotel. What time should I be there, Mrs. Haynes?" He wanted to change into more comfortable clothing also. His satchel carried most of what he needed, but he could purchase anything else at the Anderson Mercantile and Emporium he spotted across the street.

"Four thirty or five will be a good time. We'll look for you then." She grabbed Rebecca's arm and pulled her along. The rest of the family joined them and headed for the carriages across the street.

Rebecca held her hat with one hand and managed to call back, "I look forward to seeing you at the ranch, Mr. Kensington."

Geoff waved then picked up his satchel. "Rob, would you direct me to the hotel? I'll also need to procure a horse to ride later."

Rob pointed down the street. "Hotel's down the way a bit, and the stable on a little farther across from the bank. Can't miss it. You plan to rent a horse to ride out to the Haynes's spread?"

"Yes, I thought I'd do that, but I'll have to get directions first." That was one bit of information Mr. Haynes had forgotten to give him.

"Don't worry about that. My family will travel by surrey, but I prefer a horse myself, so you can ride out with me."

So, he wants to keep an eye on me. The thought amused Geoff, but he needed to get to know his competition a little better anyway. "That is most hospitable of you, Rob. What time shall I be ready?"

"I'll meet you at the stables at three forty-five. That way we can be saddled and ready to ride by four. It's about a forty-five minute ride out there."

"That sounds fine to me. Thank you." He tipped his hat and headed for the hotel.

Rob stared at Geoff's back as he sauntered down the street. The man seemed nice, but something about him didn't sit well with Rob. When Geoff had answered his question about the reason for being in Barton Creek, the man's eyes veiled over. In Rob's experience as a lawyer, that look usually meant what the person was about to say wasn't the complete truth.

Mr. Kensington may be from the big city of Chicago, but he would be surprised to find that Barton Creek was a town of people who knew what they were doing. If he had some scheme in mind to take something away from the good citizens in town, then most likely three of the most powerful men in the area would get wind of it and take care of Mr. Geoff Kensington.

The man's interest in Becky bothered him most. No matter what she said, he couldn't think of her as Rebecca. She'd always be Becky to him, and he didn't want Geoff to put ideas into her head that she was too good for this town anymore. Rob applauded her ambition to work for the newspaper. Goodness knew Mr. Lansdowne needed help with the way people were choosing Barton Creek as home. Other towns already had daily, or twice weekly with a Sunday edition, and Mr. Lansdowne wanted to keep pace with them.

Becky would make a good reporter simply because she never did anything halfway. She always strived to be the best at whatever she attempted. She'd even beaten him a few times in the horse races they'd staged before she left for college.

He'd taken the afternoon off for the festivities later, so he headed home. His sister, Caroline, greeted him, and her dimples flashed when she smiled. "How was Becky? I imagine the whole family was there."

"They were, and she's fine. Her name is Rebecca now, but I still think of her as Becky."

Caroline laughed. "I imagine she figures it's more grown-up sounding, just like you decided Rob was more fitting for a lawyer than Bobby."

That thought had not occurred to him, but he still wanted her to be Becky. He remembered the fun times they'd had at school, and it always seemed they were in competition with each other. Whether it was spelling or memorizing, one or the other of them usually won first place.

"I suppose you're right. I just hope Mother doesn't decide that Becky is beneath us in social status."

Caroline sighed. "I know what you mean. I do believe that is the reason Matthew Haynes hasn't asked Father for permission to court me." She bit her lip and lowered her gaze. "Did you talk with him at the station?"

"Yes, I did. Perhaps you'll have an opportunity to be with him this evening at Becky's homecoming party."

"Perhaps. I just wish Mother would recognize the fact that Ben Haynes, Jake Starnes, and Sam Morris are the most wealthy and influential ranchers in Oklahoma. She still thinks of them as cowboys."

Rob nodded and shrugged his shoulders. "If they're not involved in the oil business or in politics, Mother doesn't have time for them. I'm surprised she and Father are going to the party."

Amusement flashed in her blue eyes. "Humph, as mayor of Barton Creek, Father wouldn't dare miss such an occasion. Did you know Ben Haynes and Jake said they'd back Father if he decided to run for a state office?"

"Yes, he told me about it last week. Since we're getting closer to statehood, Father wants to be a part of it, and he needs all the help he can get. Their support ought to raise their standing in Mother's eyes."

At that moment his mother walked in. Her careful attention to grooming and styles caused her to appear younger than she actually was. She patted the sides of her hair, still a golden blonde. "Robert, I'm glad you're home. Your father tells me Becky Haynes brought a young man home with her. Were you there?"

"Yes, I was. Becky didn't bring him. They met on the train, and he's come on cattle business. I believe he represents some packing-house in Chicago."

A wide smile now graced his mother's face. "How nice. We must have him over for dinner some evening. I'm sure he'd appreciate a meal like he is accustomed to in Chicago."

"I'll let him know. We're riding out to the Haynes's ranch together later."

"Very good. Caroline, you will have to meet this Mr. Kensington. He sounds like the type of young man who would be a good catch." She spun around, her skirts swishing, and headed for another part of the house.

Caroline shook her head. "Mother will never stop trying to match me up with every eligible man who comes to Barton Creek, no matter how old or young he may be. I'm not likely to meet anyone who is interested in a twenty-five-year-old spinster."

"That's not true. You are a very attractive woman, and any man would be lucky to have you for a wife. Matt Haynes is blind not to see that."

She stood on tiptoe to kiss his cheek. "You're a sweet younger brother, and I wish you success with the youngest Haynes family member."

When she had left the room, Rob considered Becky. She had been fun to have for a friend when they were younger, and he'd assumed they would someday be wed. Now she had become a delightful, smart young woman, and he wasn't so sure she'd be content to stay in Barton Creek the rest of her life. One thing was for sure, he didn't plan to lose her to the charms of one Mr. Geoff Kensington.

Chapter 3

*A*lthough disappointed that Geoff had been invited to the party at the Haynes ranch, Rob decided to use the time to keep an eye on the man and perhaps learn more about him. However, on the ride out to the spread, he learned little more than he already knew about Geoff. He sat easy in his saddle as though accustomed to being on a horse, but he talked little about himself. Instead he had inquired about the land and the number of ranches and where they were located.

With so many people riding in the same direction, Rob found deeper conversation to be difficult if not impossible. Everyone in Barton Creek seemed to be headed for the Haynes place. He gave up on his attempts to ask questions. Perhaps Becky would know more about her guest and would give him information when he had time to be alone with her.

He shook himself. If he managed to get time alone with Becky, he didn't intend to spend it discussing Geoff Kensington. His interest lay more in what had happened in Becky's life the past year and why she'd been too busy to write to him.

As they arrived, Rob spotted many people he knew in the crowd. When he dismounted, Becky came out to meet them. "Rob, Geoff, I'm so glad you came together." She grasped Geoff's arm. "I was afraid you'd get lost. Thank you for riding with him, Rob. Could you take care of the horses?"

In the next moment she pulled Geoff with her toward the house.

After Rob tethered the horses at the corral, he strode that way, but he lost sight of the two. Anger and disappointment filled him and threatened to spoil his day until Matt approached.

"Well, Rob, it looks as though my sister has taken a shine to the man from the city. We'll have to see what we can find out about him. I don't want her being around any man we know nothing about."

Rob had to grin. He could trust his friend to be protective of his sister. "I hope to find some time when we can be alone this evening. I've already spoken to your father about calling on her."

A hearty laugh filled the air. "I'll say this: it's nice for you to want Pa's approval, but I do believe my sister will make up her own mind about who she will and will not have courting her. Those years away at school have changed her in more ways than one. If you do win her hand, yours will be full of her and her newfangled ideas."

Before Rob could ask Matt to explain his statement, his father called to him. "Sorry, Rob, we'll have to visit again later this evening. I have to help Pa with the meat."

Now left to his own devices, Rob surveyed the area in search of Becky and Geoff. People milled about and conversed in small groups in the grassy area in front of the house while others strolled out by the corral and stables. Finally he spotted Becky and Geoff coming from the house.

Becky laughed at something Geoff said and grasped his arm. Her hair shone in the afternoon sunlight, and the pale green of her skirt and blouse enhanced the green in her light brown eyes, but the amount of lace and embroidery on the blouse amazed him. Becky had always opted for the simplest clothing and preferred wearing trousers except to church or school. He headed toward them thinking about what other changes he would see in her.

"I know I said it at the station, but again, welcome home, Becky."

Her eyes narrowed, and Rob cringed. He should have called her Rebecca.

"Thank you, Bobby." A twinkle in her eye belied her anger.

He deserved that, but he would still think of her as Becky. A smirk crossed Geoff's face, and he covered Becky's hand with his. "Rebecca and I were headed for the stables. She wants me to see her horse, Daisy."

"I'll go along with you. I always enjoy seeing the Hayneses' stock. They have some fine quarter horses."

Although Geoff didn't appear too pleased, he said nothing, but he didn't release his grip on Becky. Rob stayed abreast of the couple as they strolled toward the corral. Becky entered the stables and quickly returned with Daisy.

She led the black mare to where Rob and Geoff waited. "Here she is. Isn't she a beauty?"

Geoff stepped over and ran his hand across the horse's mane. "Yes, she is pretty, but rather old, don't you think? I expected a much younger horse."

Becky's eyebrows shot up, and her shoulders stiffened. Rob swallowed a chuckle. No one criticized Daisy without riling her owner, and Geoff had done just that.

"I've had Daisy since I helped in her birthing when I was twelve years old. Pa gave her to me, and she's the fastest horse around these parts. Just ask Rob here. I've beat him more than a few times."

"That's true. Daisy is one fast lady." Of course he'd let Daisy win a few times just because he didn't want Becky angry with him. Still, Daisy had been a great racer in her younger days.

The horse pranced toward Geoff, who startled and jumped back. Daisy was one smart mare, and she must have sensed the man's criticism. Her head tossed back as she pulled at the reins in Becky's hands.

"Steady, Daisy. I know you're impatient for a ride." The horse nudged her shoulder. "I bet you're wondering when I'm going to saddle you and ride across the fields again." She caressed the horse's nose. "I promise to do that before I leave."

"Maybe we can have another race out in the west pasture. Perhaps Rusty will beat her this time." Rob would let her win again if it would buy him some favor from her.

This time she directed her frown toward him. "We'll see about that, Rob Frankston. Don't think Daisy isn't fast because she's older now or that I'm out of practice." She turned in a huff and strode back to the stables.

Geoff stroked his chin. "Hmm. Miss Becky doesn't appear too pleased with us."

Rob wanted to laugh, but if he did, she might mistake it for laughter toward her, and that would never do. He'd already riled her enough for one day, but then so had Mr. Kensington.

Becky returned and, without a word to either of them, headed for the house. Rob followed her with Geoff close behind. By the swish of her skirts he knew her displeasure was directed at both of them. He'd seen Becky in snits before, but they never lasted long with her. He hoped that hadn't changed.

She swiveled around with her hands on her hips. "If you two will excuse me, I see some friends I have yet to greet." She tilted her head and studied them both. "When you decide to have proper manners, I may talk to you again." With that she turned on her heel and headed toward a group of young women.

Geoff turned to him. "What did we do?"

Even though Rob knew perfectly well, he didn't care to share the reason with his rival. "That's just Becky for you. She likes to keep us guessing." Rob flicked the brim of his hat. "I'm heading over that way to see my friends. You're welcome to join me if you are so inclined."

Geoff shook his head and surveyed the area. "No, thank you. I'll look for Mr. Haynes and Mr. Morris. Might as well get to know the men with whom I desire to do business." With that, he sauntered away.

Rob jammed his hands into his pockets and rocked on his heels. So he wanted to discuss cattle business. That didn't bother him, but just let that city slicker try to make any moves on Becky, and he'd learn a thing or two. One thing was for sure—no man from Chicago would steal her away from him, her family, or Barton Creek.

Rebecca wanted to turn around and see what Geoff and Rob were doing at the moment, but pride kept her walking straight ahead. Those two. Who did Geoff think he was criticizing Daisy? And Rob thinking he'd beat Daisy with that old Rusty. She'd just have to show them a thing or two in the days ahead. Of course, with Daisy's age, she shouldn't be racing, but Rebecca would find a substitute, and then she'd show Rob who'd win a race.

Then she giggled. Having two young men seeking her attention was nice even if she didn't intend to show either one of them favor over the other, although Geoff might be the more interesting of the two since she knew little about him.

Lucy waved to her and beckoned her to come join them. Dove Anderson and Alice Morris stood with Lucy under a tree. Her cousin jiggled her little girl, Amanda, on her hip. "We wondered if you'd forget us with the attention of those two young men."

Heat rose in Rebecca's face. "We were just down to see Daisy." She held out her arms to Amanda, who hesitated then reached toward Rebecca. "My, I can't believe she's grown so much." The little girl's fingers clutched at the lace around Rebecca's neckline, then grabbed toward her hair. Rebecca grasped the tiny hands in hers and rubbed noses with the child, who giggled in delight.

Dove, holding her son Danny, said, "Children still love you, Beck—, I mean Rebecca. I thought for sure you'd go into teaching instead of journalism."

"I thought about it, but then the idea that I could write articles and make a difference in the world really appealed to me. I've always loved to write."

Alice laughed. "You'd never prove that by me. You hated those assignments in English."

"Oh, it was the ones I had to write exactly like the teacher wanted that I hated. The ones I created on my own I loved." She glanced from one young woman to the other. These were just the ones she wanted to reach with her articles about the new woman and her role in society.

"Lucy, don't you ever get tired of doing everything for your family?" She turned to Dove. "I imagine you're a big help to Luke with the store, just like his mother."

"Oh, no, since Mr. Anderson's heart attack, Luke has hired several new clerks. His mother spends her time taking care of Will and Mr. Anderson. I have my hands full with Danny and Eddie."

"Goodness, I didn't realize the store had grown that much. I'll have to do some shopping there while I'm in town."

Lucy relieved Rebecca of her daughter. "Alice has more freedom than any of us. Of course, she still considers herself a newlywed, even after three years."

Alice's cheeks turned pink. "We don't have a family yet, so I'm free to travel with Eli. We're heading up to Wyoming this summer to buy a string of horses. Eli knows horses, and I've come to love them, so it's a pleasure for me to go on these trips with him."

Rebecca clapped her hands. "That's wonderful, Alice. I'm sure you're a big help to Eli."

Perhaps she could start with Alice and Dove. Mrs. Anderson had worked in the store while Luke, Alice, and Will grew up.

One thing Rebecca did know for sure, she wouldn't be settling down to marriage and motherhood anytime in the near future. She loved her freedom too much, and she had too much work to do.

Aunt Clara tapped Mellie Haynes on the arm. "It appears that we have more than one young man interested in our Becky."

"Yes, so I've been observing. We've known Rob since we came here, and he's always liked Becky. He's even asked Ben if he could call on her now that she's home." And he'd broken her heart once, or rather his mother had seven years ago when she had such a negative reaction toward Jake Starnes.

Aunt Clara puffed out a breath. "Now that's an old-fashioned way to approach courting these days. If I know our Becky, it won't make any difference what Ben gives permission for. She's always done things her way and had a mind of her own. I remember how much she loved riding across the range chasing cattle with her pa and Matt."

"That's true, but I sense a difference in her. She has more confidence and is even more independent." Mellie squinted against the setting sun to observe Geoff Kensington as he and Rob talked. They knew nothing about Geoff except that he was in Barton Creek on cattle business. If that be true, then he wouldn't be here long enough to win Becky's affections. Then again, what did she know about young people today?

She spotted Becky talking with her cousin and her friends. Even from here her animation and vivacity stood out. So she wanted to be called Rebecca. They'd have to get accustomed to that, as well as a few other ideas she may have picked up in Boston. From what Mellie had seen thus far, her daughter didn't appear to be that excited about Rob's or Geoff's attention.

Aunt Clara tapped her chin. "Remember how she always got that moonstruck look on her face whenever Rob was around? I don't see that in her today. This may be a most interesting time for us all."

Her aunt was right about that. "I'm glad you're in town now. You can keep an eye on her for us." Since Clara had married Doc Carter, she lived in the big house that the doctor had built for her and turned his living space at his office into a nice clinic with several rooms for patients. Perhaps someday they'd have a small hospital like some of the other towns were establishing.

"I will," Aunt Clara promised. Her keen gaze went toward Caroline Frankston.

Mellie followed Aunt Clara's line of sight. Often so serious, Caroline was laughing up at Matt, obviously enjoying his attention.

Aunt Clara nudged Mellie. "And what about your son? Has he made any moves toward Caroline yet?"

Mellie shook her head. "No, and I can't imagine what's holding him back. Matt's certainly old enough to be wed."

"Maybe it's time we put a bug in his ear," Aunt Clara declared.

Mellie could tell Aunt Clara was about to go charging over to Matt, so she linked arms with the older woman to hold her back. "You leave them to figure it out for themselves," she chided.

"Perhaps you're right," Aunt Clara agreed. "But if he doesn't do something soon, he'll get a piece of my mind! Meanwhile, I aim to get some food before all the young men eat it up." She headed off for the food tables.

Mellie laughed as she watched Aunt Clara go. Turning, she gazed around the yard at all the lanterns now lighting the area as the sun fell in the west. This was beautiful country and had given Ben and her a good life. If only her two children could find the same happiness.

Mellie sighed. Her role as mother was limited now to prayer and advice when asked. Whatever happened to Matt and Rebecca in life and love was entirely in the Lord's hands.

Chapter 4

*R*ebecca eyed herself in her looking glass set above a small dressing table. She twisted her hair into one long strand then wound it into a knot atop her head. This would have to do for today. Despite the elaborate styles of the ladies in Boston, Rebecca preferred the simpler ones worn by her mother and friends. Besides, a liberated woman didn't live by the dictates of fashion.

She pinched her cheeks for more color, then dropped her hands to her lap. If she told her parents she didn't really want to go to church this morning, they would be quite unhappy and would ask all sorts of questions. Better to go and smile than to stay home and be flooded with reasons she should be in church.

Not that she didn't believe in God or the Bible; they just were not that important in her life. She had accomplished so much in the past four years, and God hadn't really played a part in it. Rebecca Susan Haynes could do quite well on her own, thank you very much. God was for those who needed somebody to call on when they couldn't take care of things themselves.

Ma's voice came through the door. "Come along, Rebecca. We're all ready and waiting."

"I'm coming, Ma." With one last pat to her hair, she grabbed up her handkerchief and small embroidered handbag. The stays in her bodice top bit into her flesh. She twisted around to get them into a more comfortable position. This was the last time she'd wear these things, but for today she wanted the women to see she kept up with the latest fashions.

Then she laughed. If that were really true, she would have spent the last hour shaping her hair around one of those frames to give it height and thickness. Such was the lot of a modern woman. She hurried out to join her family.

Throughout the church service Rebecca longed to glance at her watch. The time passed far too slowly for her taste. Fidgety children, yawning young people, and snoozing older men drew her attention from the sermon as she gazed around the room. Finally, to her joy, the sermon ended, and she could once again head outdoors.

When she climbed up into the surrey, her mother frowned. "You didn't seem too engaged in the service this morning."

Rebecca swallowed hard. Then she caught sight of Geoff Kensington and leaned forward. "Ma, there's Mr. Kensington. Please invite him to have Sunday dinner with us."

Ma waved at the young man. "Mr. Kensington, how nice to see you this beautiful day."

He nodded to them both and removed his hat. "Mrs. Haynes, Miss Haynes, it's a pleasure to meet up with you."

Ma beamed and glanced back at Rebecca. "My daughter and I were just discussing dinner. If you don't have other plans, please join us. Our niece Lucy and her husband, Jake Starnes, will be there, as well as our aunt Clara and Doc Carter."

Geoff hesitated only a moment before bowing slightly in acknowledgment of the invitation. "That is most kind of you, Mrs. Haynes. I'd be delighted to partake of dinner with you and your fine family. I'll get a horse from the stables and be right out."

Ma flicked her hand. "Oh, no need for that. We will be bringing Rebecca back to town later this evening, so you can ride with us now and when we return."

Rebecca's heart skipped a little beat. How nice to have Geoff as company on the way home. She'd forgiven him for his remark about Daisy, but since she hadn't indicated that yet, a little cold shoulder would make her forgiveness more desirable.

Rob's soul filled with jealousy when the Haynes's carriage pulled out of the churchyard with Geoff Kensington seated beside Becky. He quickly squelched it. Any display of jealousy would not impress Becky at all and might even serve to drive her away.

He should have approached her much sooner about staying in town and dining with him, but then she could have refused, saying that she wanted to be with her family her first Sunday back in town. He kicked the dirt and turned toward his home. When his father waved him over to the family carriage, Rob shook his head.

The walk home would serve as good time to tame his emotions before facing his parents and Caroline at the dinner table. Seemed like neither he nor his sister made any headway with the Haynes siblings. Caroline may give up, but he had no such intentions. Geoff couldn't be trusted.

Slumped in the wagon seat, Rebecca sighed. Ma kept Geoff so busy talking about Chicago and St. Louis that Rebecca had no chance to show any indifference at all. When the ranch came into view, she straightened up in relief. Maybe now she could have a few minutes with him. That didn't happen either. Matt and Jake both claimed his attention as soon as his feet hit the ground.

Ma grasped Rebecca's arm. "Come along, dear. Let's leave the menfolk to their talk about cattle and horses. We have a dinner to put on the table."

Aunt Clara hurried over after Doc helped her from their carriage. "I see you've invited the young man from Chicago for dinner. How nice." She followed Ma and Rebecca inside, where Lucy held a sleepy Amanda.

"Aunt Mellie, I'm going to put the baby down for her nap, and then I'll be in to help you."

"No need to hurry, dear. I have Aunt Clara and Rebecca to do that."

Rebecca blew her breath out in a puff. Cooking ranked at the bottom of the things she wanted to do this afternoon. She'd much rather be outdoors with Pa, Jake, and Matt talking about horses and cattle. She knew as much about good stock and buying it as any of the men, but Pa had let her know that was not her concern.

When Lucy joined the women in the kitchen, Rebecca slipped out and hurried to her room. She inspected her appearance and wished for some rouge for her cheeks. Ladies in Boston wore more color on their faces than anyone in Barton Creek, except for maybe Charlotte Frankston, who always kept up with the latest styles and fashions.

Rebecca snickered at the memory of Mrs. Frankston's fancy updo today. How she managed the lift she had to her hair in front and all the curls in the back was beyond Rebecca's comprehension. The woman probably had a few of those extra pieces of hair she used to supplement her own. Rob's mother also managed to keep Mrs. Weems busy with all her requests for the latest fashions. But that was a good thing now that Ruth had come to live with her mother and help with the sewing.

By the time Rebecca returned to the dining room, the table was set, and Ma went out to call the men. Soon they were all gathered around the table. Pa spoke the blessing, and Rebecca bowed her head, but instead of closing her eyes, she lifted her eyebrows and gazed across the table to where Geoff sat.

When their gazes met, he gave her a wink that let her know he'd seen her. Heat flooded her cheeks, and she squeezed her eyes shut. He'd caught her looking at him, and his wink indicated he thought her to be flirting with him. She'd have to set that straight.

As soon as Pa said amen, conversation and food both flowed around the table. Geoff held up a forkful of meat. "I must say this is the most tender cut of beef I've had outside Chicago."

Pa sliced off a chunk. "We go to great lengths to make sure of that." He looked straight at Geoff. "I think we can meet the needs of your packing company without any problem."

At the mention of business, Rebecca tuned out the conversation and observed Geoff. His clean-cut face had the appearance of one who didn't spend his days in the sun. In fact, he looked rather pale compared to the tanned faces of Matt and Jake.

Her cousin Lucy nudged her arm. "We haven't had a chance for a good talk since you got home. Maybe we can sneak away for a time this afternoon."

"I'd like that. I have so much to tell you about Boston and all that I did there."

Lucy smiled and nodded. With so many people about, Rebecca didn't see how they'd have a moment much less time for a good talk.

After dinner, Pa led the men into the large parlor. Lucy said a few words to Ma then turned to Rebecca. "Aunt Mellie and Aunt Clara are going to look after the children. With the men discussing business and probably politics, you and I can have our little visit."

Trust Lucy to make time for her cousin. Although Rebecca had known her mother hoped Lucy would tame her, the opposite had happened. Lucy turned from the socialite she'd been to a true rancher's wife when she married Jake.

The two of them strolled out to the porch and sat in the new wicker chairs there. Rebecca flopped down in one, and Lucy laughed.

"You remind me of the Becky I met the first day I came here. You plopped down on your bed like you did just now. I wondered then if Aunt Mellie thought I'd be able to turn you into a young lady." She sat beside Rebecca. "But I see you've done that all by yourself."

"Lucy, don't you miss Boston and all the things going on there? I found it to be a wonderfully fascinating city. There was always so much to do and so much to see. I don't think I could have just left it all to come out here."

"I had no choice. Papa's will was quite clear about my not getting the inheritance until I was eighteen, and I had no one to live with in Boston, so I had to come out here when your parents insisted. Yes, it was hard. I left everything I knew and loved behind, and I didn't think I'd ever fit in here."

"And then you met Jake." Rebecca's memory of those days had dimmed somewhat, but she'd never forget that winter when Jake and Lucy fell in love. It had been so romantic, but after he left to face possible murder charges in Texas, the winter became long and hard.

"Yes, I met Jake, and he's the best thing that ever happened to me. The fact that we almost didn't have a life together makes it even more precious."

"I don't know if I'll ever love anyone like that. Right now I don't have time to even think about a man in my life." If that were true, why did Rob Frankston's face keep popping into her mind? Geoff's attentions were just flattery, and he would only be here a few weeks, but she'd known Rob most of her life.

Lucy raised her eyebrows. "Oh, really? What about Bobby—I mean, Rob?"

Rebecca shrugged and shook her head. "I've known him forever. We're just good friends now."

"From the look in his eye, I'd say he has more than friendship on his mind."

"Well, he'll have to get over it." Still, it would be nice to have his attentions for such things like the church socials and Fourth of July, but then Geoff would make a charming escort too.

She shook herself. Forget them. She had more important things to do with her life than to worry about having more than friendship from either man.

Geoff listened to Jake Starnes and Ben Haynes discuss the differences in the type of cattle and stock available. Although that was his story for this trip, he had more important reasons for being here.

How long he could delay the cattle buying would depend on what kind of deal the men were willing to make.

Ben filled his pipe and reached for a long match in a container beside the fireplace. "Looks like you need to come out and inspect the herds yourself. It'll take a day or two to see my herd and then another to see Jake's. They're spread out all over the range. We don't have fences separating either of us, nor does Sam Morris. We're all together in the business. You'll find fences now on other ranches, but we're all family, so we don't have a need for them."

Geoff had learned that when he made inquiries and studied the land before coming to Oklahoma Territory. In just a few years this territory was bound to be a state, but until then they had no federal laws governing use of the land. "Didn't I hear about farmers once coming here and trying to put up fences?"

Jake crossed his legs and rested a heel on his knee. "Yes, they did. The summer Lucy and I married was a bad one for the weather. We didn't have enough rain from the middle of April until a huge thunderstorm put out a prairie fire that burned up most of the farmland and even hit Sam Morris's home. It brought hail that would have damaged whatever crops were left. Several of the farmers pulled up stakes and left before the fire."

"What happened to their land?" He had to ask to keep them from realizing how much he already knew about the history of Barton Creek. Jake and Ben were not stupid and would catch on to his knowledge if he wasn't careful.

Ben puffed on his pipe with the smoke curling up over his head. "Sam and I bought two of the farms. We use the land only for grazing. Most of it's no good for anything but grass."

"I see. That must have been a big help to you."

Jake smiled and shook his head. "You don't know Ben and Sam. They still send money to those two farmers and their families whenever they make an extra good profit on any of their sales."

So the rumors were true. Geoff's interest grew even stronger. "I must say that's mighty generous of you."

"Not really. Sam and I would not have been able to increase the numbers in our herd like we did without that land, so we feel we owe them for letting us buy it. Fire hit the Fowler ranch pretty hard, so that land sat empty until Norton, another rancher, moved onto it and set up his ranch there."

Jake leaned forward and grasped his leg with his hands. "I tend more to horses myself. We had horses back in Texas, so that's what

I have more of now even though my herd of cattle is a good size. Eli Morris and I are both horse lovers."

Geoff remembered Eli as the half-Cherokee son of Sam Morris who was married to Alice. He needed to go back over his list of ranchers and townspeople again, but at least he did know the ones Ben and Jake mentioned.

Matt leaned back in his chair. "I plan on having both on my ranch someday too."

Ben laughed. "At the rate he's going, he'll stay here and take over this one after I'm gone, and that wouldn't be a bad thing. That's what Hawk Morris is doing for his pa."

Being here in the midst of these men and listening to their talk caused Geoff to realize this was a close-knit community. They all knew one another like brothers and knew each other's business as well as their own. This venture down into Oklahoma might take longer to fulfill than he first anticipated. First thing tomorrow he must be sure his account was set up at the bank then go down to Guthrie and wire his boss about how things stood in Barton Creek.

Chapter 5

*R*ebecca awoke Monday morning in her rented room with joy in her heart. Today she would begin her career in the world of ink, newsprint, and typesetting. Ideas for her first story floated in her head. Perhaps something about the opportunities now open to women in medicine and the field of business would be a good starter to gain the interest of younger female readers, especially since Ruth had arrived with her own nursing skills.

After being home a few days and talking with Lucy and Ma, Rebecca realized that women like her mother, aunt, and cousin were happy and content in their roles. She needed to reach the younger women like Alice Morris or Ruth Dorsett. Someday women would hold positions of importance in every aspect of life, even politics, and she planned to be in the middle of it.

She smoothed the fabric of her black gored skirt. The white shirtwaist, devoid of lace and trim, suited her now in her new role. If women wanted to be accepted in business, they had to dress the part. Of course as a girl, she'd always been more comfortable in trousers, but those were not an acceptable mode of dress for young women of any age.

Hairpins secured the form for her hair to fashion the high pompadour look in front. She fastened the fall of hair in back with a large black clip because she had no time to shape it into curls or to wind it in a braid. Maybe some other morning, but this time she didn't intend to waste minutes with extra grooming.

She headed downstairs for breakfast with the other boarders. Rebecca had been fortunate that a room had been available in the Claymore boarding house. She loved the Victorian-style house Sheriff Claymore had bought for his wife five years ago when they married. Their love story was one of which legends were made. Claymore had been a bachelor many years when Catherine came to Barton Creek in search of her sister. After the reunion with Bea Anderson, the sheriff had taken notice of her and courted her for a year.

After their marriage, he bought this house for her to have as a boarding house. She had turned it into one of the best in the territory.

After a nourishing breakfast of bacon and eggs, Rebecca set off to town walking briskly. The streets of Barton Creek were much more crowded now than they were five years ago. A new school sat a few blocks from the church and was even divided into different classrooms for different grade levels. Anderson's Mercantile and Emporium now encompassed an entire city block since taking in the old post office and a storehouse. She waved at Luke as he opened the doors to his store.

Luke had attained his dream, as had Lucy, Dove, and Alice. Even Martin Fleming now did what he loved best, pastoring a church. Now it was her turn to achieve her goals in life. She stopped outside the offices of the *Barton Creek Chronicle* and breathed deeply, then stepped through the doors.

Mr. Lansdowne nodded his bald head and glanced at the big clock on his wall. "Punctual, I see. That's good."

"Yes, sir, I don't like to be late. What shall I do first?" She gazed around the room at all the equipment. The printing press took up all the space on one side of the large room. She could imagine the papers rolling off the machine. The odor of printer's ink filled her nose and whetted her desire to write.

He led her to a desk in the corner. Though small, it sported a new Underwood typewriter and a container of pencils. The stained oak surface had seen better days, but it would be her space, and that made it special.

Mr. Lansdowne handed her a list of items. "These are the people who have died since last week and the social events planned for the past week as well as the upcoming one. Get the information for the obits and visit with the ladies in charge for information about the social events. Then come back and write them up. We'll start printing on Thursday, and on Friday the finished product will be distributed."

Rebecca furrowed her brow. "But what about real news stories and articles?" Those were the things she wanted to write.

"Oh, I do those. I need someone to take care of these other things each week. I don't have time to attend every social event that goes on here, but you are single and don't have other responsibilities."

She nodded and glanced at the list. One of the social events listed a luncheon being given at the hotel by Mrs. Frankston. Probably promoting her husband for higher politics, if Rebecca had to guess. That might be an interesting function to attend. Mrs. Frankston always chose only the most influential people to her affairs, and who that might be increased her interest in the social gathering.

A young woman hurried into the building, out of breath and holding a small hat to her auburn curls. "Sorry I'm late, Papa. I didn't hear you leave."

Mr. Lansdowne shot a quick glance at Rebecca and cleared his throat before responding to his daughter. "You know I don't like tardiness. Don't let it happen again." He turned to Rebecca. "Miss Haynes, this is my daughter, Molly Lansdowne. She works here as a clerk. Miss Haynes is my new reporter."

"I know who she is. You wrote all about her last week." The girl, only an inch or so shorter than Rebecca, grinned. "It'll be fun to have another girl around here. I'm going off to school at Stillwater in the fall and only agreed to help Pa around here because Ma got tired of me messing things up at home."

The Lansdowne family had moved to Barton Creek three years ago when Mr. Lansdowne came in to take over the newspaper after the previous editor retired. "You've grown up. I remember you were fourteen when you came here. It's nice that your pa lets you help him with the paper."

Mr. Lansdowne headed for his office. "Don't you two girls stay out here too long jawing. There's work to be done." The door closed with a thud behind him.

Molly's nose crinkled when she laughed, and her green eyes danced with amusement. "Pa's old-fashioned. I don't really do anything but run errands for him and make sure he has plenty of coffee and some pastries from the bakery."

"Well, I certainly hope to be doing more than that. I'm surprised he would hire a woman for a reporter, although I think maybe my own pa might have had something to do with that." After meeting Mr. Lansdowne the first time, it had become obvious someone had helped him with the decision.

"Wouldn't surprise me one bit. Your pa has lots of influence in this town." She swirled around and held up a white bag bearing the baker logo. "I'll get Pa's coffee and pastry, then we can talk."

Rebecca sat down at her desk and perused the list again. Two obituaries could be dealt with in a short time. The undertaker's office was just down the street and should have the information. If not, she could visit the families and get what she needed. She laid the paper on the desk and sighed. This wasn't exactly what had been in her mind when she accepted the position.

Ideas for articles danced in her head as she tapped a pencil against the desk edge. She'd take care of the items on the list first, then spend her time writing those articles and impress her editor. He couldn't help but print them.

Geoff strolled out of the hotel and breathed deeply of the fresh summer morning air. The weekend had been quite productive, although he didn't get the information he actually wanted. Talking with the ranchers had been interesting, and in a few more such visits he could make his offer for the cattle.

The eclectic mixture of brick and clapboard buildings had been a surprise, but they gave character to the downtown area. The leaded glass doors on the hotel at first looked out of place but suited the furnishings the owner provided inside. In addition, the rooms were quite comfortable.

He'd half expected dirt roads with lots of dust, but he had found brick streets between the two- and three-story buildings that lined Main Street. Most small towns had not added those yet because of so many horses about, but evidently that wasn't the case here, as he'd seen more carriages and wagons than single horses.

So far the town had been a pleasant surprise, especially with Rebecca Haynes living there. The ride back to town last evening had been most enjoyable. Miss Haynes had indicated she would enjoy riding with him if he rented another horse and wanted to accompany her on Daisy.

He made his way across to Anderson's Mercantile and Emporium. From what he could tell, the store was divided into two sections. His interests led him to the windows displaying various items of clothing. A young man greeted him inside, and Geoff recognized him as the husband of one of Rebecca's friends at the welcome home party.

"Welcome to Anderson's, sir. I'm Luke Anderson, one of the owners. How can I help you this morning?"

Geoff glanced down at his dove gray trousers. "I'd like some pants a little more suitable for riding horses and conducting business with the cattle ranchers."

Luke waved his hand through the air. "Right this way. We have denim trousers and cotton shirts that are the best attire for such activities."

Shelves lined with shirts of various colors and sizes covered part of one side of the store. Jackets and suits hung on racks, and a sign indicating custom-made suits were available hung above a display rack.

Ever mindful of his job, Geoff said, "You're married to Dove, the friend of Rebecca and Lucy, correct?"

The store owner nodded and grinned. "Yes, I am. We've known Becky and Lucy for awhile now. Lucy came here from Boston back in ninety-six. When a tornado practically destroyed our town, she used some of her inheritance to help us rebuild. She's a fine lady."

That was an interesting tidbit of news. If Jake Starnes had no need of money with his wife's inheritance, then buying what he wanted may be a problem if Starnes didn't want to sell. Geoff counted on the men to be interested in making money and thus open to his offers.

Luke handed him two pairs of denim trousers and several shirts. "I think you'll find what you need here, sir."

"Thank you." Geoff checked the labels. Luke had a good eye. All the items were the correct size. "I'll take these, and I'd also like one of those hats like I've seen Ben Haynes and Sam Morris wear."

"Oh, that would be our new line of Stetson hats." He strode to a display and picked one up. He returned carrying a light tan felt hat that looked like a tall, upside-down bowl. "How would you like for me to crease it?"

"I'm not sure. I imagine like Ben does his." Geoff had never paid any attention to how a cowboy hat might be creased. They had all looked the same to him. He watched with fascination as Luke carried the hat to some type of machine and formed the hat. The machine emitted steam, and before his eyes, the tall bowl became a nicely creased cowboy hat.

He followed Luke back to the front area and the counter where he paid for his purchases. Usually he charged it all off to his company, but this time he paid out of his own funds. He would get good use from these garments later.

With bags in his hands, Geoff made his way back to the hotel and deposited them in his room. He changed into denim pants and a cotton shirt, donned his boots, and fitted the hat to his head. He surveyed himself in the mirror. Now he looked like most of the other townspeople and would blend in without calling attention to himself.

Next stop would be the telegraph station in Guthrie. He certainly didn't plan to take any chances with a nosy telegrapher who might relay information back to Ben Haynes. The operators were not supposed to tell others what went into a wire, but he didn't trust the one in this town where everyone knew the Hayneses.

Rob stood at the second-floor window of his father's law offices. He observed Geoff coming from the hotel and watched him go into Anderson's. Animosity filled his heart. He didn't quite understand why he didn't like the man from Chicago. Maybe it had to do with his interest in Becky. Even at that, the man seemed to have a secret, and Rob didn't believe for one minute his only reason for coming here was to purchase cattle. If that were the case, he'd make his purchase and leave.

Rob returned to his desk but couldn't concentrate on the document in front of him. Mr. and Mrs. Cunningham would expect their will to be ready for signing this afternoon, but his mind wandered. Becky had come back to town last night and was staying at the Claymore boarding house. Perhaps he'd go down to the newspaper office and ask her to have lunch with him.

He strode back to the window and glanced out again. This time Geoff was leaving the hotel a second time, but he was dressed in different clothes. Must be the ones he'd just bought at the Emporium. Movement down the way caught his eye. Becky emerged from the *Chronicle* office, and Geoff met her on the boardwalk.

Jealousy reared its ugly head again, and this time Rob didn't try to tamp it down. The two conversed for a few minutes, and Becky lifted her head in a laugh that he could hear from where he stood. Such a beautiful laugh, he'd recognize it anywhere, even if she wasn't in plain sight. A minute later Geoff tipped his hat and strolled toward the livery while Becky walked across to the undertaker's office.

How he wished he could know what had caused Becky to be in such good spirits with Geoff. He waited a few more minutes, hoping to see her come into view again. A horse and rider emerged from the livery, and Geoff Kensington rode toward the edge of town. Rob leaned out to watch as the rider headed south on the road to Guthrie.

Rob slumped down at his desk, all thoughts of waiting for Becky to reappear gone. His main concern at the moment centered around Geoff and why he rode toward Guthrie rather than back out to the Haynes ranch. What business did he have in Guthrie that he couldn't do in Barton Creek? The man was hiding something, and if Rob could ever find out what it might be, he could expose Geoff, and Becky would see he wasn't the man for her. For the time being, Rob had no idea how he could do anything, but rest assured, he'd keep a closer eye on one Mr. Geoff Kensington.

Chapter 6

*R*ebecca typed the last letter of her report on the Women's Guild luncheon and pulled it from the machine. One nice thing about the job was that Mr. Lansdowne had spent money on a decent typewriter. According to the catalogs she had studied, an Underwood like this one was quite expensive.

Her thoughts rambled back to the meeting she'd just attended. The ladies had all been pleasant, but after they decided to have a craft fair during the Independence Day celebration, their talk turned to the latest recipes, fashions, and new household appliances. She wanted to stand and shout and ask them why they weren't more concerned with whether or not the Territory would become a state or not. Every time she tried to approach the subject with any of the women, they looked at her like she had two heads.

She leaned forward and grabbed a pencil from the holder. Her new list would include all the women and girls she knew in town who were supporting themselves or who held down jobs.

Rebecca wrote Mrs. Weems first on the list. The seamstress had a husband who was employed by the telegraph company and didn't need her extra income, but still she made all types of clothing for the ladies in town. Ruth would be a great help to her mother. Next on the list she wrote Mrs. Anderson, but then helping your husband in a store and still taking care of your home wasn't that unusual on the prairie.

When completed, the paper held only four names of women Rebecca considered to be independent and possible partners in the quest for women's rights. If things went this slowly in other states, it would be awhile before much could be accomplished. At least Wyoming, Utah, Idaho, and Colorado had given women the right to vote.

Becky thought of her role model, Carrie Chapman Catt, who came to Oklahoma in 1898 to campaign for the suffrage movement. She gained support but was ultimately defeated by the Saloon Keepers League, who feared that if women got the vote, they would vote for temperance. Now it was up to women like Rebecca to do their part to make both men and women in Oklahoma Territory more receptive to the suffrage movement.

Someone entered the news office, and Rebecca glanced up from her desk. Rob leaned over the railing separating the entry from the office areas. A smile filled her heart and tickled her lips.

"To what do I owe the pleasure of your visit?" Rebecca stood and smoothed her skirt.

"I thought I'd drop by and see if the town's first woman news reporter would do me the honor of dining with me this evening."

"First and only right now, but I hope that will change." Her smile became full blown. "I'd be delighted to dine with you. I've heard Catherine Claymore's cooking is excellent, but the company isn't as good as your invitation." Three single men and two single women, all over the age of fifty, lived at the boarding house. Dinner with Rob offered the opportunity for conversation and for learning more about new people in town.

"Then I will meet you at the boarding house at six this evening, and we can dine at the hotel or at Dinah's."

If Dinah still cooked like she had before Rebecca left, a meal there would be most filling. The hotel may be nicer and have fancier food, but Dinah knew how to dish up good old-fashioned home cooking. "Dinah's will be just fine. Does she still serve that special steak she did several years ago?"

"She does, and many new items besides." He grasped his straw hat with both hands and bowed. "Until this evening."

He sauntered out of the office onto the boardwalk. Rebecca was sure she heard him whistling as he left. Molly tapped her shoulder. She jumped. "Oh, my, you scared me."

Molly laughed. "I know. You were so intent on watching Mr. Frankston leave that you didn't even see or hear me come in." A grin spread across her face. "He sure is a handsome man. I wouldn't mind having the mayor's son pay attention to me."

"Don't get the wrong idea. Rob Frankston is an old friend. We've known each other since our grade school days."

Molly tilted her head and smirked. "If you say so, but from the look in his eye, I'd say he sees you as more than an old friend." She turned and headed toward her desk across the way.

Rebecca shook her head. Even if Molly happened to be right about Rob's feelings, he was just a good friend who asked her to dinner. Of course when she was younger, his invitation would have sent her head to spinning. It did tug at her heart a little, but she had no time for such notions. Still it would be fun to talk over old times. She set about her tasks for the afternoon with a much lighter heart.

Rob whistled his way back to his office. At last he'd have some time alone with Becky. He'd have to try to remember to call her Rebecca. He didn't want to spoil any of the time they would have together later in the evening.

All through the remaining hours he continually checked his watch. Time passed much too slowly for him after Mr. and Mrs.

Cunningham signed their wills and left. Now he had trouble concentrating on his work, and if he didn't finish this last document, his father would be most unhappy. Finally he laid aside the papers and headed to his house to refresh himself before meeting Becky at the boarding house.

When he entered the hallway, his mother greeted him. "How were things at the office today, son?" She leaned forward for him to kiss her cheek.

Rob brushed his lips across the smooth skin of his mother's cheek. "The same as usual, a lot of paperwork. I won't be here for dinner tonight. I'm dining with Becky Haynes."

His mother's eyebrows shot up. "Oh, I understand she's living at the boarding house Catherine Claymore runs."

"Yes, she is. Wasn't she at the luncheon you attended today?" His mother never missed a meeting of the Women's Guild, but he was interested in hearing what she had to say about Becky being there since she wasn't a member.

"She was, and I don't know why Mr. Lansdowne had to send her. Nothing we do ever makes that much news since everyone already knows what went on." His mother followed him to the parlor.

"Don't you think you should be careful about seeing Becky? She asked some strange questions at our meeting today."

"Mother, we've known the Haynes family ever since we moved here. I see no problem with continuing our friendship."

She shrugged. "Far be it from me to tell you what to do, but I just think you could find someone better than the Haynes girl to pursue. You are of marrying age, you know, and it's time for you to settle down and have a wife and home of your own."

That's what he thought, but from the way things looked now, Becky wasn't interested. "And just which girl would you have me court?" He could think of no girl of the right age who would pass his mother's test, but then he wanted no other girl besides Becky.

"I'm not sure. I'll have to think on that. We have so many new families moving in, and there should be a number of young ladies who would enjoy your company."

"Maybe so, but tonight it will be Becky." He backed away a step. "If you will excuse me, I must change into a fresh shirt." Rob turned and strode from the room, hiding the snicker that threatened at the sight of the open-mouthed expression on his mother's face.

When he arrived at the boarding house, Catherine Claymore welcomed him and called to Becky. The older woman grinned at Rob. "I see you're taking up right where you left off four years ago. That's good. This girl's quite a catch."

"Yes, she is, but I'm not sure she feels the same for me as she did back then."

Mrs. Claymore laughed. "Well, I just remember how you and she looked together at church before you got all grown up. Couldn't take your eyes off each other."

Rob opened his mouth to respond, but Becky appeared on the stairway, and he snapped it shut. Her beauty stole away his breath for a moment as she stepped down beside him. Her long brown hair had been swept up on her head with one lone curl curving down on her shoulder. Her form filled the wine-colored skirt and cream blouse very well.

He swallowed hard and banished those thoughts from his mind. "You look lovely this evening, Rebecca." Yes, she looked like Rebecca now, and not the tomboy Becky.

She extended her hand to his. "Thank you, Rob." She turned to Mrs. Claymore. "Thank you for your help earlier."

Rob nodded to Mrs. Claymore and guided Rebecca outside. She tucked her hand under his elbow as they headed toward Dinah's.

Feeling her hand on his arm felt as natural as breathing. The years apart washed away, and they were once again the young couple getting ready for college.

Heads turned as they entered the restaurant, and many admiring glances were cast in Rebecca's direction. When he sat across from her in the restaurant, he saw once again the beautiful young woman she had become. With the same coloring as her cousin Lucy, Rebecca could be taken for a sister. No matter how much she had changed on the outside, inside was still the Becky he knew and loved. Somehow he would find her and bring her back.

She leaned forward now with the menu in hand. "I see Dinah has really upgraded both the restaurant and her menu."

"Indeed she has. I plan to have one of her Delmonico steaks. She told me she got the idea from a restaurant in New York City and only added it to the menu recently." It was a rather large cut of meat, but Dinah's cook prepared it to tender perfection with a nice pink center.

"Yes, I've heard of it, but it's too much meat for me. I'll have the roast beef with carrots and potatoes."

When the young woman had taken their orders, Rob crossed his arms on the table. "I didn't get much chance to talk with you Sunday at church. It was good to see you sitting with your family once again."

She worried the edge of her napkin and didn't look at him. After a few moments she glanced up. "I was there only to please them. I haven't had much time for church in my life the past few years."

"But now that you're here, you'll have plenty of free time for church." At least she lived in town, and that should make attending easier.

"I don't think so. I've found that God is wherever I want Him to be, and if I should happen to need Him, He'll be there."

Rob swallowed hard. Despite his attempt to control his feelings, his voice rose as he spoke. "Rebecca, we need God every day of our lives. Look at people here in Barton Creek. How many of them owe their lives and their livelihoods to His power and love?"

"He's not a crutch for me, and I've done quite well on my own the past four years. Those people have the strength and fortitude to take care of themselves. Each one of us must do that. We must look within ourselves for what we need to survive."

Rob sat in stunned silence. How could this be the same girl he had grown up with? "But think of Lucy and Jake and how God provided for them and for the town after the tornado in ninety-seven. And Dove and Luke wouldn't be together if God hadn't brought a miracle after the fire that destroyed the Morris home. Even Catherine Claymore wouldn't be here if God had not protected her when she was kidnapped by Indians as a child."

"Yes, God does good things when people have no control over what is happening, but when we do have control, God expects us to take care of ourselves. When things are out of control, then we can pray and seek God's help."

Rob's heart ached. He didn't have the words he needed to show her how wrong her ideas were. He wished Martin Fleming were here instead of in Tulsa, where he was the minister for a church. Being nearer their age, he might be able to explain things better than the elderly pastor at their own church.

"Besides, organized religion is much too restrictive for women. If we are submissive to men as the Bible says, we take away much of our freedom to speak, act, and live as independent creatures with a mind and will of our own."

Again he didn't have the wisdom needed to argue with that reasoning. He'd heard of women who were involved with seeking women's rights, but none had come to Barton Creek before. He frowned at her. "Are you one of the women who follow the suffrage movement?"

Her face brightened, and her eyes sparkled. "Yes, I am. I've been following Carrie Chapman Catt and the work of Susan Anthony the past few years, and they are fascinating, independent, intelligent women."

He'd heard of both of those women and how they led protests and tried to get states to allow women the right to vote. "But why would you want women to have the right to vote? Women will never be able to understand politics."

As soon as the words left his mouth he wanted to snatch them back. Rebecca's face clouded, and her fists clenched on the edge of the table.

"Rebecca, please, I'm sorry. I should never have said that. Of course smart women understand politics." His breath caught in his throat. She had to accept his apology or the evening would be ruined.

The waitress placed their food on the table then left. The steak held no interest for him now. He waited for Rebecca to at least say a word one way or the other.

Finally she picked up her fork and stabbed a potato. "I will accept your apology, but if you want to continue to be friends, you must be more tolerant of my views."

He could do that simply because he loved her, but along with the tolerance would come the prayer that she would not grow further and further away from him. Maybe he'd never have the old Becky back, but the new one needed some guidance, if not in women's rights, then in the place of God in her life. He prayed to be that guide.

Chapter 7

*G*eoff alit from his horse and led him into the livery, where Jonah met him at the door. "Glad to see you back, Mr. Kensington. Champ performed OK for you, I take it."

"Yes, he did quite well for the week. I may need him again tomorrow if my plans work out the way I hope."

"Consider Champ yours as long as you're in Barton Creek." Jonah took the reins and led the horse to a stall.

"Thank you, Jonah." Geoff turned and headed to the hotel. He remembered seeing a laundry near the hotel and decided to drop off his soiled clothing. Most of what he owned was dirty after his trips to Guthrie and Tulsa. He could have taken the train, but a ride across the Territory on horseback suited his purposes. Unfortunately, his travels had not revealed the information he sought.

The best he could do now was to hope the meetings with the ranchers gave him what he wanted to find. If his plan with Miss Haynes worked out, he would learn more about the land in which he was interested. He hadn't seen her since he'd left on Monday, but she had agreed to ride with him Saturday so she could show him more of the countryside.

He sensed someone watching and glanced up. Rob Frankston stood in the window of the law offices staring down below. Geoff lifted a hand in a wave, and Rob disappeared from the window without responding. That brought a chuckle to Geoff's throat. If competition is what worried Rob, then competition he would get. The fact that Miss Haynes was so lovely made the task a most pleasant one.

After dropping off his laundry bundle, he stowed the valise with the rest of his belongings in his hotel room. He decided on a bath to remove the grime of travel before visiting Miss Haynes at the news office.

Once refreshed and re-dressed, he strolled across the street to the newspaper. A young woman exited from the dress shop and collided with his chest.

Geoff steadied her with his hands on her arms and looked down into eyes so blue they looked like crystal. Their gazes held a moment before pink filled her cheeks.

She stepped back. "I'm so sorry. I should have been watching where I was going."

"I'm glad you didn't fall." Then he recognized her. "Ruth Dorsett, from the train. You had three young children with you."

"Yes, that's right, and you're the young man who sat and talked with Rebecca Haynes. I'm sorry I didn't hear your name."

Geoff tipped his hat. "Geoff Kensington, with a *G*, and I'm from Chicago."

She grinned then as if she remembered her errand. "It's nice meeting you again, but I must hurry to the Emporium." She lifted her skirt an inch or so and hurried across the street.

He stood and observed her for a few moments. Ruth Dorsett was a very attractive young widow. Too bad she had three children. Then he chuckled. Rebecca Haynes would keep him busy enough without thinking about another woman, especially a widow with children.

When he reached the *Chronicle* offices, the door was open, and he stepped through to find Rebecca Haynes seated at her desk staring at the typewriting machine. He cleared his throat. "May I have a moment of your time, Miss Haynes?"

She jerked around, her chair squealing in protest, and offered him a smile as wide as the open spaces on the ranches.

"Mr. Kensington, I didn't know you were back in town."

"Just arrived a short time ago. I wanted to know if our plans for tomorrow are still on your schedule."

"Yes, and I'm truly looking forward to showing you some of the prettiest country in all the southwest. Lucy and Jake are bringing Daisy in to me this evening when they come for dinner."

"That's nice of them and will save us much time tomorrow." Perhaps she'd even take him off the regular roads and show him the property he hadn't had time to see when he and Mr. Haynes last visited.

"Do you have dinner plans this evening?" Spending time with Rebecca now would give him a chance for a few questions that might not be possible as they rode tomorrow.

"Yes, I do. I'm dining with the Anderson family tonight. Mr. Anderson is doing much better since his heart attack a month or so ago, and Dove invited me to come for dinner. We have a lot of things still to catch up on from the past four years. Perhaps another time we can dine together."

"Then I shall plan on it and excuse myself so you may get back to work." He bowed slightly then headed back to the street. As he crossed to the hotel, he spotted Jake and Lucy Starnes coming into town. A glance at his watch revealed the time to be four o'clock. Rather early for dinner.

The carriage stopped first at the livery where Jake left Daisy for Rebecca, then went back to the Emporium, where he jumped down and secured the team to the railing. Jake helped his wife descend, and they conversed a few moments. Jake headed across the street to the law offices of Rob Frankston, and Lucy walked toward the newspaper office.

Mrs. Starnes must be planning to meet with Miss Haynes. That may take awhile, so he would have time to meet up with Jake and discuss their cattle transaction. With that decision he planted himself in a chair in front of the hotel and waited for Jake to emerge from his mission with the young lawyer.

The bell over the door jangled, and Rebecca glanced up from work. When she saw Lucy, she jumped to her feet and hurried to the railing. "Lucy, I wasn't expecting you for another hour."

Lucy shrugged, and her eyes sparked with excitement. "Jake had business with the mayor, so we came in early. I have hopes of getting you free from your duties a little early."

"That would be wonderful. The paper for the week has been delivered, and I don't have a story due right away." Rebecca's smile broadened as she announced proudly, "Mr. Lansdowne put my byline on one of my articles."

"Congratulations!" Lucy clapped her hands at the news.

Rebecca looked over at Molly. "Would your father mind if I left now?"

Molly waved her hand. "Go on and visit with your cousin. I'll tell Pa. He won't mind your going with Mrs. Starnes."

"Thanks, Molly." Rebecca grabbed her hat from the stand beside her desk and pinned it to her curls. "The Starneses are well remembered for all you've done for Barton Creek."

"But the Lansdowne family wasn't even here in ninety-seven when we had the tornado."

Rebecca grinned at her cousin and pushed through the gate in the railing. "Your reputation is well known, even by the newcomers." She grasped her cousin's arm. "Now, I'm so glad to see you. I miss the family more than I like to admit, and if you tell Ma, I'll say you're telling a story."

She then glanced back at Molly. "See you on Monday. Have a good time with your beau."

The girl's cheeks flushed crimson, and she turned quickly to go into her father's office. Rebecca giggled. "Arnold Garson is courting Molly, and she's torn between staying here and going off to school at Stillwater. I'm trying to convince her that she'll go much further in the world with a college education."

She stepped outside to the sunshine and spread her arms. "Hmm, it smells so good out here. When that press is running with all that ink, it doesn't smell so good inside."

Lucy wrinkled her nose and sniffed. "All I smell is the livery stable." Then she laughed. "Who cares what it smells like here. Let's go over to the hotel and have a cup of tea."

Rebecca followed her cousin across the street. "One of the things I missed after I went off to school was coming to your place and having tea once or twice a week." She had learned so much on those occasions about what it would be like in Boston and what to expect.

"If I remember correctly, you balked at first. Said you'd much rather be riding horses. It wasn't until Aunt Clara made arrangements for you to visit her brother and his family back home that you began coming more frequently. I have been pleasantly surprised at how much more mature you are now."

When they stepped up onto the boardwalk in front of the hotel, Geoff Kensington stood and greeted them. "Good afternoon, Mrs. Starnes, Miss Haynes."

Heat rose in Rebecca's cheeks. With all her attention on Lucy, she hadn't noticed Geoff seated there. "How nice to see you again. Lucy and I are just going in for a cup of tea and a pastry."

"Then don't let me keep you." He bowed slightly. "I look forward to our ride tomorrow."

Rebecca nodded and hurried inside to the hotel dining room. Lucy followed her to one of the tables.

"You have a date with Mr. Kensington?"

Rebecca settled herself in a chair. "Yes. That's why I wanted you to bring Daisy to town. I'm going to keep her at the livery for awhile so I'll have access to her." To be truthful, she missed her horse more now that she was at home than she ever had while away at school. Knowing she was near would be like having a piece of home nearby. Not that Rebecca would ever admit that to Ma or Pa and certainly not to Lucy, who might be tempted to tell them.

"Wouldn't a carriage ride have been more appropriate?" Lucy removed her gloves and raised an eyebrow.

"Then we wouldn't be able to take some of the trails over the range and see the real land of Oklahoma. Roads are too restrictive."

The eyebrow remained raised. "But you'll be riding alone, and you barely know each other."

Rebecca let her breath out in a huff. "Lucy, this is 1905, and I don't need a chaperone to go riding with a young man. Besides, you and Jake rode alone on Christmas Eve that first year you were here."

"That was different. Ben and Mellie knew we needed that time to ourselves before Jake left. If you remember correctly, that was the afternoon Jake explained why he had to leave. My heart was broken that day."

"At least that turned out OK, and he came back." The whole town had rejoiced when Jake returned and told everyone he'd not been charged for murder because the killing had been in self-defense. She'd never forget the look on Lucy's face when she saw Jake that afternoon or the one on Jake's as he hugged Lucy. She might change her mind about love and marriage if a man ever looked at her like that.

"Yes, God answered our prayers. He brought Jake back to me."

"What did God have to do with anything? Jake was already innocent before he even left Barton Creek. He just didn't know it." God couldn't have done something that was already done before they prayed about it.

Lucy waited until the waitress had taken their order for tea and pastries before answering. Her eyes narrowed as she focused on Rebecca. "God had everything to do with it. If Jake hadn't gone back, he would never have known he hadn't murdered a man. When he gave God his heart that Christmas Eve, then God started things moving that would give Jake his complete freedom."

"If you say so, but I believe people make their own choices and decide their own fate. God is there in case things go wrong." Saying it aloud after what Lucy said didn't feel quite as right as it had when she said the same thing to Rob.

"Rebecca Susan Haynes, I can't believe I'm hearing this from you. How could you have changed your ideas so much?"

"I learned a lot at Wellesley. Frankly, I don't see how you were able to leave such an exciting place as Boston. My time back East was most enlightening." She leaned forward. "Have you ever heard of Carrie Chapman Catt or Susan B. Anthony? They have such wonderful ideas about women and how we should have a voice in what happens in our lives."

"I've heard of them, but their ideas are a little too radical for my tastes."

The waitress set teacups, a small pot, and a plate of pastry on the table. "Will there be anything else?"

Lucy smiled. "No, thank you. This is fine."

Rebecca stirred her tea. "Aren't you interested in Oklahoma

becoming a state and having a voice in what will happen? Women in other western states are allowed to vote for who will serve their state as governor, senators, and representatives."

"That's best left to our men. They are much smarter than we are when it comes to how to run our country. I have enough to worry about with our children and home."

This was the same argument Rebecca had heard time after time when she tried to talk with women about the privilege of voting. Even her own parents thought her interest in being a reporter would be short-lived. They expected her to marry and settle down with a family like her cousin and friends.

"That's not what I want out of life. I want to someday write articles for a large city newspaper, articles that will help women to take a stand and think for themselves. I want to be independent like I am now by living in town rather than at home with Ma, Pa, and Matt." They should be pushing Matt to get married, not her.

Lucy sipped her tea then picked up a pastry. "You've always been different and ready to do what the men were doing rather than cooking and sewing at home."

"Yes, and I was the best roper. I even beat Matt more often than not. If Pa would let me help brand cattle and go on roundups with him, I might change my mind about journalism and stay home." But she'd never give up her quest to gain voting privileges for women.

"What does Rob Frankston have to say about your plans to move to a larger newspaper?"

"What does he have to do with anything? I haven't told him, and it's none of his business anyway. We're good friends, but I'm not going to tell him everything." She had to do something to get the idea that she and Rob would marry someday out of people's minds.

Just then she spotted Geoff Kensington greeting Jake outside. Maybe she should be paying more heed to Geoff's attentions. Tomorrow would give her the perfect opportunity.

*R*ebecca descended the stairs at the boarding house. Catherine Claymore nodded and smiled. "Now that's a right smart riding outfit."

"Thank you. Mr. Kensington and I are riding out to the ranch today. He wants to see more of the land."

"I thought he was here to buy cattle, not go riding around the countryside."

"He is, but he's also interested in Oklahoma and the fact it will someday be a state." Nearly everyone she saw said the same thing about Geoff. You'd think he was here to rob them or take away their land or something. Let them think what they wanted, she found him most attractive and charming.

At that moment the man in question knocked at the door. She opened to find him wearing denim pants, a plaid shirt, and boots. Her breath caught as she realized how handsome he was dressed as a cowboy. He removed his hat, and his smile and curly black hair gave the appearance of a young man ready for a good time.

"Ah, Miss Haynes, I see you are ready." He turned to the landlady. "Good day to you, Mrs. Claymore. I promise I won't keep Miss Haynes out late."

Mrs. Claymore cocked her head and narrowed her eyes. "I'm not her mother, but it's good for you to let me know that you won't have her out too long."

Rebecca grasped Geoff's arm. Time to get out of here and away from nosy questions and comments. "I'm sure our horses are waiting for us at the livery. Good-bye, Mrs. Claymore."

They made their way to the street, and Rebecca hooked her hand in the crook of his elbow. He placed his hand over Rebecca's. "Mrs. Claymore is a nice lady."

"She is, but she'll tell my family everything about us." She tilted her head to gaze up at him and into his dark eyes. "Still, her own story is most interesting. She was kidnapped by Indians when she was seven and lost from her family until she found her sister, Mrs. Anderson, here in Barton Creek about eight years ago."

"Not only interesting, but amazing. You must hear a lot of stories like that here on the frontier."

"And we've made for some pretty good ones ourselves. Things like how Lucy saved the town after the tornado, how the Morrises rebuilt after a prairie fire destroyed their home and almost killed Dove, and the farmers that couldn't make it because of the drought." So much happened in the old days that had been newsworthy, but nothing like that was happening around here now. Barton Creek had become a dull but busy place.

They arrived at the livery and mounted their horses. Rebecca admired the black horse he rode and led him out to the well-worn road toward her father's ranch.

"I ran into Ruth Dorsett on my way to see you yesterday. She's working with her mother."

"Yes, and she's adjusted quite nicely to life here. Ruth has inherited her mother's talent for sewing. Even though Mrs. Weems is using the sewing machine for much of her work, she and Ruth still use hand-stitching for detail, and Ruth's is some of the best I've ever seen. I plan to have several new items— Oh, dear. Here I am running on about something that doesn't interest you at all." After all her plans to be an independent, intelligent young woman, she'd reverted to the old Becky, who didn't know when to stop talking.

"I'd enjoy listening to you talk no matter what the subject. You're one of the most animated women I've ever been around. Your enthusiasm for whatever the subject might be is quite fetching."

His eyes crinkled around the edges as he smiled. Heat rose in her cheeks at his amusement, but at least he hadn't laughed at her. He certainly knew how to charm females. Some other men she knew could take a lesson or two from him. "Thank you. Sometimes I just rattle on about nothing, but you're more interested in what our land is like than the latest fashions."

"Yes, and I understand that your father's and Jake's lands run together, and Mr. Morris's borders both of them."

"That's right. Jake's ranch was part of ours until he bought a large parcel from Pa when he and Lucy married. Pa was excited to have Jake as a neighbor and a nephew. He says Jake is one of the best cowboys he's ever known and knows more about horses than most anyone in these parts except maybe Eli Morris." She stopped Daisy and leaned on her saddle horn. The sky, a brilliant blue this day, seemed to go on forever. A few stray clouds drifted across, casting little shadows as they passed between the sun and this spot.

Geoff peered upward. "I understand now what they mean by a 'tall sky.' I've never seen such blue in or around Chicago. Makes me glad I came out here. That and the people I've met." His grin sent great delight to her heart. Perhaps he wouldn't be so hasty to dismiss her ideas for the rights of women.

They rode on farther in silence. Rebecca drank in the beauty around her. The heat of summer had not yet sucked the life out of plants and trees. A few stray wildflowers lent their color to the landscape. How she'd missed this country, although she hated to admit to that fact.

They slowed at the creek, and Rebecca paused to allow Daisy to lap at the water. Geoff did the same for his mount. "Where is the portion that the farmers gave to your father, or rather sold?"

"I'm not really sure. That all happened when I was much younger and didn't pay attention to that kind of thing. I know it's west because the fires that year came from the northeast and didn't reach any of our land. Pa was most grateful for that."

She turned Daisy in that direction. "If we follow the creek, we should come up to it somewhere. This one winds around and joins up with the one outside town and flows on to the river. The only bad thing about it is that heavy rains cause flash floods. I only remember that happening a few times, and what there was of town had streets filled with water, and the livery was flooded."

"But it was drought that caused the farmers to leave."

"Yes, two years in a row without much rain destroyed their crops. Pa says the land isn't any good for crops. He barely gets enough grass out there for the cattle that wander over to that section. I don't know why he's holding on to it. Even the creek water isn't fit to drink there." She glanced over at Geoff, whose face was now an unreadable mask.

She furrowed her brow and contemplated what could be hiding behind his bland expression. What could he possibly be thinking about?

She shook her head and wheeled her horse around. "I think it's time to head back to town, don't you?"

Geoff took one last look around, then tipped his hat. "Lead on!"

Mellie stepped down from the wagon. "I'll be in Anderson's store or Mrs. Weems's dress shop when you finish your business." Ben waved to her and headed across the street. When she entered the store, a new clerk greeted her.

"Good day, Mrs. Haynes. How can I help you?"

The face was familiar, but Mellie couldn't quite place it. So many new people moving in made knowing folks much more difficult these days. Then she grinned in realization of the identity of the young man speaking to her. "I remember now; you're Tommy Perkins. I didn't know you were home."

"Yes, ma'am, I finished school and came back here to work for the summer. I plan to move to Oklahoma City in the fall and find a job there."

"That's nice. I know your mother is glad to have you home since Sarah has married and moved to Tulsa." She handed him her list. "These are the items I need today. If you'll take care of the staples and spices, I'll find the canned goods."

She carried her basket to the shelves of canned fruits and vegetables. This was so much easier than doing the canning at home. More variety was available in the store cans. What she made herself had to be grown first and then go through all the processing.

"Mellie Haynes, you're just the person I want to talk to."

Mellie turned around to find Catherine Claymore standing by the counter. "Oh, and might it have to do with my daughter? What is she up to now?"

"As a matter of fact it does. I was about to send Will Anderson out to your place, but then I remembered you usually come to town on Saturdays. If you plan on seeing Rebecca, she's not in town. She and that Geoff Kensington fellow rode off over an hour ago. Seems he wants to see more of our country, as he put it."

"Then it's good he has Rebecca to show him around. He had dinner with us last Sunday, and of course he was at the welcome party." As much as she liked Rob Frankston, Mellie was glad to see Rebecca interested in another young man. For some reason her children couldn't make up their minds about the Frankston siblings.

"I thought you'd want to know they are not chaperoned. It appears that is not the custom these days, but I can't say that I approve." Catherine's mouth puckered like she'd eaten a sour ball.

"Now, Catherine, they're both adults, and it should be perfectly all right for them. He's a guest in our town, and we must show him every courtesy." A little apprehension crept into her heart. They really didn't know much about the Kensington fellow except that he was interested in buying cattle. Rebecca should be more careful, but telling her daughter to be careful would do as much good as telling the wind to stop blowing.

"You're probably right, but it just seems to be a little too risky for me. I'm glad I don't have daughters to worry about these days. With my two stepsons grown and out on their own, I imagine they are courting young ladies themselves. Mr. Kensington was nice enough to tell me he'd have Rebecca home before too late in the evening."

Mellie reached for a can of tomatoes for her basket. "Now see, he's being very considerate. If I'm not worried, then you shouldn't be either."

"I know. I just keep remembering Rebecca the way she was when I first arrived. I thought then that she was one of the prettiest thirteen-year-old girls I'd ever met. And she was so high-spirited and full of life. Made my heart glad just to watch her." She walked toward the door. "Tell Mr. Haynes I said hello."

"I will, and thank you again for your concern." Mellie chuckled to herself. Rebecca would be furious to know Catherine had said anything about her being with Mr. Kensington. Her daughter had always been and probably always would be free-spirited with a mind of her own. They'd tried to tame her, with little success.

She finished filling her basket with the items she needed and placed them on the counter for Tommy to add to the other goods he'd assembled. She'd have to tell Ben where their daughter was. Most likely he would have wanted to stop by and see her before they left town.

Rob waited on the boardwalk for Mrs. Haynes to come out of the store. He'd gone down to see Rebecca and learned that she was out on the trail with that Kensington fellow. He hoped to gain a little more information about Geoff from Mrs. Haynes.

He spotted his sister coming out of the bakery. Matt Haynes met her, and they exchanged a few moments of conversation. He couldn't understand what was taking Matt so long to ask Caroline to marry him. Caroline may not be the beauty that Lucy Starnes or Dove Anderson or even Rebecca might be, but she was pretty with her blonde hair and fair complexion.

Rob only knew that if he had his way, he'd be asking Rebecca to marry him before the first of the year, but with that young woman, one never knew just where he stood in her affections. For years he'd thought their relationship was secure, but since Rebecca went to college, everything had changed.

Mrs. Haynes stepped through the door, and Rob jumped to help her with her parcels. "That's a heavy load you have there. I'll take these for you." He took two of the bags and fell into step beside her.

"Why, thank you, Rob. How very thoughtful." She walked down to the wagon. "We can put these things in the back here. Mr. Haynes is off on errands, and I have a few more for myself."

"Could you spare me just a moment? I have a few questions for you."

"Of course I can. What would you like to know?"

Rob stammered around a moment before getting his words out. "I–I was wondering what you might know about Geoff Kensington. I can't find out anything about him." His cheeks felt as hot as the coals in a stove on a winter day.

"I do know he and Rebecca have gone for a ride on the trail today, but we only know that he is a cattle buyer from Chicago. Mr. Haynes and Jake Starnes have been talking with him about that. Why? Is there something we should know?"

"Not really. I just have this feeling about him. He's not all he says he is, and I think there's more to his trip down here than he would care to admit at this time." Maybe he should resort to some of the resources he had in other places.

Mellie placed her hands on her hips. She was by no means a short woman, but she still had to peer up at him. "That's a serious statement you've made there. Do you know something you're not telling me?"

"No, ma'am. It's just an observation, and I'm letting my feelings for Becky cloud my judgment." He stepped back. "If you'll excuse me, I'll let you get on with your errands."

He turned and walked away, but Mellie stopped him. "Rob, I have had the same first impression of Geoff Kensington as you have. I don't intend to meddle in my daughter's affairs, but if you can learn more about Geoff Kensington and his business in Barton Creek, I'd appreciate your telling me what you find."

Rob noted the signs of worry in the lines of her face. "I promise you that if I find out anything that would be harmful to Becky, I'll let you know."

"Thank you. That's all I can ask."

He watched her cross the street to Mrs. Weems's shop before heading back to his office. His list of former classmates and a few friends may reveal who would be the best ones to inquire into the background of the man from Chicago.

Chapter 9

*O*n Monday, Geoff made his way to the land office. After Saturday's ride he was curious to find out how much land Ben Haynes and Jake Starnes actually owned, and the boundaries of that land. What he saw on the excursion on Saturday didn't reveal the information he sought.

A smile crossed his lips. Although he failed in one area, he had succeeded quite nicely in the other. Miss Haynes had agreed to have dinner with him, and that pleased him. The more time he spent around the attractive reporter, the more he admired her spirit and enthusiasm. Rob Frankston may have been her friend for many years, but he was much too ordinary for a girl like Rebecca.

She needed a man who would let her be herself. Even if she had rather liberal ideas about women and the right to vote movement, she was a delight to be around, and he'd be dumb not to cultivate her admiration while he was here. He'd already wired his superiors that he'd need more time, even the entire summer to complete the assignment. They had given permission for Geoff to remain in Barton Creek after the cattle sale.

The clerk in the land office greeted him and inquired as to his business. When Geoff explained his mission, the man behind the counter rubbed his chin. "Well, I can show you, but don't think you'll have any chance of buying one bit of that land. Those men have been most protective of it since they acquired it from the farmers."

"I don't plan to buy the land, but I did want to see just how widespread their holdings are. I want to be sure they can deliver the product when we make our deal." If he knew the boundaries, he could ride out and see for himself just what was on that land where no crops would grow.

"I wouldn't worry about them delivering the cattle. They're men of their word. Why, I don't know any men around here who people trust more'n Ben Haynes, Jake Starnes, and Sam Morris."

"I'm sure they are, but I'd still like to see their land holdings."

The clerk pulled out a map and spread it across the counter. "This here's the west boundary. That was Dawson's farm. The North Branch Creek runs through there before it joins up with Barton Creek and comes on to town. Ben says the water ain't no good in some parts."

The part about the water interested Geoff. That's what he wanted to see for himself. He laid a sheet of paper beside the map and began making a crude drawing of what he saw on the map. He made note of landmarks he could use to find his way to what he hoped was there.

Geoff folded his drawing and slipped it into his pocket. "Thank you for your help."

The clerk nodded and turned to other business. Geoff strolled outside to bright sunshine. He made his way to the stables and asked Jonah to saddle up his horse. In a few minutes he set out to investigate for himself what he hadn't been able to see before.

The sun still shone from the eastern sky and hadn't yet reached the steamy temperatures that would come later in the day. He hoped to be finished with his ride and be back in town by early afternoon. He didn't know why, but the heat here seemed to bear down and become much less bearable than the same temperature in Chicago.

A few miles out of town, Geoff pulled out the map. He glanced around at the landscape then checked the drawing. Familiar land-marks let him know he was headed in the right direction. After an hour or so of riding and checking, he recognized the stand of trees that lined the creek on Ben Haynes's property. If he followed the creek, he would find the farmer's land.

The creek flowed well this time of year and had at least two feet of water in most spots. Good spring rains had provided plenty of water. He stopped to let his horse have a drink and had one himself from his water flask, then he wet his kerchief to wipe his forehead. He removed his hat and ran a wet hand through his hair. Movement from the east caught his eye.

He shaded his eyes and pushed his hat back on his head. Two riders approached. As they drew nearer, he saw that one of the riders was Matt Haynes. The other one looked like the cowboy called Hank.

Matt called out to him. "Kensington, what are you doing out here all alone? You should have come up to the house and had one of the men or me come with you."

Geoff squinted up at the young man. "I thought I'd look around for myself. Didn't want to bother you or interrupt your work."

"You wouldn't have been a bother. Besides, there aren't any cattle out here on this range. We could've saved you some time and effort."

Geoff wasn't looking for cattle, but he couldn't tell them that, at least not yet. "I wondered about that. Pretty barren around here."

Hank tipped the brim of his hat. "Yep. This is the land the farmers had and couldn't grow crops. C'mon with us and we'll take you back to the herds." He nodded back the way they'd come.

"Pa will be glad to see you. He was planning to come into town and find you anyway."

Geoff had no choice but to follow. His quest to see what was down the creek would have to wait for another day. At least the day wouldn't be wasted if he visited with Mr. Haynes and moved forward with the cattle sale.

Rebecca read through the list of events for the week. No one had died, so she had no obituaries to write. Today the committee for the July Fourth celebration planned to meet at the town hall. Memories of past celebrations filled her thoughts. So many fun times in the past involved Rob Frankston.

Perhaps Geoff would remain in Barton Creek for the celebration. If she told him about the fun and invited him to attend the festivities with her, he'd have reason to stay around. She grabbed her notebook. First she needed to attend the meeting and find out what the committee planned.

She slipped in the back of the meeting room at the town hall and took a seat. The chairman had just called the meeting to order and now led the group in prayer. Rebecca shook her head at the idea of prayer before they began. The group didn't need God to tell them what to do. They had minds of their own to figure it out.

Finally they got down to business, and each subcommittee made its report. As Rebecca took notes, she bit her tongue to keep from making comments. She could have stayed in the office and written this article. Nothing new had been added to the celebration for the past ten years as far as she could tell.

These people had no imagination at all. She remembered some of the celebrations she'd attended in Boston with her cousins there. Wonderful speeches, parades, bands, and even one reenactment made them much more meaningful. Having ice cream and games and a few speeches by local people grew old after awhile. Even the fireworks lacked the color and excitement of Boston.

Finally she could sit still no longer. She raised her hand and was recognized by the chairman. She stood and let her gaze travel among the committee members. Mrs. Frankston wore a frown that indicated she didn't appreciate the interruption. Rebecca swallowed hard. "The program you are discussing is the same thing we've done as long as I can remember. Why not do something different? Have you considered inviting outside guests to come in as speakers or having a play or skit to depict one of the important events of that time or having a band to play some of the new patriotic music?"

Mrs. Frankston frowned and pursed her lips. The chairman looked at the mayor's wife and cleared his throat. "We've always had this program, and it has worked quite well in the past. Why should we change it?"

Rebecca took a deep breath and chose her words with care. She didn't want to offend anyone. "I understand, but with so many new people coming in, it would be nice to have more variety and something for everyone."

Mrs. Frankston stood and glared at Rebecca. "Now we know you've been away in the city back East, but this is Oklahoma Territory, and we do things a certain way. I've heard about some of your grand ideas about certain things, but we're all quite happy with the way things are."

"Mrs. Frankston and the rest of you, I'm not suggesting you abandon what has been done in the past, but add to it with some of the things I suggested, or even your own ideas. Barton Creek is growing, and our ideas and activities need to grow with it."

Mr. Fleming from the bank nodded and stood. "I see Miss Haynes's point. It may be too late to implement very many new events, but we might consider them for the future." He grinned at Rebecca. "I particularly like the idea of more music. We could advertise and see just how many musicians we have and perhaps come up with a small band."

Mrs. Frankston still glared icicles at Rebecca, but if they liked any of the ideas, that would take away the rejection emitting from the mayor's wife. Other committee members agreed with Mr. Fleming, and a buzz began among them. The chairman called for order.

"Now that we have some ideas flowing, let's have each subcommittee meet and see if you can come up with any new activities. We can meet again on Friday of this week. That will give us time to implement some of them before the Fourth, two weeks from tomorrow." He pounded his gavel. "This meeting is adjourned until Friday at this same time."

Rebecca closed her notebook and headed for her office. The end of the meeting may not have been according to parliamentary rules of order, but at least it got the men and women thinking about what could be done to make things more interesting.

When she stepped outside, a bulletin posted on the community board caught her eye. On closer inspection she saw that it advertised a meeting in Guthrie for women interested in knowing more about the federal government and the rights of women in America today. A suffragette meeting right here in Oklahoma, and it would be on Thursday evening!

Rebecca's nerves tingled with excitement. Not only did she want to attend the meeting, but she also wanted to write about it and prove to Mr. Lansdowne that she was a good reporter. She certainly didn't plan to write death notices and society tidbits the rest of her career.

Once back at her desk, she typed up the notes she'd taken at the meeting. Anything from the coming Friday meeting would have to wait until the next week, and she didn't intend to miss that gathering to see what ideas had been born, if any.

When finished, she leaned back in her chair and considered the flyer she had read earlier. The trip to Guthrie would be in the evening, which meant an escort would be needed. Normally she would attend meetings like this alone or with a friend also interested in the movement, but common sense reminded her that no trip to Guthrie at night would be safe for a woman alone, no matter how independent she might be. Rebecca bit her lip as she contemplated whom she could ask to escort her.

The bell over the door jangled, and Rob Frankston walked in. He grinned at Rebecca and removed his hat. "I was hoping to catch you here and ask if you'd take time to have lunch with me."

The solution to her dilemma stood in front of her—that is, if he would even consider going to such an event. Maybe he'd be more receptive to the idea on a full stomach. "I'd be delighted, Rob." She reached for her hat and pinned it to the curls atop her head.

Rob's spirits soared at her answer. Finally an opportunity to have time with her presented itself, and he would make the most of it. "Will Dinah's be all right, or do you prefer the hotel?"

She stepped through the gate and grinned up at him. "Dinah's will be fine."

He tucked her hand under his arm and walked with her out the door. She breathed deeply then exhaled. "The day is beautiful, don't you agree?"

At the moment he'd agree if she said the sun was purple. Everything about her was so alive and vibrant. The pale yellow blouse she wore accented her greenish eyes and brown hair. She'd been pretty as a young girl, but now she was beautiful like her cousin Lucy.

In Dinah's they sat at a table by the window. Rebecca gazed out to the streets. "Barton Creek has grown so much. So many more buildings around town, and when I went into Anderson's the other day, he had more customers than I ever remember."

"Yes, Father is quite proud of how we've grown while he's been mayor. He's planning to aim for a higher political position when we finally obtain statehood." Then the law firm would be his completely and have enough business to support a wife and family. But he didn't dare mention that to Rebecca.

"I'm not surprised. I do hope Oklahoma will give women the right to vote so that we can have a say in those elections."

Rob swallowed the retort that had almost escaped his lips. He didn't want to ruin his precious time with her by squabbling about something so trivial as women voting. Although, as he considered the young lady across the table, he had to admit that women like Rebecca would make very intelligent choices. She was one who always thought through every decision she made. She may appear impulsive to others, but he knew from experience how quick-thinking she was.

She leaned forward. "That brings me to something I would like to ask of you. A speaker will be in Guthrie on Thursday night talking about women's suffrage, and I need an escort. Would you accompany me?"

His heart skipped a beat, and the palms of his hands dampened with perspiration. At least an hour to Guthrie and an hour back plus the meeting would mean a sizable amount of time with her. No matter what the subject of the talk might be, if he sat beside Rebecca, he didn't care. "I'd be honored to go with you. What time will it be?"

"The speech begins at seven, I believe, so we'd need to leave by six at the latest."

A plan took root and spread its tendrils through his heart. "If we could leave at five or even a little before, we could have dinner in Guthrie and be on time. I could borrow Father's carriage."

A smile lit her face, and she almost bounced in her chair. "That would be delightful. I can plan to leave a few minutes early from the newspaper. Too bad the trains don't run in the evening, or we could have a train ride there and back."

That fact didn't bother Rob at all. Sitting on a train with soot blowing in to soil his clothes and the wheels making enough noise to hinder conversation did not lend the most ideal of conditions for having Rebecca alone. The fact that they would travel alone may raise a few questions, but Becky wouldn't have agreed if that were to pose a problem.

At that moment Geoff Kensington stopped at the table. "How nice to see you, Miss Haynes, and you too, Rob." His eyes held a haughty expression as if to put Rob in his place.

Rob refused to let someone from the city disparage him and deemed a nod to be the only response needed for such a greeting. However, Rebecca smiled up at him with a twinkle in her eye that caused green tentacles of jealousy to curl like a vine around his heart.

"Oh, Mr. Kensington, I didn't expect to see you here."

Rob hadn't either. Mr. Kensington could just as well have eaten at the hotel. Or perhaps he'd seen them come into Dinah's and decided to join them. Either way, he wished the man would be on his way. The way Geoff looked at Rebecca as though she were a prime side of beef heated his blood and sent it to his face. The smirk on Geoff's face indicated he was fully aware of his effect on Rob.

He breathed deeply to control his tongue just as Dinah set their meal on the table. Now the man would have to leave.

Geoff bowed toward Rebecca. "I'll leave you to your meal, but I did want to ask if you plan to go to the women's meeting in Guthrie, and if so, if I might escort you."

Now the heat rose in Rebecca's cheeks and tinted them red. "I do plan to go, but Rob has offered to escort me. Perhaps some other time."

"I see. Well, that's my loss. I should have asked you sooner." He bowed again. "Enjoy your meal." He backed up and hurried away to another table.

Rob stifled his chuckle. He had one up on the city slicker, and somehow he would make Rebecca forget all about the man from Chicago, no matter what it might take.

Chapter 10

*O*n Thursday afternoon, shortly before five, Rebecca checked her reflection in the looking glass Mr. Lansdowne had installed on the wall of the bathroom for her and Molly. She pinned stray tendrils that had escaped the mass of curls at her neck back into place, then pinched her cheeks to give them a rosy hue.

If she hadn't been so quick to think of Rob as the one to go with her tonight, she could be waiting for Geoff Kensington to escort her to the suffragette meeting. Although he scoffed at her comments concerning the rights of women, he was by far the most interesting man she knew in Barton Creek.

Still, an evening with Rob couldn't be considered a waste. With him she always relaxed and said whatever was on her mind. He knew her too well for her to be putting on airs and trying to be the sophisticated young lady that she displayed for Geoff. To be truthful, she didn't even mind when Rob called her Becky.

With a sigh and one last look in the mirror, she hurried out to her desk to retrieve her purse and her hat. Another flyer describing the meeting tonight lay next to her typewriter, and she picked it up to read it again. She had never heard of the woman speaking, but the flyer said she was a member of the National American Woman Suffrage Association, and Rebecca longed to be more active in the group she had joined as a senior at Wellesley. Perhaps she would learn more about what she could do at the meeting tonight.

Mr. Lansdowne had finished the paper that now awaited

delivery in the morning, and the printer was quiet. He walked out from his office and grinned at Rebecca. "I see you're ready to go. Which one do you have as an escort this evening?"

Heat rose in Rebecca's cheeks. "Rob Frankston is taking me over to hear a speech in Guthrie. We plan to have dinner first. That is why I'm leaving a few minutes early." If she told him the true reason for going to Guthrie, Mr. Lansdowne might laugh at her and never let her write an article.

"Interesting. The only speech I know of in Guthrie tonight is by that woman who promotes women's suffrage. Is that where you're going?"

Put like that, she couldn't possibly ignore the question. "Yes, I just thought I'd go over and see what she has to say."

"Hmm, and Rob Frankston is escorting you?"

At Rebecca's nod, Mr. Lansdowne chuckled and turned back to his office. Although he kept his voice low, she still heard his comment. "I wonder if that boy knows what he's getting himself into tonight." Then he chuckled again and closed his office door.

She wanted to stamp her foot and give her editor a piece of her mind, but she stopped the words from erupting from her mouth. She'd show him by writing a story he couldn't turn down.

Molly had kept her head down and her mouth closed during the exchange, but now she glanced up at Rebecca. Her blue eyes sparkled with interest. "I think I would like to hear a speech like that sometime, but Ma and Pa would never allow it. Please take good notes and tell me everything about the meeting tomorrow."

Rebecca nodded and headed for the door. "I'll do more than that, Molly. Just wait until I write my story. Good evening."

Molly's squeal of delight followed Rebecca through the door. She had no more than stepped out to the boardwalk than Rob appeared at her elbow.

He doffed his hat and grinned. "All ready to go, I see." He

offered her his arm. "The carriage is ready at the livery, and I've wired ahead for reservations for us."

She grasped his arm as they made their way to the livery stable. Jonah had rebuilt his business so that he had compartments for all citizens who wished to store their vehicles and horses in his establishment since only the larger and newer homes in town had carriage houses. He had hired several young men who kept the stalls clean.

Once they were in the carriage and headed out of town, Rebecca allowed her enthusiasm to gush forth. "I'm so glad you agreed to accompany me tonight. I thought this evening would never come, even though getting the paper ready to deliver tomorrow kept us quite busy today."

"I'm pleased to do it, Rebecca. We've had so little time together since your return."

"Yes, that's true, and I fear it is my fault. Having a career does keep one busy." Guilt inched its way into her heart. She'd had plenty of time for Geoff Kensington, but not for her longtime friend. Of course, at one time Rob had been more than just a friend, and that's what kept her from spending more time with him now. She wasn't ready for that path.

"Yes, I suppose it does. It's surprising how many people have need of a lawyer's service these days. Father has very little time to devote to our practice with his mayoral duties, so all the clients expect me to handle their affairs."

"And that's good for you, of course." She twirled a parasol over her shoulder to ward off the rays of the late afternoon sun. Once she would have relished letting the sun beam on her face, but now she protected it as often as possible. She may like to ride the open range, but she didn't intend for her complexion to age and wrinkle like so many of the ranchers' and farmers' wives did. Sometimes she wished she had skin like Dove's. Her Indian heritage lent just enough color to her features to give Dove a smooth, tanned appearance all year round. Creamy, pale complexions may appeal to many, but Rebecca envied the soft light brown of Dove's skin.

"Now what would have you in such deep thought, Miss Haynes?" Rob turned to stare at her with a twinkle in his eye.

"Oh, I was just thinking about all the changes since we were in school. We have telephone service, and most places have water running directly into their homes. I'll be glad when electricity comes to town. So many more conveniences come with it."

"Yes, God has certainly been good to Barton Creek. We don't have the crime that Guthrie and Oklahoma City seem to have, and our people are friendly and care about one another."

"What does God have to do with it? I seem to remember when our town wasn't like that."

Indeed, it had been his mother and Mrs. Anderson who had stirred up feelings of prejudice and animosity when Jake was in trouble, and when Luke fell in love with Dove, and the Fowler family had caused all kinds of trouble. God had made a mess of those situations.

"No, Barton Creek hasn't always been the ideal place, but look how we've grown. God has sent just the right people to help make us what we are."

"Oh, you mean God let Ruth's husband die so she could come out here and live with her parents with three small children to mother? That's not a loving God to me. I remember the preacher always telling us how much God loves us and watches over us, but from what I've seen the past few years, that's not exactly true." Her hands clamped hard around the handle of her parasol.

Rob said nothing. He had to figure out a way to make her see how God had taken care of everyone through all the bad times. When they finally arrived in Guthrie, she bounced on the seat beside him.

"Look at all these buildings and people. It's as busy as cities I saw back East."

Rob had to admit it appeared that over half the population crowded the streets and walkways in this town. Conversation, the clomp of shoes on the sidewalks, the creak of wagon wheels, and the whir of carriages spinning down the street all added to a cacophony accented by loud music blaring forth from a building that looked like it might house a saloon. He noted each street until he found the one he wanted by the restaurant, being careful not to nudge another carriage in his haste to find the place they were to eat.

One of those new horseless carriages called a motor car chugged its way down the street. Horses shied away from the noise as the driver honked his horn. Rob fought to control the reins. "I didn't realize they had those new cars in Guthrie."

Rebecca shook her head. "I didn't either, and it's amazing how much bigger Guthrie is now than when it sprang up during the land rush. With this many people, there should be a wonderful crowd for the meeting tonight."

He found a spot where he could hitch the horses then alit to help Rebecca down from the carriage. They entered the restaurant, where they were seated almost immediately. He sat and watched Rebecca as she gazed around at the Victorian setting. The clink of crystal and silverware added to the atmosphere, along with the low hum of voices in conversation.

"This is as nice as any place in Boston. Thank you for thinking of it."

Rob swallowed hard. Rebecca had no idea how beautiful she looked with white lace about her throat and the whimsical blue hat atop her head. Set at a jaunty angle, the white feathers swished as she moved her head while talking.

All too soon the dinner ended, and they made their way to the hall where the meeting would be held. Rob quickly made note of the fact that very few men accompanied women. The high-pitched chatter of the women all around him continued as he and Rebecca found their seats. Her eyes danced with excitement, and she extracted a pencil and pad from her purse.

"Taking notes for the paper?" No matter what she wrote, he could bet that convincing Mr. Lansdowne to print it would be more difficult than any case he argued in court.

"Yes, and I'm thrilled at the turnout here tonight. This is amazing. We saw crowds like this back East, but I never expected it here tonight, especially after the suffrage bill was defeated in 1899. But we've come a long way since then, and I'm sure Carrie Chapman Catt would be pleased."

Rob wouldn't know about that, but if this is what Rebecca wanted, he'd have to learn more than he knew now.

At that moment a woman rose and came to the podium. All voices quieted and waited for Katherine Newsome to speak. Rebecca listened closely to Miss Newsome's words.

"Suffrage is extremely important for all women. It will give us full rights of citizenship in that we will have a voice in the election of our candidates for national as well as state leadership. Suffrage will also give all women access to better educational opportunities and allow us to pursue careers once open only to men. Not only that, it will afford better working conditions for those women who must work to provide for their families."

Rebecca's head bobbed in agreement with the words from the stage, but, despite his resolve to listen, Rob only half heard the speaker as he admired the woman beside him. Women had been fighting over voting rights for more than fifty years. Some states that had endorsed and allowed it had reversed their policies even while others embraced it. Now the suffragettes wanted every state and territory to allow women the right to have a say in who ran the government.

Rob could see no problem with the right of women to vote. After all, they were citizens and affected by government rulings just as men were, and Rebecca herself had convinced him that women were intelligent enough to vote wisely. He just didn't see how women in predominantly male vocations could be successful. Homes were an important part of society, and a woman should spend time in overseeing the happenings of her family. Taking care of a husband and children seemed to him to be the most important job a woman could have. Of course, some women had to work, like Mrs. Weems and her daughter, but they had their own business.

He remembered some of the things he'd read about while studying law. Some companies and factories in the north and east didn't always provide the best working conditions for their employees, some of them women, and the suffrage movement also aimed to improve those conditions. He was very much in favor of that part of the movement.

When the speaker mentioned the fact that within a few years Oklahoma would be a state and women deserved a voice in who would represent the people, women all over the room cheered and clapped. Rob observed that the men appeared uncomfortable, as though they didn't want to be seen there. Their wives probably dragged them against their will.

The woman ended her speech to a standing ovation. Rebecca

bounced on the balls of her feet and clapped loudly. She glanced over at Rob, who had stood also. "Isn't she the most marvelous speaker?"

"Um, yes, she is." He nodded then leaned over to whisper, "I think there is a soda fountain nearby where we can pick up some ice cream."

Her hazel eyes still sparkled with excitement. "Later. I want to try to meet the speaker and see what other suggestions she might have for me to use in Barton Creek."

Before he had a chance to respond, she pushed her way through the women standing in the aisles and approached Miss Newsome. With the advantage of his height, he saw the speaker smile and nod her head at something Becky said. He stood waiting, then sat down as the auditorium emptied. Becky might be awhile.

Finally he pulled out his pocket watch and gasped. They must leave quickly if they wanted to get ice cream and return to Barton Creek before Mrs. Claymore's curfew. That was one lady he didn't care to cross by getting Rebecca home late.

He started down the aisle toward her, but she waved good-bye to the speaker and headed toward him. "I'm sorry, but she was just so interesting, and she gave me some good ideas on getting the women in Barton Creek involved. Do we still have time to get that ice cream before we go home?"

"Just barely, unless you want to ring the bell and have Mrs. Claymore come down to open the door for you." He figured they had about fifteen minutes to spare.

He purchased the treat for her then led her back to the carriage. Once settled, he turned the horses toward Barton Creek.

Becky finished her ice cream and wiped her hands on a paper napkin. "Rob, what did you really think about tonight's speech?"

"Very interesting. Personally I have no objections to women voting in our elections. I also understand the need for improving working conditions for women in factories across the country. What I can't understand is why women would want to leave the security of a home and family to work. Being the wife of the mayor is a full-time job for my mother."

"But for some women, staying home is a waste of talent. Of course, some have no choice and must work to help their husband with their income and expenses."

"And if there is no need for an additional income?" He couldn't imagine letting his wife work and leaving the children with a nanny.

"Then she should pursue what interests her the most. If that interest is in her family, then that is her choice. But don't you see? Women should have that choice."

Her argument held logic, and he understood her passion for women's rights. Still he found it hard to accept a woman working if she had a man to provide for her.

He rather enjoyed discussing such things with Rebecca, but he still thought of her as the young Becky he knew from childhood. She was intelligent and sincere in her desires to further the cause of women, but she was still Becky and always would be. Even if she rebelled, he could only think of her and call her by that name.

The only thing to mar the evening and cause a nub of worry to cross his heart was the fact that Becky seemed to have hidden away her deep spiritual beliefs from her younger days. As he watched her in the moonlight, he could see that former self deep inside her, but for some reason she repressed it. His greatest desire at the moment was to find that Becky and bring her back.

Chapter 11

*M*ellie sealed the letter she had just finished and put it aside to mail when she went into town. At the moment she had a more important mission. Much as she wanted to respect the privacy of her daughter, she was concerned about Becky. A visit with Lucy might shed some light on Becky's behavior these few weeks past, since Becky was more likely to confide in her cousin than her mother at this stage in her life.

After removing her apron, Mellie found her purse and headed out to the barn. Ben had hitched up the wagon before he left when she had expressed her desire to visit with Lucy. Thankful for the few clouds in the sky, Mellie donned a bonnet then climbed up to the wagon seat.

Half an hour later she drove up into Lucy and Jake's yard. She took a moment to admire the two-story brick-and-stone house Jake had built. The porch wrapped around three sides and supported a roof from which three dormer windows projected to indicate the three bedrooms upstairs. Baskets and pots of bright red geraniums lined the porch, and a bed of multicolored zinnias filled a flower bed below the porch railings.

Lucy opened the door and stepped out on the porch, holding baby Amanda in her arms. "Good morning. I'm glad to see you, but what brings you out this way?"

Mellie alit from the wagon and tied the reins around the post by the walk leading to the house. "I wanted a visit to see my great niece and nephews, but I also wanted a visit with you."

Lucy held the door open. "Wonderful. I have lemonade in the ice box and cookies I baked yesterday."

Mellie grinned and remembered the time when Lucy had more problems with cooking than a rabbit had babies. Since then she'd become one of the best cooks in Barton Creek. "That sounds like a winning combination." She stretched out her arms for Amanda, and the little girl giggled and fell into them.

"I'm so glad you named her for your mother. I do believe she looks like her already. Her hair and eyes remind me of Amanda. With you and Jake as parents, she can't help but be a real beauty as she grows up."

Color filled Lucy's face as she poured lemonade into glasses. "If she does, I hope the beauty isn't in her face alone. I pray she has the beauty inside that I saw in Mama and in you when I came to Oklahoma."

"I'm sure she will." Mellie glanced around. "Where are the boys? They're usually anywhere they think there might be food."

Lucy's laughter still rang out like music, as pretty as she was. "Jake took them out with him this morning. They were only going to be riding around the range to see where the cattle are grazing. He'll be back at noon with them, and those boys will be ready to eat whatever is on the table. And I hope they'll also be ready for a nap."

Mellie grinned and nodded as she clapped Amanda's hands together, and the child giggled again. "You have a wonderful family, Lucy. I'm so proud of you and Jake."

Lucy sat down across from Mellie and handed Amanda a sugar cookie. "Now that's out of the way, do you want to tell me the real reason for your visit?"

Heat rose in Mellie's face. She hadn't intended for her concern to be so obvious, but Lucy had always been the astute one. "It's Becky." She held up her hand as Lucy's mouth opened. "I know, I know. She wants to be called Rebecca, but she's still my Becky. Anyway, Catherine Claymore tells me she went out riding last Saturday with that Geoff Kensington. And that last night Rob took her to a women's suffrage meeting in Guthrie."

Lucy sipped her lemonade then leaned over to wipe crumbs from Amanda's face. "Those two must keep her really busy," she laughed.

"I'm glad she hasn't completely abandoned Rob. He's a good influence for her." She had visions of planning their wedding when Becky returned, but those dreams were on hold for who knew how long now. If only there were a way to find out more about Geoff Kensington, she would feel much better about his relationship with her daughter. "Still, I can't imagine why he would take her to a speech on women's suffrage."

"I admit Rebecca has some modern ideas about women and their role in life. I've been thinking about it, and the Bible does tell us that a woman is to be a helpmate for her husband. Perhaps that means that a woman should also have a say in what happens in the country that will have an effect on her way of life, but it does sound rather radical."

Mellie bit her lip and hugged Amanda to her chest. "I'm not nearly as worried about her work with the women's suffrage movement as I am about her spiritual condition. She seems bored in church, doesn't want to attend the young people's Sunday school anymore, and gets evasive whenever I try to talk to her about God."

Lucy rolled her glass between her palms and tilted her head. "I know what you mean. She said some things that concerned me, and I've been praying for her."

Amanda reached out toward her mother, and Mellie handed the

child to Lucy. "I think she'd listen to you and Dove if you talked to her and found out what's really going on in that head of hers as far as her faith is concerned."

Lucy snuggled her daughter then handed her part of a cookie. "I could ask Dove to go with me to see Rebecca. We could invite her to have lunch with us. Maybe the two of us can guide Rebecca back to the roots of her faith."

"I would feel so much better if you did that. I don't want to be a prying, controlling mother, but I do love my daughter and don't want to see her trod a path that will only lead to sorrow and pain."

Lucy tapped her chin. "If you can come and watch the children for me on Tuesday, I will go into town and see if Dove and I can entice her to have lunch with us."

"You know I'll come to stay with your little ones anytime you ask. It's as though they are my grandchildren since neither of you have parents to be here to love on them." Mellie had thought of Lucy more like her daughter than a niece ever since Amanda and Charles had been killed and Lucy had come to live on the Hayneses' ranch.

Lucy said nothing for a moment, and Mellie reached over to grasp her niece's hand. "I know, I still miss them too." Then she pushed back from the table. "It's time for me to go home and take care of my men, and I know you have chores to do as well." Mellie gathered up her bonnet and headed for the door with Lucy following her.

"I'll be here before eleven on Tuesday to give you plenty of time to drive into town for your visit with Becky." She stopped on the porch and turned to hug Lucy. "I knew I could count on you to do something to help ease my mind."

A few minutes later she guided her wagon and team on the road home.

Rebecca walked beside Geoff to the boarding house. He had met her as she left the newspaper office and offered to escort her home. This was the first time she'd had an opportunity to be alone with him since their ride last Saturday. He hadn't even been in town over the weekend. "You seem to be keeping busy. I've barely seen you this past week."

"Yes, I've had business on other ranches around the area. Oklahoma City is growing and offering many opportunities for business. Just five years ago it had a population of around twenty-five thousand, and now it's more than double that. Hard to believe that many people have come out here to live."

"It's funny that I've never visited any cities or towns here but Guthrie, and yet I've been to Boston and towns around that area as well as Providence, Rhode Island, and of course the area around Wellesley. My aunt and uncle even took me to New York City one time. It's time for me to see more of Oklahoma."

"And I'd be happy to escort you. We could take the train down to Oklahoma City and have dinner or go early in the day and see the sights there and return by evening."

The idea of going on a trip with Geoff, albeit a short one, sent shivers of excitement through Rebecca. Such a great opportunity to get to know him better as well as see more of the area. "That sounds like a splendid idea."

"Then let's set aside time next Saturday for our excursion."

"I look forward to it. I'm so glad the train to Oklahoma leaves early in the day." A carriage or wagon ride as far as this one would be didn't appeal to Rebecca at all. Even with Rob, the short trip to Guthrie had become quite uncomfortable by the time they neared home.

"Which reminds me. How was the meeting in Guthrie?" He grasped her hand resting on his forearm and squeezed it.

Heat rose in her face at the gesture. Such a simple question accompanied by the intimacy of his hand on hers sent her thoughts flying around her head like bees in a flower garden. She swallowed hard and said, "It was quite interesting. The speaker was excellent and made some very good points about women and their right to vote. She also pointed out all the opportunities suffrage would bring for women. I can only hope that Oklahoma will see the light and allow women their rights when we become a state."

The paper sitting in her desk drawer at the newspaper office sent tendrils of anger coursing through her heart. Mr. Lansdowne wouldn't even look at it, much less think of putting it in the paper. She pressed her lips together to keep from saying words she might regret later.

Geoff chuckled and glanced at her. "That look tells me something is bothering you. Is there anything I can do?"

"Not really. Mr. Lansdowne won't print an article I wrote about the meeting. He thinks the whole idea of women voting is ridiculous." The more she thought about it, the angrier she became. "It's not like we want to rule the country; we just want to have a voice in what goes on in it. If we have a government for the people and by the people, it should be for *all* the people and not just the males. I wish I could get more women here in Barton Creek to feel that way."

"Have you tried organizing a meeting and perhaps having a speaker come here?"

"No, I haven't, because I can't get even one woman to listen to what I have to say. I thought Ruth Dorsett would, but she says she's too busy taking care of her children and helping her mother to worry about who gets elected to what. I hope President Roosevelt will be more receptive to the ideas of NAWSA." He'd only been in office a few months since the election, but he had the experience since he'd taken over after McKinley's assassination. She still wasn't quite sure of his views yet, but he must be good as he'd won with more votes than any other president since Monroe.

"Tell me what NAWSA is again."

"It's the National American Woman Suffrage Association. To think that women had the right to vote when our country was founded and then those rights were taken away slowly but surely. Mark my words, someday our Constitution will give us back those rights." It may not be in the next few years, but it would happen in her lifetime.

"Now that wouldn't surprise me a bit if the ladies in the movement have your enthusiasm and spark towards suffrage."

"And you wouldn't be against it?"

"Of course not. Our own government advocates equality for all, and I'm sure that was meant to include women."

His smile melted her heart like ice left in the heat. Here was a man who understood her feelings and believed in them. He probably wouldn't object to her having a career either if she were his wife. Her head jerked. Where had that thought come from? Still, if she did decide to marry, Geoff might make a wonderful husband.

His hand over hers grew warm, and she was grateful they had reached the boarding house. A few more minutes and she'd be imagining more than marriage to Mr. Kensington.

He doffed his hat and bowed. "Thank you for a lovely walk. Perhaps we can have dinner again soon to discuss our trip for next Saturday."

"Yes, of course. That would be lovely."

He bowed slightly then walked away. Rebecca entered the house, and immediately the aroma of pot roast and apple pie accosted her senses. The smell led her to the dining room, where Mrs. Claymore had set the table.

The landlady glanced at Rebecca and grinned. "Judging by that smile on your face, I would say you have had a very good day."

"Yes, I did, and it's all because of Geoff Kensington." He had listened to her and not made fun. The more she was with him, the more she realized she could easily fall in love with him.

Mrs. Claymore laughed. "Well, I say whatever put that bloom in your cheek scores one in my book. It makes my heart glad to see you happy."

"Thank you, Mrs. Claymore. I do believe he will make me very happy." Rob Frankston wouldn't like it, but then he had no say whatsoever in how she conducted her life. He was too old-fashioned for a modern girl like her. She headed upstairs to freshen up before dinner with visions of her trip with Geoff next Saturday dancing in her head.

Chapter 12

*T*he bell over the door to the news office jangled, and Rebecca glanced up from her work. Dove and Lucy entered and smiled at her. "Good morning, you two. What brings you over here?"

Lucy shrugged her shoulders and grinned. "It's been awhile since we had a visit, so Dove and I decided to see if you'd have lunch with us."

Rebecca looked down at the watch pinned to her blouse. "Oh my, where has the morning gone? No wonder my stomach rumbled a few minutes ago." She opened a drawer and extracted her needlepoint handbag. "Molly, I'll be back shortly. When your father returns, tell him— Oh, never mind, I'll speak with him myself later."

She settled her white straw hat on her curls then stepped through the gate to join her friends. "I'm so glad to see you both. I haven't had time to really catch up on the news from home or town except what I read in the paper."

Dove and Lucy both laughed at the little joke. Then Dove said, "I understand you made quite a speech at the committee meeting for the Independence Day celebration. Mrs. Fleming and Mrs. Anderson could talk of nothing else last week."

They walked out of the offices together into the stifling heat of a June afternoon. Rebecca fanned her face. "I'm glad we're not going far. I don't like it so hot. As for the committee, I just thought it was time for something different, but when they met again last Friday, it was the same old stuff." She let her breath out in a whoosh. "I don't think this town will ever change. Granted they did form a band and the park is prettier than it was eight years ago, but it seems they could at least have had a speaker from Guthrie or Oklahoma City or one of our representatives. Don't you all get tired of hearing Mayor Frankston every year?"

Lucy nodded then waved at Ruth Dorsett when they reached Mrs. Weems's shop. "He is the mayor after all. Mr. Fleming is going to say a few words, and I understand Alice is to sing."

"That's right, but they'll have ice cream and baked goods just like always." Rebecca shook her head. "That committee couldn't come up with an original idea if it bit their noses."

Dove covered her mouth with her fingers to stifle her laugh. "Rebecca Haynes, you do have a way with words. Anyway, I'm glad they're still having the activities for the children. I can enjoy the other events knowing that Danny and Eddie have someplace to play. Danny's been talking about what he and Micah will do for days."

Lucy stopped and glanced back at the dress shop. "You all go on in and get a table. I'm going to see if Ruth will join us. I've wanted to get to know her better, and this would be a good time for all of us." She turned and headed toward the dress shop.

Rebecca and Dove stepped into Dinah's and were led to a table near the window. Rebecca smiled at the young woman seating them. "Thank you, Elena. Lucy and Ruth will be joining us."

She had no need to look at the menu, as she already knew it from the times she'd come before. Dinah herself came out of the kitchen and headed for their table. She wiped her hands on her apron.

"How good to see you, Miss Haynes and Mrs. Anderson. Our pot roast is especially good today, but we do have a new menu for lunches now. We've added a few sandwiches and some salads for the hottest part of the day." She handed Rebecca a menu. "These are our new selections for lunch."

Rebecca eyed the list before her. "Now that sounds like a wonderful idea. I'll have one of the sandwiches." She glanced at the menu and realized Dinah had added several items to the back page as well. "I've changed my mind. The chicken salad sounds good, and I'll have a glass of sweet tea with it."

Lucy and Ruth joined them, and all four women ended up with the same order. Rebecca giggled. "Well, that will make it easy on our serving girl." She smiled at Ruth. "It's nice that you could join us. How are your children?"

"They're adjusting well. Mama and Papa dote on the twins and make them feel so loved that the loss of their father is beginning to fade. Not that I want them to forget him, but I want them to have a happy childhood." She glanced over at Dove. "And Billy loves playing with Danny."

Dove laughed. "Those two boys are a handful, and they will be even more so when we add Charley and Micah to the mix in July."

Rebecca grasped Ruth's hand. "It's wonderful that you and the children are making friends."

Dove and Lucy exchanged glances, and Rebecca narrowed her eyes. Those two were up to something. They didn't just happen to decide to ask her to eat with them. But having Ruth there puzzled her. If Dove and Lucy wanted to ask questions, they would not have invited Ruth.

No time to think about such things now. Elena brought their tea and a basket of muffins.

A few minutes later, Elena served their lunch, and Rebecca welcomed the plate set before her. She started to pick up her fork, but Lucy intervened by grasping her hand.

"Let's say grace, ladies." She bowed her head and said a brief prayer of thanksgiving for the meal before them.

Heat rose in Rebecca's cheeks. She had dropped the habit of praying before meals and usually arrived at the boarding house table just after it had been said. God knew she was thankful, so she didn't have to tell Him all the time.

Lucy arranged her napkin on her lap and leaned toward Ruth. "So tell me, how do you like our church?"

The young woman clasped her hands on the edge of the table. "I like it a lot. Reverend Daly preaches such good sermons. In the months after Henry's death, our pastor was a great comfort to me. Without the Lord, I don't know how I would have made it through those dark days."

Rebecca gazed at Ruth. "You are a strong woman, and you had great strength to get through your husband's death and great courage to pick up and come here with such young children."

Ruth blinked then bowed her head. Rebecca barely heard her answer. "My strength comes from my faith." Then she raised her eyes and looked squarely at Rebecca. "Without God, we are nothing. Without Him, I would never have had the courage to come this far alone with three small children."

Rebecca shrugged. Another woman depending on something other than herself to make changes in her life. "Whatever you believe for yourself is fine, but I'd rather be independent and know that if no one else is around, I can depend on my own strength to do what needs to be done."

Dove and Lucy exchanged glances again then looked down at their plates. Rebecca's eyes narrowed. "All right, ladies, tell me the truth. Ma sent you into town to check up on me, didn't she?"

Lucy's eyes opened wide. "Well, she was concerned because you seemed bored in church and haven't come to Sunday school."

"Ma worries too much. You can tell her I'm fine, and I'll be in

Sunday school next time if it will make her happy." She picked up the basket of muffins. "Would anyone care for a muffin to go with their salad?"

For the rest of the lunch, Rebecca was careful to steer the conversation away from herself. No matter what her mother may think or want her to do, Rebecca refused to give up her independence.

Rob started across to the news office to see Rebecca but stopped when she walked out with Lucy and Dove. They must be planning an all-female lunch hour. He shrugged and turned toward home. A home-cooked meal had more appeal now.

Someone tapped his shoulder. He turned to find Geoff Kensington behind him. "Hello, Kensington. What can I do for you?"

"Oh, I just wanted a chance to speak with you."

"And what business would you have with me?" Distrust for the man again filled Rob. Nothing Geoff had done warranted such suspicion, but Rob considered himself a fairly good judge of people, and his instincts told him to beware.

"Would you care to join me for lunch at the hotel? On me. I can tell you more about my business then."

Rob hesitated then decided that anything more he could learn about Geoff would be to his advantage. "Yes, thank you, I would like that."

He followed Geoff into the dining room of the hotel, where the hostess seated them. Rob glanced at the menu then ordered a steak with potatoes.

Geoff chuckled. "Can't live in a cattle ranching town without eating your beef, can you? Ever tried lamb? They prepare it to perfection here to my great surprise."

"I've had lamb, but it doesn't appeal to my tastes." He closed the menu and leaned back in his chair. "Now what is the business you want to discuss?"

Again Geoff chuckled. "Not one to waste time, are you?"

After the serving girl took their order, Geoff placed his forearms on the table and leaned toward Rob. "I need a lawyer to represent my interests here in Barton Creek."

"What?" That was the last thing Rob expected to hear from Geoff. He recovered from the shock and asked, "What interests might those be?"

"I'm here to purchase cattle from Ben Haynes and Sam Morris, and I'm interested in perhaps purchasing a horse from Jake Starnes. I plan to be in Barton Creek longer than I first expected and would like to have my own mount."

"I remember your purpose for being here. You do know that our firm represents all three of those men in business as well as their personal affairs."

"I assumed so since yours is the only law firm in town, but I figured your father represented them and you could represent me."

Rob narrowed his eyes. His distrust of Geoff grew even stronger. "I'm handling most of the affairs of those men now. Since I've joined the firm with Father, he has spent more time with his mayoral duties, so I cannot represent both sides." Geoff was smart enough to know that already, so there was no reason to even discuss it.

"I see. Then I must look to Guthrie or Oklahoma City for an attorney."

"Yes, you will." Rob wished he could pull away the veil over Kensington's eyes. The man was completely bland and revealed nothing of himself.

"Speaking of Guthrie, how was your trek over there last week?"

Rob held back the smile that wanted to grace his lips. So now Geoff finally got to what he really wanted to know. He debated whether to embellish his story with glowing accounts of his time with Becky or to stick with the facts. Actually the trip was none of Geoff's business, but Rob restrained a rude reply.

"It was an interesting speech, I must say. The suffragette women have some strong arguments. To hear Rebecca talk, women will soon be voting for the president himself."

This brought a derisive laugh from Geoff. "Surely you don't believe in all that folderol. It's just a bunch of females sounding off because they can't have their way."

If he talked like that to Becky, she'd send him packing right away. That might be one way to get her out of his clutches. "Maybe so, but they do have some good ideas. Of course I tried to reason with Becky, but she is one stubborn woman."

"Wouldn't it be better to just go along with her and say you support the cause? Seems to me that would sway her opinion in your favor."

Now what was he up to? "You have a point, but Becky and I have known each other since childhood, and she'd see through anything I might tell her if it isn't the complete truth."

The waitress brought their food, and the next few minutes were spent paying attention to the meal. Rob bowed his head for a quick blessing but noticed that Geoff picked up his fork and began eating immediately. Another reason to keep him away from Becky. With her faith on shaky ground, she needed someone to guide her back to it.

Geoff swallowed a piece of meat then said, "I might look into law firms in Oklahoma City on Saturday. Rebecca and I are planning an excursion to that city on the Saturday morning train."

The piece of beef in Rob's mouth grew larger and threatened to choke him. He clenched his hand around his fork to keep from punching the man in the nose. So that was the reason for this lunch. Becky couldn't be planning to go on such a trip with Geoff.

It wasn't like her at all, but then he didn't really know what the new Rebecca might be willing to do. He swallowed the offensive piece of beef and sipped his water to help it down. "I see. With all the changes and growth there, that should be an interesting day."

"Yes, I expect it will be. We'll return on the evening train from there. Rebecca is excited to be going. She told me she hasn't traveled much in Oklahoma, so this will be a treat for her."

Why couldn't the man quit talking? Rob didn't want to hear anything else about the trip, but if he let his jealousy be too evident, Geoff would not leave it alone. A glance at his pocket watch reminded him he had a business to take care of. "Thank you for the lunch, Kensington, but I must return to my office. I have a client coming in soon, and I want to be prepared for him."

"Of course. I understand." He stood as Rob headed for the exit. If he didn't leave now, he might wipe that smirk off Geoff's face despite being in a public restaurant.

He hurried across the street to his office, but none other than Mrs. Carter, the doctor's wife and Becky's aunt, waylaid him before he got there.

"Rob, wait a minute. I must have a word with you."

He paused and waited for the plump little woman to catch up to him. "Good afternoon, Mrs. Carter."

She fanned her face, and the feathers on her hat bobbed up and down. "Pooh, call me Aunt Clara. Everybody else does." She paused for breath. "I've seen my niece with that Kensington fellow a number of times around town. What I want to know is why you haven't proposed marriage to her to get all this other nonsense out of her head."

"Mrs.— I mean Aunt Clara, you know as well as I do that Becky is an independent young woman, and one doesn't propose marriage just like that. She does have some radical ideas, but I believe it's best to let her get it out of her system. When she sees that she'll not have any luck around Barton Creek, she'll abandon them."

At that moment Becky exited Dinah's. She started across to the news office but stopped when she saw them. She marched over to where they stood. "Aunt Clara, if you and Rob are discussing me, you can just stop right now. And you can tell Ma that I will go to Sunday school when I feel like it and not because she expects me to go."

She turned to Rob and poked her finger in his chest. "And you, Mr. Frankston, can keep your opinions about me, whatever they are, to yourself. I won't have you, Lucy, Ma, or anyone else telling me what I can or cannot do."

With a flounce of her skirt, she turned and almost ran to the news office.

Rob raised his hands and shrugged. "What was that all about? How did she know we were talking about her?"

Aunt Clara shook her head and laughed. "Now that's our Becky, always wanting her way."

Rob furrowed his brow and stared after Becky. "But I think our best bet is to pray that she will see how important God is in her life. I believe she'll come around when the Lord ordains it."

Aunt Clara wrapped her hand around his arm and patted it. "I pray so, Rob, I pray so." She narrowed her eyes thoughtfully. "I still believe the best way with that girl is to give her freedom, Rob. If she comes back to you, you'll know for sure you have her whole heart. If not…" She shrugged, then turned and walked back toward her home.

Becky had certainly stirred up a hornet's nest since her return. He prayed she would not look to Geoff Kensington to find love and acceptance. No matter what she did, his love for her would not diminish.

He glanced back over his shoulder and found Geoff standing

on the boardwalk outside the hotel. He leaned against a post in a most casual pose, and his smirk had intensified to the point it made Rob stop and clench his fists. No telling how much Geoff had seen of what happened in the streets with Becky and Aunt Clara. One day Rob just might take a swing at that face and ruin it with a broken nose or black eye.

The door slammed behind him as he entered his office.

Chapter 13

On Saturday morning Rebecca stood with Geoff at the train station ready to board for the trip to Oklahoma City. Excitement and anticipation created flutters in her heart. What an adventure she expected for today. Rob had complained about her being gone all day with Geoff, but she reminded him that he had no claims on her, and Geoff knew how much she wanted to visit the city.

She hid a smile as she remembered Rob standing on the boardwalk outside Anderson's Mercantile as she and Geoff passed by on the way to the station. His frown and arms crossed over his chest spoke of his disapproval and perhaps jealousy, which sent a shiver of delight through her. She'd never had the interest of two men at the same time and found it to be an intriguing situation.

The train whistle blasted forth a shrill reminder to board. The conductor held out his hand to help her up the steps to the car. Geoff followed her to a seat near the rear of the car. She settled herself on the padded wooden bench. "The smoke and soot don't seem to be as heavy this far back in the car."

Geoff bowed then sat beside her. "Whatever you say is fine with me. I look forward to our time together today. I want to know so much more about you and your interests."

Today he wore his dove gray pants, a white shirt, and a dark gray coat. He was as handsome in them as he was in his more casual clothes. She remembered the strength in his hands as he held her arm or hand, and the heat rose in her face at the thought of how good it felt.

She glanced down at her handbag. "And I will delight in knowing more about you. I've looked forward to this trip ever since you mentioned it. I'm so thankful the train schedule to Oklahoma City includes one in the morning and the evening."

She gazed up at him and felt herself drowning in the dark blue pools of his eyes. Her body tensed at the realization of how long they would be together. The ten o'clock train would get them to their destination by noon. Then they'd have the entire afternoon for sightseeing and dining before the return on the seven o'clock trip back to Barton Creek. She'd never been with one man for that long and didn't know what to expect. Still she looked forward to whatever Geoff had planned for the day.

She turned her attention away from him to her surroundings. The noise and crowded conditions of the train gave little opportunity for serious conversation, but Rebecca enjoyed watching the people and thinking about where they were going and why.

She leaned toward Geoff. "I can't believe so many people are going to Oklahoma City."

He grinned and shook his head. "Don't you know it's like going into town every Saturday when you live out on a farm or ranch?"

"I suppose so. I know I enjoyed all our trips into Barton Creek when I was growing up, and Guthrie and Barton Creek still have plenty of places to buy things."

"There's a lot more to see and do in the city than in Barton Creek. And some of these people may be going on down to even Fort Worth and Dallas, or they may change trains and go on to Denver and other points West."

Of course people traveled more by train now than they had even a few years ago. After all, she had come all the way from Boston to Barton Creek just a few weeks ago. She'd have to get accustomed to the idea that the West didn't end with her hometown. So many places to visit and so many new things to try whetted her appetite to see and experience everything possible. Even though Mr. Lansdowne wouldn't publish her story about the suffrage meeting, maybe he would print one about Oklahoma City and all it had to offer.

At that moment she was glad a notebook and pen were in her handbag. Perfect for taking notes. One of these days her editor would recognize her talents and allow her articles to be printed in his paper. Until that time, she would find interesting subjects and keep writing.

When they arrived at the station in the city, Geoff surprised her with a rented horse and buggy with a driver. As he helped her to board, he said, "I've rented this for the day as it will make seeing all the sights much easier. Where would you like to go first?"

Rebecca raised her parasol against the sun. "Let's ride through the downtown area, and of course I want to see the offices of the *Daily Oklahoman*. I read copies of it every day in our office. Then wherever you think we should go will be fine."

Her eyes opened wide at the crowded, noisy streets. Motor cars chugged down the streets, and a streetcar carried passengers to an unknown destination. The clang of the trolley bell rang out, and the horse leading their buggy shied and cantered sideways. Rebecca grabbed Geoff's arm, and he wrapped his other one around her.

"Don't worry, the driver can handle the horse. The noise simply startled him."

Rebecca nodded then realized his arm still held her in an embrace. Heat rose in her face, and she pulled away from him, at the same time hitting him in the face with her parasol. "Oh, my, I truly am sorry." She lifted her fingers to the welt now appearing on his cheek. "I hope it doesn't cause too much pain. The sudden shift in the carriage was unexpected."

Geoff chuckled and placed his hand over her fingers. "It's quite all right. Just a little scratch like that won't cause any pain." He glanced at the offensive parasol. "I must say that would make a good lethal weapon if you ever needed one."

The heat on her cheeks increased. She must be redder than the hot embers glowing in Ma's stove after dinner. She slipped her hand from under his and turned to face straight ahead. The intense look in his eyes completely unnerved her. She gazed around for something to offer in conversation.

"I see poles and lines. I knew they had electricity here and telephones, but so many of them stagger my mind."

"Yes, Oklahoma City is getting quite cosmopolitan. But then you've been in Boston, so this shouldn't surprise you."

"You're right, but that was back East where things are far ahead of us. I just didn't expect to see so much progress right here in the Territory. Why, we're not even a state yet." She pulled out her notebook and began jotting down impressions.

"So you brought your work with you?"

She glanced up from her writing to see his raised eyebrow and a smile on his lips. "And why not? This is a wonderful opportunity to write an article about the city."

"I hoped you'd find my company interesting enough to hold your attention for the day."

Heat rose in her cheeks yet again. She had offended him. Her thoughts swung from remorse for hurting his feelings to desire to get good information for a story. After all, she really had no feelings toward Geoff except friendship, and as a friend he should understand her desire to succeed in her chosen field.

The sun's rays bounced off the brass trim of the carriage and blinded her for a moment. She turned her head and blinked her eyes, but spots still danced in her vision. Geoff's hand grasped her arm as she struggled to focus.

"Are you all right? I didn't intend to make you cry."

He thought he'd offended her. She turned back, laughing in his face. Men had such big egos. Everything was about them. "You didn't. It's the sun. I do find your company interesting, but so much is new here. I wonder if they have a group of suffragettes here."

Geoff leaned back against the seat. "I have no idea, but I'm sure you're going to find out." One thing he'd learned about Rebecca, she had very set opinions and ideas when it came to women, but he would much rather she leave them behind when they were together.

"Of course I am. If they do, then I can come down here to meetings and find out what progress is being made for our rights."

"Don't you ever think about anything else? You talk about women's rights or your job as a reporter every time we're together. I have no objections concerning the rights of women to vote or to do anything else for that matter, but I simply cannot understand why they want to bother themselves with politics." Most women he had known didn't care one way or the other about the workings of the government. As long as they were well fed and had a nice home, they were satisfied.

"Yes, I do think about other things, like the orphans on the streets of the big cities like New York and Chicago, how children and women are used like slaves in so many factories, and how some men seem to think women are simply an ornament on their arms to make them look good."

Geoff's eyes opened wide. That pretty little head held more

information and ideas than a history book. Perhaps he'd underestimated her. He hoped to gain more information from her about her father and his land, but he would have to change his tactics or she'd see through him quicker than a hound after a fox.

"I had no idea you even knew about such things. You truly amaze me."

Her cheeks tinged with pink. "I did more than simply study fine arts courses at Wellesley. We had many projects in which we were involved. I have never liked to see anyone suffer at the hands of another person."

"Yes, I can see that." The carriage stopped, and Geoff realized they were at the newspaper building housing the *Daily Oklahoman*. This would be a good place to change the avenue of their conversation.

"We're at our first destination. That is, if you're still interested in a tour."

"Of course I am. I can relay to Mr. Lansdowne some of the things they are doing here to get out a daily paper."

He helped her to step down then walked with her up to the building. The receptionist at the front desk took great delight in telling them about the paper and finding someone to give them a tour.

An hour later they boarded the carriage, and Geoff directed the driver to a restaurant on the way to Wheeler Park and Zoo. "I think you will find the zoo a most interesting place. They have gone to great lengths to landscape the park grounds and provide animals for the zoo."

Rebecca peered up at him with furrowed brow. "How do you come to know so much about Oklahoma City? I've lived in Oklahoma most of my life, but you know more than I ever did."

"I've been down here and to Tulsa since my arrival in Barton Creek. My company has many interests, and I've been doing research for them." Before she could inquire as to the type of research or what his company was planning for this part of Oklahoma, he pointed to the restaurant where they were to have lunch. "They have wonderful food here, and I'm sure you'll find their beef is some of the finest in the state."

At that moment, he decided the rest of this day would be to simply enjoy being with Rebecca. He had plenty of time to find out what he needed to know about the Haynes land.

Rob paced back and forth in front of the boarding house. Becky had said she'd be gone all day with Geoff, but Rob hadn't believed she'd actually spend the day in another city with a man she'd known only a few weeks.

With the Fourth of July celebration coming up in three days, he wanted to be sure that Becky attended all the festivities with him and not Geoff. However, he couldn't be sure that Geoff hadn't already claimed her for the day.

Rob couldn't imagine spending the day with anyone other than Becky. Except for last summer when she had not come home between semesters, they had been together at all the celebrations since they were children.

He stopped in his tracks. He should go back to his office and work, even though it was Saturday, and wait for the train to return. If Becky knew he'd been waiting at the boarding house for her, she'd get the idea he was jealous. Of course he wouldn't admit it to her, but jealousy did rear its ugly head. He didn't want anyone else to gain her favor and possibly win her hand in marriage.

Ever since he'd been fifteen, he'd imagined Becky as his bride even though his mother thought he could do much better. His sister had decided the same thing about Matt Haynes, but now they were both in their mid-twenties and Matt hadn't made any indication marriage was on the horizon. Rob prayed he and Caroline were not doomed to love two people who would not return that love.

He settled himself at his desk and looked over the will requested by a couple who had recently moved to Barton Creek. He wrote it to their specifications and prepared it for them to sign on Monday. When he placed it into his drawer, he glanced at his watch at the same moment the train blew its warning as it approached the station.

Instead of racing down to greet the train, he stayed at his desk. If Geoff had already asked to escort Becky on the Fourth, then it wouldn't matter whether he saw her tonight or not. She had promised her mother to attend Sunday school tomorrow, so he would take his chances with her there. It wasn't likely that Kensington would attend church, as he hadn't since that first Sunday in town.

Rob moved to the window and peered down at the street.

A couple walking arm in arm came into view, and he recognized Becky's hat right away. Once again jealousy wove its way into his heart and pounded its rhythm. Becky laughed and tilted her head back in pleasure at something Geoff said.

"Lord," he whispered aloud, "You have led me to believe Becky is the one You have appointed for me. If I am wrong, then I need a sign. Until then I won't give up in pursuing her love." His words hung in the air as he watched them continue down the street to the boarding house.

Chapter 14

*M*ellie scanned the church yard for Becky. She'd promised to attend Sunday school today then go home with the family for dinner after church. After Lucy's report, Mellie had become even more concerned about her daughter's lifestyle. The fact that she had spent an entire day out of town with a man to whom she wasn't even engaged worried Mellie.

"Ben, I don't see Becky anywhere. She promised me she'd be here."

"Then she will be. And what happened to calling her Rebecca?" Ben helped her down from the carriage.

"I'm in no mood for her new ideas and what she wants to be called, although I probably will call her Rebecca when she's around. Still, she had no business going off alone on a train with that Kensington fellow." She peered around again, but still no Becky.

Ben grasped her hands. "My dear, you have to let her go sometime. I know it's hard. I can hardly stand the thought of her being away from home and living in the boarding house."

"She's still so young and impressionable. That Mr. Kensington could fill her head with all kinds of ideas." Mellie still had no new information on him even though she'd asked her relatives back East to find out what they could.

She blew out her breath. The temperature had already risen to about the eighty-five degree mark before even ten o'clock in the morning. At this rate it would be well into the nineties by the time church let out. The long-sleeve shirtwaist she'd worn this morning now clung to her back, and she wished she'd chosen to wear a lighter-weight skirt. At least her straw hat shaded her eyes from the glaring sun.

Of course summer in Oklahoma always meant hot temperatures, and right now she'd give anything for a glass of cold liquid to cool the anger overheating her.

She turned to peer down the street and caught a glimpse of her wayward daughter headed toward the church like she had all the time in the world.

"There she is, Ben. I hope she has a good explanation for being late. At least she wasn't with Mr. Kensington."

At that moment Rob drew near and tipped his hat. "Mrs. Haynes, I understand Becky is supposed to go out to the ranch for dinner today."

"Yes, that's right."

He rolled the brim of his hat with his fingers. "Do you mind if I invite myself?"

The boy looked so sincere and just a little nervous. Sure signs of a young man in love. She grinned and patted his arm. "Rob, you are always welcome at our place. We'd be glad to have you join us today."

He ducked his head and backed away. "Thank you, and please don't say anything to Becky about it. I'll talk to her later." Rob turned and walked back to the church.

Ben shook his head and laughed. "Now what was that all about?"

Mellie punched his arm. "As if you didn't know. Now shush, here she comes."

Becky crossed over to the churchyard and waved. Mellie's heart swelled with pride at the sight of her beautiful daughter. She wore a pale green dress of lightweight fabric that swished about her feet. The lace trim of her collar matched the lace on the sleeves, and tendrils of hair escaped to brush against her neck. The brim of her white straw hat dipped to expose the pink and green flowers adorning it.

"Good morning, Ma. I'm sorry I'm running late." She leaned over and kissed Mellie's cheek. Then she winked at her father and hugged him. "You're looking good today. Must have been a good week."

"It was, and it's even better now that you're here. We've missed having you out at the ranch."

Becky linked her arm with his to walk into church with Mellie close behind. How her heart rejoiced to see her daughter smiling and going into church. No matter how old Becky was, she'd always be their little girl. She may be smart and sophisticated with her college education, but here she was still Becky Haynes.

Seeing her now with her father brought back memories of the two of them riding across the prairie together. Becky had always been as one with Daisy, moving in total synchronization. How Mellie longed to see that once again.

As they entered the church, Mellie searched the congregation for signs of Mr. Kensington. He had not been in church since the first Sunday he'd been in town. If he wasn't a Christian, she didn't want him keeping company with Becky, but as Ben reminded her more and more often, Becky was an adult and had to make her own decisions. All Mellie could do was pray that her daughter would remember the Bible teachings of her youth and not be attracted to the man, no matter how charming he might be.

After the adults were dismissed from Sunday school, Mellie settled herself in the pew with her family. How good it was to have all four of them sitting there with Aunt Clara and the doctor right behind them. Lucy and Jake and their children sat across the aisle and completed the family circle.

Lucy's favorite verse came to mind, and Mellie smiled. Yes, the Lord had made this day, and she would rejoice and be glad in it no matter what came their way.

Geoff waited by the entrance to the hotel until all the members were inside the church. They'd be busy there for awhile, which gave him time to go out to the ranch and check out again that land the farmer sold to Ben Haynes. Most likely the cowboys wouldn't be out riding herd today, so he would not be deterred as he had been before.

Jonah had Geoff's horse ready and waiting when he sauntered over to the stables. Geoff thanked him and slipped him a few extra coins for the trouble of working on a Sunday.

The livery owner thanked him then said, "I'm glad to help out with my horses anytime. I fear the day when those new horseless carriages may come in and put me out of business."

Geoff mounted his ride. "They are the thing these days. Saw quite a few of them in Oklahoma City, but don't worry. Men will always need horses. Machines may break down, but a good horse will go for a long time and not be near as costly."

"Sure hope you're right." He scratched his chin. "You said you'd only be out a few hours, so let me know when you return so's I can meet you and take care of Champ for you."

Geoff nodded and waved before taking off. As he rode past the church, he heard the hymn singing. The strains of the familiar melody "A Mighty Fortress Is Our God" brought back memories of the days he attended church with his parents. How long ago that had been. After suffering under his father's strict discipline according to the Bible, he'd abandoned all things to do with church when he left home. Now he had little time for religion and all its teachings. Life had been good for him without his paying attention to God, so he saw no need to seek His favor.

He nudged his horse to a faster gait in order to get to his destination more quickly. He wanted to be sure to have enough time for a thorough inspection of the land in question. If his suspicions held true, he'd have good news for his boss.

Half an hour later he reached the area where the farmer's land met the Haynes property. Although it was now all one spread, Geoff still thought of it as belonging to Dawson, the one who had sold out to Ben. He reached the creek and began his trek along the same route he'd started when he had been stopped by the Haynes men.

Something didn't look quite as it should. He pulled out the map and unrolled it to check his location. According to the map, the creek should be going to the right in a curve then back around and down toward town. This part veered off to the left in a straight line back to Barton Creek.

He dismounted and searched the ground around the area. Finally he spotted what looked like a dried-up creek bed. Rocks and debris formed a trail that led him to the right. He held the horse's reins in one hand and walked the path of the rocks. In less than a hundred yards he came upon what he'd been searching for.

The ground all around him oozed with a black substance that choked out anything within its reach. For as far as he could see, patches of the black goo dotted the earth. Dead trees, broken and bare, stood as testament to the fact that the black stuff smothered the grass and any other plant that may have once been there.

He stooped down to dip his finger into the substance then lifted it to his nose. The unmistakable odor of petroleum filled his nostrils. Geoff jumped to his feet. It was here, just like they suspected. Oil. He could barely contain the excitement that rose in his chest. Tomorrow he'd ride into Guthrie and relay the good news to his company. Then he'd wait for instructions as to how much to offer Ben Haynes for the land.

Rebecca barely listened to the sermon. Her mind wandered as she contemplated the women in her family and in the church. They all seemed to be quite content with their lives. None of them wanted to discuss matters of government and the laws that affected their well-being.

As outspoken as Aunt Clara may be, she still believed a woman's place was in the home taking care of her husband. Of course, she had married so late in life that having her own man to take care of after so many years of caring for someone else's children was a blessing.

The number of women in church actually surpassed the number of men, which gave Rebecca pause to consider. If men were to be heads of their household, then they should be the ones leading the way for the spiritual growth of the family. Since many of the men in town didn't deem it important to be in church, their wives took up the slack. Of course, to Rebecca's way of thinking, it shouldn't make any difference one way or another what a family's relationship was to God as long as they believed He existed.

Rebecca sighed and let her shoulders sag. Too many people used their religion as an excuse to lean on God when they should stand on their own two feet and take care of themselves. A finger poked her in the back, Ma's familiar reminder from childhood, and she automatically straightened her shoulders. Some things never changed.

After sitting through an hour of Sunday school before the

service, she thought the morning would never end. In all the years she'd been attending, the preacher hadn't improved much. When the service finally ended, she stepped outside to breathe fresh air. Too many bodies in a warm room on a hot day didn't lead to pleasant aromas. Now that she bathed almost daily, the thought that all these people cleansed their bodies much less often caused her stomach to roll.

A hand grasped her arm as she descended the steps. She jerked her head around to find Rob next to her, grinning like he had a great secret.

"Rob Frankston, you scared me half out of my wits grabbing my arm that way."

His grin didn't fade and his brown eyes sparkled with mischief. "I'm sorry, but I had to catch you before you hurried away."

"And what is so important that you couldn't wait to speak to me until later?" Whatever it was better be important. Her stomach rumbled now in anticipation of the dinner Ma had prepared for the family.

"I meant to ask you before now, but we haven't had the opportunity. Would you allow me to be your escort for the celebration on Tuesday?"

Rebecca's eyes opened wide. She'd completely forgotten about the Independence Day festivities, and she was supposed to cover them in detail for the newspaper. She groaned. "I'd love to, but I have to work."

"Can't you work and enjoy the fun at the same time?"

Nothing was said about her not joining in with everyone else at the games and other events, so she may as well accept his offer and have fun while taking notes. "You're right. I can do both. We'll have to see everything so I don't leave anything out of my story."

"That's fine with me. Shall I meet you at the boarding house, or do you have to report to the office first?"

He led her to where her family waited. "Meet me at nine at Mrs. Claymore's."

Ma grinned down from her perch on the front seat of their buggy. "Good day, Rob. Would you care to join us for dinner out at the ranch?"

Rebecca narrowed her eyes and peered at her mother as Rob accepted the invitation. Ma's joy at his acceptance angered Rebecca. They were trying to run her life again. She should've thought earlier and invited Geoff to dinner or even to go with her to the events on the Fourth.

She pasted a smile on her face and nodded to Rob. "I'll see you in a little while." She lifted her skirt and placed a foot on the step up just as he placed one hand on her back and one on her arm to give her a boost up. The strangest sensation spread itself through her arm and along her back.

It must be the heat, that's all. "Thank you, Rob." Rebecca settled herself on the seat and looked down at him. He still grinned at her then flipped his straw hat on his head and snapped the brim with his fingers. Once again that strange feeling coursed through her veins. She shook herself and looked away. After all, she had to remember this was only Bobby Frankston, the boy she'd known most of her life.

Chapter 15

*G*eoff headed back for town, but took a different route, hoping he wouldn't get lost in the process. He had spent more time at the site than he had intended, and now didn't want to risk running into any of the Haynes family on his way back to Barton Creek. With the telegraph office closed on Sunday except for emergencies, Monday was the soonest he could get a message to his company.

A fair price had been agreed upon for the cattle, and Geoff hoped the same could be done for the land. Just in case Ben didn't want to sell the old Dawson property, the company was willing to offer a price for drilling and carrying off the oil that was there. They wanted to do what was best for all involved. The only problem would be if Ben Haynes decided he didn't want any type of drilling to take place.

Oil had become a profitable product of Oklahoma land, and those in Tulsa and surrounding areas who had cashed in on the black substance had reaped great rewards. Of course, some people weren't willing to have the rigs on their land, especially near their homes, but as money rolled in, more and more were willing to sacrifice a little beauty for profit.

If rumors were to be believed, a huge undrilled oil deposit lay somewhere near Tulsa. If so, the entire face of the territory in northeast Oklahoma would be changed. That's what the ranchers and farmers feared most, the effects the new industry would have on their land.

Perspiration trickled its way down his neck and between his shoulder blades. He removed his hat and wiped at his brow. He had forgotten how scorching the sun's rays could be at midday. At least his hat shaded his eyes from the worst of the glare.

He consulted his map once again and noted he was now on Haynes's land. Best he get on his way and not be caught again by either of those men Ben called Monk and Hank. They most likely wouldn't believe his story about checking out the cattle again.

The sun glinted on something in the distance, and Geoff squinted against the glare. As he drew nearer, he spotted three men riding toward the north. The glint must have come from something on one of their saddles. Afraid it might be cowboys from the Haynes's ranch, he skirted into a stand of trees, being careful to keep them in sight so as not to run into them.

They drew closer but were still too far away to identify. He remained hidden but realized the men were not cowboys. They didn't sit in the saddle the way men accustomed to riding would. Then they headed straight for the land Geoff had just left. His curiosity itched to ride behind and see what they were up to, but common sense told him to leave and get back to town. But something deep inside told him the men were up to no good.

All the way back to the livery stables, he debated whether or not he should alert Sheriff Claymore. If he did, the lawman would ask all kinds of questions as to why he was out that way in the first place. If he didn't, and something happened out there, Jonah would remember this morning and let the sheriff know.

When he dismounted, Jonah appeared from one of the stables, and Geoff decided on a compromise. "Hello, Jonah." He handed the reins to the stable owner. "Did anyone else rent horses today?"

"Nope, just you. Why?"

"I saw three men riding out around the Haynes's place and wondered. They didn't ride like cowboys and were going off in a direction away from the ranch."

Jonah scratched his chin in the way he did when he was thinking. "If they headed northwest, ain't nothing that way 'ceptin' that tainted land ol' man Dawson tried to grow corn on."

That "tainted land" as the old man called it held one of the best deposits of oil Geoff had seen in his business of finding such sources. It might even be bigger than Spindletop down in Beaumont, Texas.

"I see. Well, I just thought I'd ask. Seemed a little odd for anyone to be out there on a Sunday morning."

"You were out there." Jonah pulled the saddle off the horse and plunked it down on a stand.

Geoff didn't skip a beat. "Yes, I was. I want to see as much of this territory as I can. Why, I may even decide to settle down here in Barton Creek myself." Which wasn't entirely the truth, but it wasn't a complete lie either.

Jonah peered at him through narrowed eyes. "That so? Wouldn't have anything to do with one Miss Becky Haynes, would it?"

Geoff laughed. Nothing got past the old man. "It might and it might not. Only time will tell. Thank you again for your services." Still chuckling, he headed back to the hotel.

Sunday dinner with her family brought back memories Rebecca thought she'd placed in the far reaches of her mind. The conversation and exchanges among those present formed a pleasant backdrop for her reverie. Even Rob joined in the banter with her brother, Matt.

Rebecca gazed around the family circle. Lucy and Jake sat with

Charley and Micah between them and Matt and Rob across from them. Matt had maneuvered the seats so that Rob had the chair next to her. Listening now to his voice sent ripples of excitement through her stomach and swept away her appetite. This had to stop. She hadn't had these feelings around him since they were in school. Why were they happening now?

Ma spoke to her and Rebecca blinked. "I'm sorry. What was that, Ma?"

"I asked what you were working on at the newspaper."

All eyes stared her way, causing heat to rise in her cheeks. "I'm not writing anything special right now. I'll be covering all the activities for the July Fourth celebration though."

Lucy raised an eyebrow. "What happened to the story you were going to write about the meeting you went to in Guthrie?"

Rebecca bit her lip. "Nothing. Mr. Lansdowne didn't think it worth the space to print it. He's just too old-fashioned to see how important it is for women to have a voice in our government with their votes."

Silence greeted her statement as all movement except from the two little boys ceased. She glared at them and asked, "What?"

Ma shook her head and patted Rebecca's arm. "Dear, it's just that women voting is such a radical thing. What do we know about how things should be run?"

Rebecca clenched her teeth and swallowed the retort on her tongue. She pushed back her anger and said, "Ma, you and Lucy run households and take care of your families. You plan and prepare meals, take care of spending money for groceries and things needed for the home. You plant gardens, grow food, then can and preserve it for winter, in addition to keeping your family in clothing. Who better to know how things should be run than women who organize and take care of their homes?"

Lucy cut a piece of meat for Micah. "That may be so, but

running a country is entirely different from running a home. I'm doing things my mother had no idea about doing, but it doesn't qualify me to pick the person who governs our nation."

"But don't you want to have a voice when it comes time to make decisions about Oklahoma becoming a state and who will run it? For that matter, doesn't it make a difference to you who runs for mayor or sheriff of Barton Creek?"

Pa's guffaw brought snickers of laughter from Matt and Jake. "My child, if Mayor Frankston ever has anybody running against him, it would turn this town upside down."

Her hand went to her mouth. The mayor was Rob's father. She had to learn to watch her words and not say whatever popped into her head. She watched him out of the corner of her eye, but his face remained passive and unreadable. Just once she'd like to know what was really going on in that mind of his.

"I'm sorry, Rob. I meant no offense. I was only speaking in general terms."

He reached over and covered her hand with his. "No offense taken. I knew what you meant."

His gaze held hers, and for a moment she saw something there that unnerved her, but it was gone in a flash. Surely she had imagined it. She slipped her hand from under his and clasped both of hers in her lap. What was wrong with her today?

Talk about the events of next Tuesday took over as conversation resumed. No matter what she tried to think about, the feel of Rob's hand on hers and the momentary look in his eyes filled her mind. She braced herself and forced her brain to think of what she wanted to do in life. Pa, Jake, and Matt may laugh at her ideas now, but someday she'd prove them wrong, and women would have as much say in who was elected as the men did.

Rob may not understand Becky's reasoning for her beliefs, but he understood her passion. He'd seen it in her when she was thirteen and had defended Jake against all those in town who believed him to be a murderer. That was one reason he loved her so. Her loyalty, honesty, and passion for what was right gave her something he'd seen in few women, and he never wanted to do anything to stifle it.

After dinner he watched her play with Charley and Micah. How good she was with children. Visions of her playing with their children filled his mind, and he was transported to the future when she would be his bride.

The sound of his name spoken by Mr. Haynes ended the reverie. "Excuse me, Mr. Haynes, what did you say?"

"We have an agreement with Geoff Kensington. Could you draw up a contract for us to sign?"

"Of course. Will Mr. Morris be a part of the deal?" His heart swelled with pride and gratitude. Two of his father's biggest clients were now putting their trust in his ability to handle their business. "I'll get right to work on it tomorrow. Of course, with Tuesday being a holiday, I won't have it completely ready until Wednesday."

"Good enough." Then he leaned over and whispered, "Why don't you take Becky on a stroll down to the corral. I think you two need some time together."

Heat crept up Rob's neck. "Thank you, sir. I'd like that." He glanced toward Becky, and her eyes were directed straight at him with uncertainty and questions.

He moved to her side and held out his hand. "Rebecca, I should be leaving soon. Would do me the honor of walking down to the corral with me?"

Pink filled her cheeks and she lowered her eyes, but she stood and took his hand. "Yes, I would like that."

A few minutes later they stood near the corral, and a young filly loped across to the fence to where they were. Rebecca held out her hand and the filly nuzzled it. "Pa named her Star Bright because of that white marking between her ears. I rode her once, and she's as fast as Daisy ever was."

Rob leaned against the post with one foot on the bottom rail and his arms resting on the top one. "You sounded so sure of yourself at the dinner table, Becky. You truly believe in all that you said."

She gazed up at him with her greenish-brown eyes and smiled. "I was, and I apologize again for the remark about the mayor."

He clenched his fists to keep his hands and arms where they belonged and not around Becky. "Like I said, no need for that. I understood your point."

She reached into a bucket of oats and fed a handful to Star Bright. "I noticed you didn't laugh when Pa, Jake, and Matt did. I thank you for that."

He'd never laugh at her in front of her family, or anyone else for that matter. Mr. Lansdowne must be blind not to see the sincerity of her beliefs. He hadn't read any of her articles but what were printed in the paper, and he had the feeling those didn't reflect her true talent or writing ability.

"Some of what you said made sense. I think I'll look more into it and learn what makes you so passionate about it."

"You'd do that?" She reached over and hugged him. "Oh, that would make me very happy." Then just as quickly she stepped back. "I'm sorry, I shouldn't have done that."

"I'm glad you did." It was time for him to leave before he did something to ruin this new development in their relationship. He strolled over to where his horse waited by the hitching post.

He stopped and turned to find her very close behind him. The lavender scent of her hair reached his nostrils, and he wanted to pull out the pins and see it cascade about her shoulders as it had when they were young. Instead he clutched the reins of his horse, but he still leaned toward her. Then he straightened. If he didn't leave right now, he just might spoil everything by kissing her.

Becky blinked twice and stepped back. He swung himself up into his saddle and tipped his hat. "Good day, Becky. Thank you for a most enjoyable day." He clicked the reins and rode away. He'd come too close to doing today what he planned for the Fourth. A whistle filled the air as he trotted down the road toward Barton Creek. The Fourth of July this year would have more than one reason to be the most memorable day of his life if all his plans succeeded.

Chapter 16

*R*ebecca stepped out onto the porch of the boarding house. She spotted Rob headed her way and waved. Such a beautiful day for the festivities planned. The town had taken on a carnival atmosphere with all the bunting and flags waving in the air and the game booths set up around the park.

Mayor Frankston and the committee had actually managed to add a horse race to the Fourth of July celebration, and the fact that they had listened to her suggestion gave her satisfaction. After Pa said she could ride Star Bright, she'd asked Jonah to add her name to the race participants just before the deadline. She had known Rob would enter, but Geoff's name on the roster had been a surprise. He'd been gone most of the day yesterday, and she had no chance to question him about it.

Rob tipped his hat. "Good morning, Rebecca. Are you ready to see what the day has to offer?"

"Yes, and Mr. Lansdowne is allowing me to write up the article covering all the events."

"So that means you'll be taking notes all day."

She grinned and poked his arm. "Not all day. I can remember most everything since I've been attending these celebrations so long." She squinted up toward the sky. Maybe she should have worn her wide-brim straw hat to ward off the sun's rays. As much as she enjoyed wearing hats, she hadn't wanted to be hindered in any way, and a hat sometimes did that.

Rob offered up his arm. "Then let's make our way down the street and see what this affair has for entertainment today."

"Let me get my parasol. This sun is going to be hot even with the clouds. I'll be back in a moment." She turned and hurried back inside and upstairs to her room. A few minutes later she stood on the steps and opened up the yellow-and-green parasol that matched her yellow summer dress.

They sauntered down the street now filling with Barton Creek citizens of all ages. Every building along Main Street saluted the holiday with red, white, and blue decorations. Some businesses, like the bakery and the diner, remained open to entice customers in to sample their wares.

In past years a barbeque dinner at noon provided participants with food for a nominal fee, but the crowds had grown to a size that could no longer be accommodated. Now families planned picnic outings or a meal at Dinah's to sate their appetites. In addition, booths offered various temptations to sample during the day. The Ladies Guild of St. Martin's church provided a beautiful array of homemade cakes and other sweets along with stands for lemonade and iced tea.

Rebecca smiled and nodded at both familiar and unfamiliar faces along the way. "I'm still amazed at how many new people have come to Barton Creek in the past ten years. So many people I don't know."

"Our population is up to over five thousand now. It's great for business, but I'm hoping for someone to join Father and me in our law firm to help with all the clients we're getting."

"I heard Aunt Clara say that the doc is expecting a young doctor to arrive soon to help take care of some of his load, and Ruth is helping him out several days a week. She said that some days he doesn't finish seeing patients until nightfall."

"Growth means more work, but without growth we have no

progress. I, for one, am certainly glad to see it all happening here. I feared Guthrie and Oklahoma City would be more attractive than our town."

They paused in front of the livery. Rob stepped up to check the entry board for the races later this afternoon. He gasped and turned to Rebecca. "Your name is on the list. When did you register? I didn't see it there yesterday."

"It wasn't there." She grinned and swallowed a chuckle at the look of disbelief on his face. "I had Jonah enter me just before the deadline. I didn't want you or Geoff to know who your competition would be."

"But you can't; I mean, women aren't allowed in the race."

She snapped her parasol closed and placed her hands on her hips. "And just why not, Mr. Frankston? I didn't see anything in the rules that prohibit me from riding in the race."

His voice sputtered, but he came up with no real answer. Finally he shook his head. "Whatever you want to do is fine with me, but don't expect me or any of the others to give you any sympathy and hold back."

"And just what makes you think I'd want you to do such a thing?" The nerve of Rob to even think she'd need or even want special consideration. She'd win and show them all what a woman on a horse could do.

He held up his hands in mock self-defense. "Never said you did, but you'll have some stiff competition, so you'd better be ready. After all, Daisy isn't as young as she used to be." Then he laughed. "Let's see what other surprises might be lurking around the next corner."

Rebecca pushed open her parasol once again. "All right, but remember what I said." And wouldn't he be surprised to see her on Star Bright instead of Daisy.

They walked together to admire the various displays of hand-crafted items and artwork done by local citizens. Before the booths closed for the day, she planned to purchase a few items she'd seen, especially the painting of a mustang rising up with forelegs to the sky against a backdrop of mountains. It would be a great reminder of one thing she really loved…horses.

Alice Morris hailed her from across the street. Rebecca waited for her friend and Eli to catch up. "Good morning, Alice, Eli."

"Oh, Rebecca, I was hoping to speak with you today." Alice glanced back at her husband then at Rob. "Do you two mind if I steal her away for a few minutes?"

Rob laughed and shook his head. "Don't mind a bit. In fact, I have something I want to discuss with Eli." The two men turned and walked away.

Alice fell into step beside Rebecca. "I understand you went to that meeting in Guthrie and that you worked with the suffragettes back East."

"Yes, I did. Why?"

"I've been reading some of Catt's writings and talked with a few women when we went up on our last trip to buy horses in Wyoming, and I'm interested in hearing what you have to say."

Rebecca's heart skipped a beat. Someone besides herself actually wanted to know more about the works of the women she admired. She grasped Alice's arm. "Let's go across to the bakery and get out of this sun. We can talk there."

Once inside the bakery Rebecca ordered a pastry and glass of tea, and Alice did the same. They chose a table in a corner where they could talk more freely. Alice leaned forward with her fore-arms on the table. "Last spring when we were in Wyoming, I met some women, and we discussed voting for women. They are quite happy with having a voice as to who gets elected, but they said it was a real fight to get it."

Envy for Alice's ventures into the far West nudged Rebecca. If only she could get around like that and talk with women who had the privilege of voting, she could write articles that would make Mr. Lansdowne sit up and take notice. "It's so important for women to have a say in who runs their country or state. I want it for the Territory so that we can vote for statehood, and then vote for the leaders we send to Washington or to our own capital to propose new laws."

With an interested audience, she could talk for quite awhile about suffrage and the right of women to do what they pleased with their lives. Rob would have to wait. If he really wanted to spend time with her, he wouldn't mind.

Rob and Eli strolled down to a concession stand and bought bowls of ice cream. Although older by only four years, Eli's early success as a rancher amazed Rob. The half-Cherokee man had taken the land given to him by his father and turned it into a highly regarded horse ranch. Jake Starnes and Eli now supplied horses for the army at Fort Smith in Arkansas and Fort Davis in Texas.

"I noticed you entered the horse race this afternoon. Did you know Becky signed up too?"

Eli's mouth gaped open. "You're not serious? Does she know that Jake and I are entered?"

"I would assume so. She gave Jonah the money to enter just before the deadline so no one would know until today that she planned to race." Not that it would make any difference at all to Becky who was in the race. She only cared about her horse and what she could get Daisy to do, and Becky believed she would win. "Did you know Geoff Kensington entered too?"

This time Eli almost choked on a bit of ice cream. "You're kidding. Where would he get a horse fast enough to beat all of us?"

Rob shrugged and glanced back down the street to see if Alice and Becky were in sight. "I think the one Jonah rented him is the horse he'll be riding. Jonah says he's a mighty fine horse, and fast too."

"Not as fast as my Firestorm or Jake's Black Prince. Daisy is about past her prime. Surely Becky realizes that."

"I don't think she does. Daisy will always be a winner in Becky's eyes. I hate to see her disappointed today. Just so you know, she doesn't expect any special consideration as the only female in the race."

Eli laughed and shook his head. "Don't think that'll be a problem. I plan to ride to win, and I'm sure the others will too. Even being Jake's cousin by marriage won't bring her any favors. Jake and I have a little wager on our part."

Rob finished his ice cream and tossed the container into one of the trash receptacles that dotted both sides of the street. His father didn't want litter ruining the looks of his town. He cocked his head at Eli. "And what sort of bet do you have going?"

"If he wins, he gets the pick of the next bunch of horses I bring back. If I win, I get one of those saddles he's so proud of."

"And if neither of you wins?"

"Doesn't matter who wins the race. This is just between the two of us. If one of us wins the race, that will be a bonus. The money will always come in handy." Eli tilted his hat to the back of his head. "Did you know Jake is having a rodeo out at his place this fall? He says they have them down in Texas on the horse ranches as a contest for the cowboys to let off steam. He's advertised it around some of the other towns."

"Didn't I see something about that in a flyer or a sign somewhere around here?"

"Probably did. I think he's beginning to promote it in Barton Creek now. We have enough riders from the ranches close by to have a good show."

"Then I suppose we'll be hearing more about it in the coming days." Rob lowered his voice to a whisper. "Here come the ladies. I wonder if Becky knows about the rodeo?"

Becky twirled her parasol and peered up at Rob. "From what I know of you two, you've been talking nothing but horses."

"Yes, and especially the race today."

Alice grabbed Eli's arm. "Did you tell him about the wager between you and Jake?"

Becky's eyes opened wide. "You and Jake are riding today?"

Eli shrugged and grinned. "Yep. He'll be on Black Prince, and I'm riding Firestorm."

The corners of Becky's mouth turned downward. "Those are two of the fastest horses around." Then she straightened her shoulders and grinned. "But my horse will beat you both. Wait and see."

Rob didn't plan to burst her bubble of confidence, but even he knew Daisy didn't stand a chance against the horses of Jake and Eli. He'd have to come up with something extra special to cheer her up after losing the race. His present plans might not be enough.

Eli pulled a watch from his shirt pocket. "My stomach and my timepiece say it's time to eat. Care to join us at the hotel?"

Rob glanced at Becky, who gave a slight shake of her head. "No, we plan to eat at Dinah's today. Maybe we'll catch up to you at the concert before the race. If not, then good luck in the race."

Alice entwined her arm with Eli's and the couple strolled across to the hotel. Rob turned to Becky and extended his hand. "Shall we head for Dinah's now?"

She grinned and hooked onto his elbow. "Yes, I'm ready. Besides I need to build my strength for this afternoon. I plan to give you boys a run for your money." The music of her laughter filled the air.

Rob didn't care a bit about winning the race, but he hoped Becky would make a good showing. She prided herself on her skills with a horse, but it had been four years since she'd really ridden Daisy in a good race. Her eyes sparkled with excitement, but his legs wobbled like a baby learning to walk. If only she knew the effect she had on his heart every time they were together.

Geoff sauntered over to the livery to check the entries for the big race. His boots had grown more comfortable each time he'd worn them, and he much preferred the Levi pants he now wore to the business trousers he usually had on.

He scanned the roster and stopped short when he reached Rebecca Haynes's name. It hadn't been there when he last checked yesterday. Surely she didn't plan to race Daisy against the mounts of Morris and Starnes. Even his rented horse could beat Daisy. He didn't care whether he beat out Eli or Jake, but he did want to come in ahead of Rob Frankston.

Another poster caught his attention. "Good morning, Jonah. What is this?" He held up the paper.

Jonah peered at the writing and grinned. "Oh, that's a rodeo Jake Starnes is planning for a competition for the cowboys on the ranches. I think he's planning to have some bronco riding with those unbroken horses he brought back from Montana or Wyoming or wherever he went."

Geoff had heard of rodeo competitions among the cowboys on different ranches, but most of them had been in Texas and up in the northwestern states. He'd seen a show put on by Buffalo Bill Cody. The choking smell of the dust, the band, the roar of the crowd, the pounding of hooves as performers reenacted Custer's Last Stand, and the sound of Annie Oakley's shooting filled his mind with wonderful memories. Of course, a rodeo competition like this couldn't compare, but it would still be an interesting event if Jake Starnes was organizing it.

"You ain't planning to enter that, are ya?" Jonah spit a stream of tobacco toward a pot near the door.

Geoff cringed as the wad made a splat in the container. Such a nasty habit. "Of course not. I'm no cowboy. I'll watch the others take chances with their lives." He turned and walked out to the streets where townspeople milled about and visited the various booths and exhibits.

He spotted Rebecca and Rob as they left Dinah's. Rob said something to her, and her laughter rang out so that it reached even Geoff's ears. She was such a beautiful young woman. He couldn't understand why she thought she had to compete with the men in this race—other than the fact that she had a competitive spirit.

Even though Miss Haynes wasn't on his arm today, he looked forward to the race this afternoon and putting Rob Frankston to shame.

Chapter 17

*R*ebecca breathed deeply and smiled with her eyes closed. She let the sounds of music, children calling to one another, and the laughter of people around her wash over like a soothing rain. This was home, and she had missed it last year when she had stayed in Boston for the summer. The celebration there had been something extra special, as the city was the hub of Revolution activity leading to independence, but it couldn't compare to what they had right here in Barton Creek even with its same program year after year. These were her people, her family.

Rob grasped her hand. "It's a beautiful day, and I can see how happy you are to be here. I'm happy you're here too. I missed you last summer."

For some reason that statement satisfied Rebecca more than the delicious meal they'd just consumed at Dinah's. Her heart did a little tap dance, but she quickly brought it under control. Regaining her feelings for Rob was not a part of the plan for her life. She must be more careful and not encourage him.

He nodded toward the park. "Let's go on over to the bandstand. I can hear the band practicing, so that means the concert will start soon."

"I can't wait to hear them. It sounds like they have a much larger brass section, which will be wonderful for the Sousa marches."

They approached the park and found a good place to sit and wait for the concert to begin. Mayor Frankston had done an amazing job with the layout of the park and the location of benches and walkways. He and the town council wanted to name it in honor of a Cherokee chief in the area before settlers moved in, but Mrs. Frankston and a few other prominent citizens had squelched that idea so that it simply stood as Barton Creek Town Park. Not very original in Rebecca's estimation, but then she didn't have an alternate name either.

Rob left for a moment then returned with two ice creams in a rolled cookie. "Here you go. The guy called these 'cookie cones.' Said he got the idea at the St. Louis World's Fair."

Rebecca licked her treat and nodded. "It does make it easier to eat, and you can eat it all and not waste any. Remember the summer we first had ice cream? Mr. Anderson brought in some new freezers and donated the ingredients."

Rob swallowed a bite and grinned. "Yes, that was the fundraiser for the farmers. Didn't do much good though. Most of them up and left anyway."

Another memory flickered in Rebecca's mind. That had also been the day the Fowler boys had caused such a ruckus. One tried to attack Dove Morris and the other one stole the money raised. At least everything had turned out all right, but she'd never forget Mrs. Frankston's ugly behavior that day when she accused Hawk Morris of the robbery and called Mrs. Morris the mother of thieving Indians.

She glanced at Rob beside her. How different he was from his mother. He didn't have a mean bone in his body. He genuinely liked people and tried to help them in whatever way he could. His sister, Caroline, had been in love with Matt since they were fifteen, but Matt couldn't or wouldn't see it. Perhaps he, like Rebecca, couldn't quite grasp the idea of Charlotte Frankston as a mother-in-law.

Her head jerked. Where had that idea come from? She didn't

plan on marrying Rob or anyone else for that matter for a long time. She'd let her guard down again with memories from the past. If she didn't stop that, she'd never reach the goals for her future.

Rob wiped his hands with his handkerchief. "Did you see there's going to be a shooting contest before the race?"

"Yes, but what's the sense of doing it? Everyone in town knows Hawk Morris is the best shot of anyone around."

"True, he has won every year, but there's always someone thinking they can be better than Hawk this year. Six men have signed up to try and beat him, including Jake."

"I wish him good luck, although I understand he was pretty handy with a gun before he became a cowboy. Beat that cheater down in Texas to the draw." Jake may be good, but Hawk was so good he could go off and star in any Wild West show even though he preferred helping his father run the Morris ranch. That was a full-time job now that the herd had grown so large and they had so many more cowboys working for them. Today's contest would be interesting with Jake entered. She sighed. "I guess I'll have to miss it today since I'll have to change clothes to get ready for the race."

Rob stared at her a moment as if to make a comment, but at that moment the band played a fanfare, and Mayor Frankston stepped to the podium, forestalling any remark.

The mayor held up his hands. "Friends and fellow citizens of Barton Creek, I welcome you here today for the celebration of our nation's birth." He stretched his hand toward the American flag to his right. "Now let us all say our Pledge of Allegiance."

As one voice the group recited, "I pledge allegiance to my Flag and the Republic for which it stands, one nation, indivisible, with liberty and justice for all." Then the band struck up the familiar strains of "America," and every person sang, "My country, 'tis of thee, sweet land of liberty, of thee I sing," words that had come to mean so much to Americans everywhere.

Rob grabbed her hand and began to sing in a rich baritone voice. Rebecca turned to peer up at him. His voice had matured since she'd been gone, and now his notes were clear and pure with the beauty of the song. It seemed as though every day she learned something new and different about Barton Creek and her old friends.

After that the mayor again stepped up. He waved his hands for quiet, and when the crowd settled, he grinned broadly, hooked his thumbs in his suspenders, and moved his head back and forth to gaze across the crowd. "Today I have an important announcement to make."

Cheers rose up from the crowd, and the mayor held up his hands. "Doctor Carter has a new assistant coming, and they will be running the clinic together. Since Doctor and Mrs. Carter are living in their new home, they plan to expand the clinic at its present location. This means new and improved medical facilities for those in Barton Creek."

The crowd roared and clapped again, and Rebecca gasped. She had no idea Doc had hired an assistant or would be expanding the clinic. Of course, as the local reporter and Clara's niece, such announcements shouldn't come as a surprise. She wondered why she hadn't heard the news earlier.

Strains of a Sousa march filled the air as the band played, and Rebecca recognized it as "Stars and Stripes Forever." She couldn't keep her feet still and tapped out the rhythm on the dirt path under the bench.

A new thought occurred. Ruth had helped Doc a few times already in his work, so perhaps she'd be hired as the nurse for him and the new doctor. What a wonderful opportunity that would be for Ruth and her children.

The next song picked up as soon as the first one finished, and the music continued for several more. All around her people sang and laughed as the excitement of the day rose. Rob leaned over and whispered, "If you're going to race, you'd better get ready."

"Oh, my goodness, you're right. I'll see you down by the stables in a few minutes." She turned and hurried back to the boarding house to change into her riding attire. Pa had promised to have Star Bright at the stables ready for the race, and she was anxious to see what the horse could do.

The race would begin at one end of Main Street, where the brick ended and dirt began as the road headed out of town. The two-mile course would stretch one mile out of town to the prairie then across ranch land and circle back the one mile to the finish line down by the church.

Daisy did her best when kicked into high speed after the halfway mark. Rebecca hoped this would hold true for Star Bright. Racing a new horse didn't seem as good an idea today as it had earlier when her spirit of competition took over.

She changed into her split skirt then frowned. Much as she hated to revert to her childhood days, she decided to wear the denim pants so popular with the cowboys. Better to be comfortable and have more freedom in the saddle than to be a young lady today. She dropped the split skirt and pulled on the pants. The only problem was that the jeans made for the male body didn't exactly fit her slim frame.

Indecision faced her as she chose a shirt to wear. All this time she'd been trying to show her family how she had matured and grown into a young woman, yet here she was back to how she'd been all through her school years in Barton Creek. She clenched her teeth and grabbed a shirt. The thought of competing against the men roused in her that feeling of seeking equality and proving she could do anything a man could do and still be a lady.

After shoving her feet into her boots, she let her hair fall loose then gathered it into a ponytail at the neck and secured it with a ribbon tied into a large bow. Then she planted her tan felt hat firmly on her head and headed for the stables. The gunshots from the sharpshooters' contest rang out in the air. With race time so near, this must be the last match. Since he was kin, she hoped Jake would outshoot Hawk.

Rob watched the shooting contest with interest, but at the same time kept on the lookout for Becky. The last pair stepped up to the rail and prepared for the final round. The winner of this match would be the winner of the contest and given a sharpshooter medal and a one hundred dollar prize.

Just as he figured, Hawk and Jake were the final contestants. Each man had two guns with six rounds in each one. Identical targets were lined up for each man. The one who hit the most number of targets with the greatest accuracy in the fastest time would be declared the winner.

In a few moments gunshots filled the air. Targets went down at lightning speed, and Rob gasped. He'd never seen such accuracy as the targets fell one after the other. Jake was giving Hawk his first real competition. The crowd cheered and passersby stopped to observe the action.

In a matter of minutes it was all over. When the judges went down the range to check the results, Hawk and Jake shook hands to let people know this was a friendly competition and not one of rivalry. The judges returned, shaking their heads and checking their score sheets.

The three men stood in a huddle conferring with each other. Rob glanced again at his watch and realized the race was due to start very soon. A decision would have to come quick, or the race would be delayed.

Finally the men walked over. The head judge held up his hand for quiet. "Today we've had a most amazing display of shooting we've ever seen. Only one second separates the two. Our sharpshooter for 1905 is Jake Starnes."

Rob shouted then clapped wildly. A cheer rose from the crowd and filled the summer air. Jake and Hawk shook hands.

Hawk grasped Jake's shoulder. "If someone had to beat me, I'm glad it was you. Now c'mon, you have a race to run, and if you race as well as you shoot, Eli will have a run for his money."

The two men laughed and headed toward the end of the street. Rob followed and spotted Becky with Daisy. Then he jerked his head around. That wasn't Daisy. Becky was up to something! He hurried toward his own horse and grabbed Rusty's reins. Becky strolled to his side, Star Bright trailing behind her

"Where's Daisy? I thought you'd be riding her?" This put a whole new slant on today's race.

Becky laughed and patted Star Bright's forelock. "You know Daisy's too old for racing. Star Bright is my ride for the day."

"I suppose you think you can beat all of us who have experienced horses?"

"You bet I can."

He had to grin at her confidence. "We'll see about that." Of course he might slow down a bit to let her think she was beating him until the last minute.

She nodded her head toward Jake. "I understand my cousin beat out Hawk. I hoped he would."

"That's right. You should have been there. Jake beat him by only one second. Best shooting match this town has ever seen."

"Wonder if he'll include one in that rodeo he's working up?"

Before Rob could respond, the race starting official called out, "Mount your horses, men, er, uh, and lady."

Becky laughed and hoisted herself into Star Bright's saddle. Rob did the same with Rusty, and they lined up at the starting point. He glanced down the way and saw Jake and Eli as well as Geoff and a number of other men from town. Ten riders and horses should make this a very exciting race, especially with Becky in it. He prayed she wouldn't make too bad a showing. His first inclination was to wish Geoff to fall off and be disqualified, but he realized that wasn't exactly the Christian thing to do. But he did hope Becky would at least come in ahead of Geoff.

A few minutes later a gunshot sounded and the race began. As he figured, Hawk and Eli were among the leaders going out. He knew Becky's strategy from the past but wondered if she'd use the same tactics today. After all, Star Bright wasn't Daisy.

Across the rangelands and back to the dirt road, Rob concentrated on keeping ahead of Geoff, who stayed close. Becky trailed behind Geoff, but when Rob turned to check, she didn't appear worried or tense. That told him to watch out—Becky would make her move soon.

At each quarter-mile mark, judges observed the race to make sure no one broke the rules. One of the riders from town went down as his horse stumbled and fell. Rob managed to avoid a collision and raced ahead.

Then, just as she'd done so often in the past on Daisy, on the last turn back toward town, Becky kicked Star Bright into full speed and the horse flew by Geoff and then him. Becky's golden brown hair bounced on her shoulders as she ran at full stream. A laugh started deep down in Rob's gut. That scheming girl was up to her old tricks. He pushed his heels into Rusty's flanks and sped off to catch up to Becky.

He managed to get even with her, but with one look at him, she flipped her reins from side to side and Star Bright forged ahead. The finish line came into view. Becky wouldn't make it first, but she was still ahead of Rob.

The crowd roared again as the nine riders crossed the line drawn across the road. Eli pulled up in first place with Jake coming in second and Becky a close third. Eli waved his hat in the air. "Looks like I get me a new saddle."

Rob pulled up beside Becky. "Sorry, you didn't win."

Becky laughed. "I didn't think I would against Eli or Jake. Their horses are much stronger and faster than Star Bright, but I accomplished my goal." A big grin spread across her face, and her eyes sparkled with amusement. "I wanted to beat you and I did, so that's my reward."

He wanted to reach out and hug her, but he'd save that for later. "You sure did. Just like old times. Star Bright is going to be a great horse for you." Rob didn't mind losing to her as long as he could be ahead of Geoff, and he was.

Geoff joined them when the racing judge handed Eli the trophy and the check for winning. "That's a fine horse, Rebecca. I had no idea she'd be that fast."

"She may be new to racing, but she didn't let me down. I thought Jake or Eli would win. Those two men have more knowledge about horses in their little fingers than I have in my whole body."

That was true, and it made their herds the best in the state. At least all the competitions today had been friendly and nobody's feelings had been hurt. So far the day had gone much like he planned, and he hoped it would continue that way.

Becky peered up at Rob. "I'm going to change back into my other clothes. Shall I meet you somewhere?"

Before he had a chance to reply, the thunder of hoofbeats filled the air along with shouts from the men riding in. Rob grabbed Becky's hand and ran to where the men stopped. He recognized the rider as Hank, the foreman of the Haynes's ranch. Ben Haynes raced up to the cowboy.

The man didn't get off his horse but shouted to Ben and the crowd. "We've been out to the range, and someone has killed a dozen or so of our herd. We need to get back out there."

A gasp then murmurs rose among those standing within hearing distance. Mr. Haynes ran to Becky. "Honey, I need Star Bright to take me back out to the ranch. I came in with your ma in the surrey. Get it and bring her home soon as you can."

Becky stepped back and handed her father the reins. "Of course I will. Go find out what's wrong, and I'll go find Ma."

He mounted Star Bright and was joined by Matt and Sam Morris. Jake, Eli, and Hawk followed the others, and the men galloped away.

Tears streamed down Becky's face. "Who would do such a cruel thing?" She brushed a tear from her cheek. "I have to find Ma. I'm sorry, Rob, but we have to get home."

She turned and headed to the center of town, and Mrs. Haynes ran to meet her. They conferred a minute, then Becky led her to where the buggy was tied. Rob stood still and watched as they came down the street and then headed out to the ranch. His shoulders drooped, and he kicked the dirt. He turned to go home. Such a terrible ending for a perfect day, and now his surprise would have to wait for another time.

Tendrils of fear worked their way through his mind. He prayed the slaughter of these animals was some horrible mistake and not the beginnings of an all-out assault on the ranchers.

Chapter 18

*R*ebecca's heart thudded all the way home. She ran the team at the safest speed she could as Ma held on to the side rail and said nothing. By the look on her face, Rebecca knew her mother worried that whoever had killed the animals might still be on the ranch.

When they arrived, Matt waited for them. He paced back and forth in front of the corral and rushed toward the surrey when Rebecca drove up. "Thank goodness you're here. Sam Morris lost cattle too. Pa, Jake, and Hank went out with the crew to see what other damage may have been done, and Mr. Morris went with his men back to his own land."

Ma hopped down and grabbed Matt's arm. "How many did we lose?"

"I don't know for sure. Hank found at least a dozen of ours. Monk went to check farther out on the range." Matt secured one foot in a stirrup then swung his leg over his saddle. "Pa left Star Bright saddled. He won't like it if you go out there, but I thought I'd let you know in case you have any ideas to head in that direction."

She wasted no time running to the horse and jumping up onto her back. Ma called to her, but Rebecca only waved and raced after Matt. Whatever was going on, she wanted to be in the middle of it. She had as much right to know what happened out on the range as any member of her father's crew, and since it concerned her family, knowing became even more imperative. Her instincts as a reporter kicked in and set off her determination to get as much information as possible.

When she reached the spot where her pa stood with Jake, the stench of blood caused her to gag and cover her nose and mouth with her kerchief. The sight of the beautiful cattle cut open and bleeding brought tears to her eyes and boiling anger to her stomach. Whoever did this was cruel and heartless. Flies swarmed around the carcasses. Rebecca swung down from her mount and ran to Pa, who hugged her.

"You shouldn't be out here. This isn't a sight for your eyes."

"I had to come." She peered over his shoulder and let the tears dampen her kerchief. "Who could have done something this awful?"

"We don't know, but we've been looking for clues. So far we've found nothing but a bunch of horseshoe tracks that go in every direction. Whoever it was didn't want to be followed. It's hard to distinguish our prints from theirs."

Jake slapped his gloves against his thigh. "These men knew everyone but a small group of cowboys would be in town."

Rebecca pulled the kerchief from her mouth and nose. "Did anyone let the sheriff know?"

"Yes, when Sam learned some of his were slaughtered too, he sent Hawk back to get him, but I'm sure he heard about it after we left."

No sooner were the words out of his mouth than Sheriff Claymore rode up with several men he'd deputized. He asked the same question as Rebecca had earlier. Pa shook his head and pointed to the tracks that were now almost indistinguishable in the dirt. "All we have is a mess of tracks that take us nowhere."

Sheriff Claymore surveyed the scene and rubbed his chin. "I'm sorry this happened, Ben."

Monk rode up with two other cowboys. "Found about half a dozen more dead in the southwest pasture. I think that's all we lost. Don't know about Morris."

The sheriff jerked around to Ben. "Sam's herd was attacked?"

Pa nodded and waved at Monk and Hank. "Let's get this mess cleaned up. Three of you go out and take care of the others. Matt, you go with them. Becky, go on back to the house and let your ma know what's going on."

That's not what she wanted to do, but Ma did need to know. She'd be worrying herself sick about something happening to Pa. At the moment she didn't even mind the slip in calling her by her childhood name. Other things were more important.

As she rode back to the ranch house, Rebecca remembered how good it had felt to race this afternoon. She had to admit that this country was in her blood, and she cared more about her people, and their ranches and cattle and horses, than she'd realized.

Geoff rode back to the livery in deep thought about the turn of events that ended the festivities of the day. Surely this wouldn't affect his deal with the men. Perhaps he should ride out to the Rocking H and let Mr. Haynes know he'd buy whatever the man had to offer. As for the other matter, it could wait until the vandalism with the cattle was taken care of.

Jonah greeted him when he arrived at the stables. "Did I hear right? Someone killed a bunch of Ben Haynes's cattle?"

Geoff dismounted and handed the reins to Jonah. "Yes, you heard right. That's all I know."

"Now who in tarnation would do something like that? Don't make no sense 'tall. Cattle rustling would be more like what you'd expect, and we ain't even had none of that, and that's a blessing."

Jonah led the horse to a stall, and Geoff called out, "Don't unsaddle him. I'll be back after I clean up to ride out to the Haynes's ranch."

Jonah nodded and waved, so Geoff headed for the hotel. Soon as he changed into another shirt, he planned to find Rob and check whether he had the contract ready, and then Geoff would ride out and let Mr. Haynes know that the cattle deal was still on the table.

People still milled about enjoying the remaining festivities. Geoff stopped in the middle of the street and gazed down toward the church. He'd been in town less than a month, but he had come to admire the people here. They did business with both an open-hearted honesty and a wise shrewdness, a pairing that he found refreshing.

In his hotel room, a new realization dawned on Geoff. Those men he spotted Sunday morning didn't belong out where he saw them. This could be a rival company's way of getting Ben Haynes to be more willing to sell that land with the oil. His stomach soured, and he sat on the bed to think. Mr. Barstow had said another company was interested, but they may not be as patient to wait for the right circumstances to make an offer for the land or for drilling rights.

He jumped up to finish cleaning up. His trip out to the ranch took on more importance.

In a few minutes he had washed off the grime from the race and changed into a clean shirt. Except for Sundays and business meetings, he hadn't worn his suit in Barton Creek since he arrived, and he probably wouldn't put one on again until the day he left town. He much preferred the Levis and cotton shirts of the cowboys, but he would have scoffed if anyone had told him that a month ago.

When Geoff walked out of the hotel, Rob hailed him. "Geoff, I need a word with you."

"I was on my way to find you. I wanted to find out about that contract with Haynes and Morris. Is it ready?" He met the young lawyer in the middle of the street.

"Yes, that's what I wanted to talk to you about. The signing is tomorrow, but are you still planning to go on with it?"

"Yes. I'm on my way out to the ranch now to let them know the deal is still on if he wants to continue. I wanted to find out how many cattle are involved in this slaughter."

"I don't imagine it's too many. If it'd been something like the water being tainted, then the loss would have been substantial. There's bad water on his land, but he keeps his herd away from there."

Geoff knit his brows. Haynes had told others about the land where the creek had been diverted. "Oh, I didn't know he had bad water anywhere. Is that why the creek is diverted?" He gulped and wished the words to be back in his mouth. He didn't want people to know he'd been out there yet, but Rob didn't seem to pay notice.

"Yes, it's on the property that once belonged to a farmer named Dawson. It's the main reason he couldn't get crops to grow. Between that and the drought, he had to sell out. Ben and Sam went in together on it. They and a bunch of others went out and dug new trenches to reroute the creek around the land on that really bad section."

The statement piqued Geoff's interest. More than a few knew about the oil that marred the land for farming. "Out of curiosity, what is wrong with that section of land?"

Rob removed his hat and raked his fingers through his hair. "Mr. Haynes says it's oil, but he's not sure how much. He's waiting to see what happens over at Red Fork in Tulsa. They're bringing good amounts now, but he's concerned with the effect it will have on the land."

How anyone would want to wait with the oil industry booming as it was remained a mystery to Geoff. "Doesn't he understand the potential for the wealth that comes from oil fields? Tulsa is booming now since it became involved in the oil industry."

"Yes, he does know, but he's more concerned with its effect on the cattle industry. He's been to Tulsa along with Sam Morris. They want to make sure it's all compatible and the herds won't be harmed."

Geoff interest took a new turn. "Has he had any offers to buy the land? Would he have talked to anybody about drilling there?"

Rob's laughter rang out, and several people turned to stare. "Sell? That's the last thing Ben or Sam wants to do, and he hasn't told me if anyone has asked. If the oil is plentiful and the section valuable, they plan to send half the profits to the Dawson family. When Dawson sold him the land, Ben knew why no crops would grow, but Dawson didn't. Even when Ben tried to explain, the farmer wouldn't listen and just wanted to leave."

"How do you know so much about it?"

"My father drew up the contract for the sale and the provision to Dawson of any profits from the oil wells they might put there. It also provided a clause to keep Ben and Sam from selling the land. I think he wanted to make sure the Dawson family shared in any profits as long as possible. I'm handling the affairs for Ben now that I'm working with Father. His mayoral duties are taking far more time now that the town is growing so fast."

Geoff made a mental note of Rob's knowledge. This was the man he'd be dealing with if any headway was to be made with Ben Haynes or Sam Morris. Mr. Barstow had given him authority to either buy the land outright or secure the mineral rights, but getting them might be more difficult than either of them first believed.

If only he could persuade Ben and Sam to see the value of the oil and what it could do for their town. It had grown in the past few years, but an oil strike could create jobs and bring in more people. Geoff had come to love this town and its citizens, and he wanted to make sure that whatever transpired would be in the best interests of all concerned.

"I'm going to get my horse and go on out to the ranch. I'm hoping we'll still meet in your offices tomorrow to finalize our cattle deal." He also planned to ask about the Dawson land if the proper opening arrived. All would depend on the extent of the cattle loss and the money involved there. His main concern now was that another group may be using unscrupulous tactics to force Ben Haynes to do something about the land.

Less than an hour later he found himself on the porch of the Haynes's house. He followed Rebecca into the living room and sat across from her on the sofa. He took in again the expanse of the room with its upholstered furniture and massive fireplace. Two chairs made of leather sat across from the sofa, and a large kerosene lamp sat on a table nearby. Sun poured in through the nearly ceiling-high windows on the southwest side of the house as the sun lowered in the sky.

Rebecca leaned forward. "I don't know when Pa and the others will be back. I'm sure you're concerned about how this will affect your cattle sale."

"Yes, I wanted to assure your father that I plan to buy the same number we agreed upon earlier. I didn't want him to worry that I might back out."

"He'll be glad to hear it. More cattle were discovered dead in another part of the range, and even Sam lost a lot of his herd."

Mrs. Haynes, ever the thoughtful hostess, brought in a tray with coffee and set it on a table. "I'm sorry Ben isn't here to meet you. This has been a harrowing day."

"Yes, it has. The circumstances this afternoon certainly marred the festivities." He paused. "I talked with Rob Frankston before coming here, and he will have the contract ready for tomorrow just as planned."

Geoff glanced across at Rebecca. Her blouse bore the signs of the dust from the race, and strands of hair had escaped its tie at the back to fall free on her shoulders. The tiredness, worry, and frustration clearly showed in her eyes and the droop of her shoulders. His first instinct was to sit beside her and wrap his arm around her shoulder in comfort, but he restrained himself.

He searched for a way to remove the worry from her face. "That was a fine run you gave Jake and Eli in the race. Star Bright proved herself a quite good racer."

Rebecca managed a smile and her eyes brightened. "Yeah, she'll be just as good as Daisy ever was. I knew I probably wouldn't beat those two, but my goal was to come in ahead of you and Rob. And that I did."

Heat rose in Geoff's face. "Well, I didn't make a very good showing, but it was fun and a welcome break in the day. I understand Jake won the shooting contest too. I thought Hawk would win that one."

This time Rebecca's laugh rang out, cheering him with the idea that he'd taken away a little of her sadness.

"Only one second of time separated the two. I've seen what Hawk can do with a gun but have only heard about Jake's gun expertise. He outdrew a gambler in Texas who was cheating and drew his gun first."

"I don't think I'd want to take either of those two on in a gun fight."

Before Rebecca or Mrs. Haynes could comment, Ben and Matt strode into the house. Mr. Haynes's eyes opened wide when he spotted Geoff. "What are you doing out here?"

Geoff rose and extended his hand toward the rancher. "I wanted you to know that I still plan to go through with our cattle deal tomorrow. I hope your loss wasn't too extensive."

Ben grasped his hand. "Thank you. No, the loss was minimal considering the hundreds of head of cattle we have. It'll mean a little less at auction, but it won't break us. I just can't figure out who would do such a thing or why. We're all puzzled."

"I understand Sam Morris's herd was attacked too." Geoff sat again as Ben sank into one of the leather chairs.

"Yes, and that's hard to understand, but he's like me. We'll salvage what we can of the carcasses and go on with our ranching like before."

Geoff nodded. Since Sam owned part interest in the Dawson property, he understood the reason if his suspicions were correct, but he couldn't let Ben know that.

Rebecca jumped up then wrapped her arms around her father's neck. "I'm just so glad it wasn't any worse and that whoever it was wasn't after you or our men."

Ben patted her back and kissed the side of her head. "Me too, baby; me too."

Matt leaned over the pot on the table. "I smell coffee, and I could sure use some about now."

"Food or drink, they're always on your mind." Mrs. Haynes poured him a cup. "I have supper cooking, Mr. Kensington. Can we interest you in staying?"

Rebecca shook her head and stood. "Ma, I have to get back to town before dark. I have a story to write and a job to do tomorrow."

"But you need to eat before you go. Tell her, Ben. She needs to stay, and Mr. Kensington too."

"Yes, Becky, you can take time to eat. You'll still be able to get back to town and write your story."

She lifted her head and sniffed the air. "Ma, do I smell apple pie?"

"Indeed you do. Baking always helps when I'm nervous or worried."

"Then I guess I'll have to stay." She glanced at Geoff. "Ma's apple pie is too good to pass up, and I can always wait until tomorrow morning and write at my desk."

Mrs. Haynes clapped her hands and smiled. "Now that's settled, couldn't you spend the night too? Some of your clothes are still in your room, so you'd have something to wear tomorrow. I don't want you to go back to town alone at night."

Geoff reached over and placed a hand on Mrs. Haynes's arm. "If I may be so bold, I'd be happy to accompany Miss Haynes back to town. We can leave after supper and get back before it's too late."

Mrs. Haynes appeared to think about that a moment before nodding in agreement. "Yes, that would be all right, I suppose. I didn't want her out alone in the evening after all that's happened today." She reached toward Rebecca. "Come, help me put supper on the table."

Rebecca followed her mother to the kitchen, from which delicious aromas of cooking roast beef and spicy apple pie wafted into the room. Not only would he have a good home-cooked meal under his belt, but he'd have the pleasure of Rebecca's company on the ride back to Barton Creek. A day interrupted with tragedy now drew to a more enjoyable ending.

On the ride back to town Rebecca shut out the events of the past few hours. She'd remember enough to write a story about it for Mr. Lansdowne, but that was tomorrow. Tonight she wanted to think about good things only, and Geoff Kensington was a good thing.

She cut her gaze to him and observed him in the saddle. His ride was as easy as any she had seen, and his clothing seem suited to him now. At first Geoff had appeared to be just another man from the city, but his muscles and good body build were more evident in the tight denim pants and cowboy shirt. How would it feel to have those strong arms around her? She blinked and pushed the thought away.

Geoff turned toward her. "You've been very quiet since we left the ranch. I'm sorry this has been such a hard day for you."

His concern touched her heart, and her eyes misted over. "Thank you for caring about us and coming out to reassure Pa you'd still buy the cattle."

"It was the least I could do after all your pa has done for me. Besides, if I hadn't come, you wouldn't have had an escort back to town, and this is one trip I'm glad to make."

Rebecca swallowed hard and blinked away the tears. His smile touched something deep inside her. She could come to care a great deal about this man if she let herself.

Their attention turned back to their ride, and nothing more was said. Thoughts of Geoff ran through her mind until she pushed them away, concentrating instead on what she'd write in her story. No matter how attractive Geoff was, she couldn't let him distract her from her job.

Chapter 19

*R*ebecca's fingers flew across the keys of her typewriter. All of the events of yesterday filled her head with images, words, and ideas. She'd organized her notes in such a way last night that she now had the makings for three articles. Nothing could distract her this morning, not even Molly's incessant chatter about nothing in particular and everything in general.

By the time the clock struck the ten o'clock hour, she had all three finished and proofed. She leaned back in her chair and stretched her arms over her head. What a day the holiday had been. Nothing like it had ever happened before, and Rebecca hoped it wouldn't happen again anytime soon.

Molly set a cup of coffee on Rebecca's desk. "You look like you could use a little pickup refreshment about now. I've never seen you concentrate so hard on your writing."

"Thank you, Molly." Rebecca sipped the soothing brew and blinked her eyes to focus on something besides the fine print of her articles. "These are important stories for me, and I'm hoping your father likes them well enough to use them for Friday's edition."

"I'm sure he will." Molly grabbed up a white sack with the red bakery logo. "I have a couple of cinnamon buns from Peterson's Bakery if you're interested."

Rebecca's stomach rumbled and she grabbed for the bag. "I'm always ready for one of Mrs. Peterson's cinnamon buns." She reached into the bag and breathed in the rich smell of spice and sugar. One bite, and a little bit of heaven rolled across her tongue with its velvet smoothness. After devouring the last morsel, she wiped her hands on a handkerchief.

"You do know how to pick up my spirits, Miss Molly."

The young woman grinned and ambled back to her own desk. Rebecca pulled the last sheet of paper from her machine and stacked it with the rest for the article on the racing and sharp-shooting events of yesterday. The other two articles, one in general of the day's activities and the other about her father's loss, lay ready to present. She breathed deeply then gathered them up and headed for Mr. Lansdowne's office. She knocked on the slightly open door.

The editor glanced up from his work and waved her in. "What do you have for me?"

"Three stories about the different events of yesterday, including an article about the new doctor and clinic and what happened to my father's cattle." She laid them on his desk.

"I had planned to write about some of that myself, but seeing as how you've already done so, I'll take a look at them later." He waved his hand in dismissal. "Now get on with the work I assigned you."

Disappointment caused a lump to lodge itself in Rebecca's throat. She turned and headed back to the outer offices. He'd rejected the article written about the speech she attended in Guthrie, and it now lay in her bottom drawer. The story about Oklahoma City was in a pile somewhere on Lansdowne's desk, but it would probably never be printed either.

With a huge sigh, Rebecca returned to her desk. May as well check out deaths for the week and see if any meetings were scheduled before Friday's deadline. No deaths, but the Evangelistic Women's Missionary Society was meeting on Thursday to discuss a mission-type project. Rebecca shook her head. No telling what those ladies would find to do for the members of their church.

She stood and stretched then strolled over to the front window to gaze down Main Street. Geoff Kensington left the hotel and headed across for Rob's law office. She leaned farther to see her father's horse hitched in front along with Matt's and Sam Morris's. They must be there to finalize the contract for the cattle. Once his transaction was finished, Geoff would probably be leaving Barton Creek.

To say she'd miss him would be an understatement. He'd been an interesting companion on several occasions. Still, with his business concluded, he had no real reason for staying around. He'd made life much more fun, and he didn't argue with her about religion like Rob did.

Surely something else would come along to occupy her time. Rob would most likely be seeking to spend more time with her, but she wanted more adventure than he offered. Still, she couldn't deny that deep down Rob stirred up those old feelings from their younger days, feelings she had to squash down every time they rose or she'd never reach her goals.

"Miss Haynes."

Rebecca jerked around at the sound of her name. Mr. Lansdowne stood at his door. He beckoned her to come to his office. Her knees shook so that she had to grab the rail to keep from falling. The tone of his voice gave her no clue as to whether he was angry or pleased. The knots in her stomach threatened to undo her, but she stiffened and walked into his office.

His thick black eyebrows formed a straight line across his brow, and he peered at her over his wire-rimmed glasses. "Have a seat, Miss Haynes."

She sank as gracefully as she could manage into the straight back wooden chair across from him and waited.

After a moment, he spoke. "What makes you think you can write?"

Her heart plummeted to the depths of despair. Rejection again. She swallowed hard and said, "I learned well in school, and it's a joy to put words on paper."

A grunting sound came from his throat, and he held up one of her articles. "Well done, Miss Haynes. I'll use them all in Friday's edition."

Rebecca's breath came out in a whoosh. All three in one edition was three more than she ever dreamed he'd use. "Thank you, Mr. Lansdowne. This means a lot to me."

He grunted again. "Don't think it's going to be a habit of mine. I hired you to take care of the things I don't have time for." Then he dismissed her with a wave of his hand.

Rebecca carefully closed his office door behind her. Then she danced and swirled her way to her desk on her tiptoes. Molly giggled and clapped her hands without them touching so her father wouldn't hear them celebrating.

Molly ran over and hugged Rebecca. "I knew you could do it. I'm so happy. This calls for a celebration. Think I'll run down to Peterson's and get a cake." She giggled again then ran out the door.

With Molly on another of her bakery runs, Rebecca slumped down in her chair and fanned her face. Excitement again coursed through her veins, and she even looked forward to the missionary meeting. What a glorious day it had turned out to be.

Ben Haynes and Sam Morris greeted Geoff when he entered Rob's office. He removed his hat and shook hands. "Any new clues or ideas about what happened yesterday?"

"None whatsoever." Ben slapped his hat against his thigh. "The sight of those animals out in the sun still makes my blood boil. This is worse than rustling."

Sam nodded in agreement. "If I get my hands on whomever is responsible, they'll wish they'd never heard of me or stepped foot on my land."

Ben clapped Sam on the shoulder. "I feel the same way, but we'll let Claymore handle it for now. Let's get on with our business."

The men sat down, and Rob stood behind his desk. "Here is the contract as we discussed it last week. The cattle will be taken to Guthrie and loaded onto rail cars and shipped to Chicago to the Barstow Packing Company."

Ben peered at Geoff. "That's a long way for these cattle to travel. We usually take them down to Fort Worth to the stockyards there."

"I understand, and it would be more convenient if our company were located in Fort Worth, but with one or two of your men riding with them, they should be fine."

Sam spoke up. "I'm sending Hawk and one of our drovers to oversee our livestock. Are you going back with them?"

Geoff hesitated. His excuse for staying behind could not be revealed yet, but he had to have some reason to give them. His mind whirled then settled. "Actually, I plan to stay in Barton Creek. I have let Mr. Barstow know, and he says I can handle business from here. I've come to like your town and may even settle down and buy my own place." He didn't know what Mr. Barstow might say, but the reason sufficed for now.

Ben chuckled. "Wouldn't have to do with that daughter of mine, would it?"

Heat rose in Geoff's face. Rebecca was certainly one of the drawing cards, but not the one that most interested him at the moment. "She's a fine-looking young woman, and I admire her spirit."

Rob cleared his throat. "Let's get on with the contract." He pushed several papers toward the men.

Geoff noted the set of Rob's mouth. Of course, Rebecca was Rob's girl, and he saw Geoff as his competition. He held his amusement in check. No sense in creating anger or jealousy in him at this point. Too much was at stake.

After Ben and Sam signed their names in the appropriate places, Geoff signed his and pushed it back toward Rob. He stood and extended his hand toward Ben. "It's been a pleasure to do business with you."

Ben shook his hand and nodded. "Glad we had what you needed. If you'll excuse us, we have another matter to discuss with Rob."

"Of course. I'll meet you tomorrow at Guthrie when your men take the herd there."

He stepped out to the hall and closed the door behind him but didn't leave. Curiosity as to what Ben and Sam had to say to Rob overrode his conscience. Their voices became audible as he waited outside the door.

Ben's words reached Geoff's ears. "Sam and I are concerned about three men who visited us last week. We haven't told anyone because it didn't seem important, but in light of what happened yesterday, it may be."

Sam spoke next. "We don't know who the men are or who they represent for sure. For all we know, they gave us fake information, but the truth is they asked about Dawson's land and offered to buy it and take it off our hands."

Geoff's ears perked up. That must be the three men he spotted out that way on Sunday. They were interested in the oil that made the land unsuitable for farming. He'd have to be careful now as to how he approached them with his own interest in the land.

"Are you telling me that you and Ben suspect these men may have had something to do with the slaughter?"

Sam's voice rose in anger. "That's what I think, and it's what I want to tell Sheriff Claymore when we leave here, but we need to make sure our papers are airtight and those men can't find some loophole to get that land."

Geoff heard shuffling of papers then Rob's words. "It's airtight, Father made sure of that. If these men are trying to make you sell, they have a strange way of doing it. But I do think you need to let the sheriff know."

Chairs scraped across the floor. Geoff had heard enough, and he headed for the stairway and downstairs. Out on the street, he checked his watch. Not quite noon. He had time to go over to Guthrie and send a wire to Mr. Barstow. As he hurried toward the livery, an idea began to form and then take hold. Maybe he had a plan that would not only allow him to stay in town but also pave the way for Ben and Sam to agree to selling the rights to drill on their land.

After Ben and Sam left, Rob filed the papers from the cattle sale. He sank back into his chair and contemplated the meeting just completed. The prospect of Geoff staying in Barton Creek didn't sit well with him. The only reason he hadn't been truly worried before now about Becky was the fact that Geoff was only to be in town a few weeks to conduct business.

He'd have to step up his plans to convince her that her faith was still important and that she could find happiness here rather than in some big city. Just because Geoff appeared to be attracted to Becky didn't mean that Becky would fall in love with him.

Holding on to the belief that the true spirit of the girl he loved still lay buried beneath the sophistication she wanted everyone to see, he swiveled his chair and leaned over to gaze out the window at the town he loved. He saw Molly enter the bakery then reappear a few minutes later with a white bag. She was heading back to the newspaper office.

Rob had a few minutes to spare, so a visit with Becky seemed in order. He grabbed his hat and headed downstairs.

A few minutes later when he walked into the *Barton Creek Chronicle*, he found Becky and Molly giggling over a cake. He cleared his throat, and both girls jumped. "What's the occasion?"

Becky patted her chest with her hand and scowled at him. "Rob Frankston, you scared me half to death. You should make some noise or something." She grabbed a cloth and wiped at her hands.

"Sorry to frighten you, but the door was open and you two were having such a good time. What are you celebrating?"

Becky face went from a scowl to a wide grin, and she grasped his hands. "Mr. Lansdowne is running three of my stories in Friday's edition."

"He is? That's grand. It's what you've dreamed about." He squeezed her hands and pasted on a smile he hoped looked sincere. Although his heart rejoiced for her, dismay also filled him as he realized successes like this could ultimately take her away from him. Still, he wanted her to be happy.

"Is this a tea party or a newspaper office?"

All three stopped and turned toward the voice. Mr. Lansdowne peered over his glasses at them. He held a cup toward Molly. "I need more coffee. And a piece of that cake you brought from Peterson's."

Rob swallowed a grin as Molly dipped her head and went over to grab his cup and fill it with coffee from the black pot on a small stove in the corner. He waited until Mr. Lansdowne had both coffee and cake in hand before speaking. "Mr. Lansdowne, I'd like to place a small ad in the paper for Friday."

The editor waved his hand with the cake in the air. "Don't tell me, tell Molly there. She handles all the advertising." He scowled again then entered his office and closed the door.

Molly giggled. "His bark is worse than his bite. He complained, but he had that sparkle in his eye that told me he was amused by the whole thing." She tilted her head at Rob. "Do you really want to place an ad, or was that an excuse for being here?"

Rob had to laugh at her astute assessment. "Caught, but now that I said it, perhaps I will take out an ad just to prove I had good reason to be here."

Becky grasped his arm. "Oh, Rob, that isn't really necessary." Then she frowned. "Just why did you come?"

"Mainly to see you and to let you know the sale is complete. Your father and Mr. Morris just left my office."

"Oh, that's good. Geoff assured Pa he would follow through."

The look on her face spelled disappointment mixed with pleasure. He hoped the prospect of Geoff leaving wasn't the cause for the downcast expression she wore.

"The deal is done and the cattle will be delivered tomorrow to Guthrie." He stepped back. "Now if you ladies will excuse me, I must get back to my office. I'll write up my ad and bring it to you later." He bowed slightly and said, "Miss Haynes, Miss Lansdowne, it's been a pleasure, and congratulations again for your stories."

He turned and left the office at a rapid pace. But instead of going back to work, he turned toward home. Right now he needed a good home-cooked meal, and Ruby, the family cook, would surely have an excellent one prepared.

The memory of Becky's face as she told him about her stories filled his mind. If only he could be the one to bring that same look of joy and happiness. No matter how long it took, he wouldn't stop trying.

Chapter 20

*G*eoff sat at a table in the hotel dining room in a quandary as to what he would do now that the cattle sale was done. The herd had been safely delivered and loaded onto the train at Guthrie yesterday. He'd already been back over there this morning to see if a return wire had arrived from Barstow in response to the one he sent.

It had, and from the sound of it, his boss had not been happy with the delays in his main interest, the oil on the land owned by Ben and Sam. He chastised Geoff for not already making the offer, as Barstow was more interested in the oil than in buying any more cattle. He had instructed Geoff to use whatever means necessary to acquire the land.

Those men who approached Ben last week may be the ones responsible for the cattle slaughter. Perhaps they thought that if they hurt Ben enough financially, he'd be forced to sell the land to them. Mr. Barstow might resort to such tactics if he didn't get his way, but Geoff would never carry out orders like that. Knowing what the deal with Dawson stipulated, he doubted Ben would be at liberty to sell the land anyway.

Since he did value his job with the oil company, Geoff would try to win Ben's and Sam's trust and friendship, then tell them of the proposition he had for them. That may not be to Mr. Barstow's liking, but he'd face that later.

He paid his tab and walked outside to bright sunshine and the beginning of another hot afternoon. The first thing he had to do was to come up with some reason to be back on Haynes's ranch land. Sunday would be his best bet, as the family would be at church along with most of the ranch hands. He had to find something to do with himself until that time.

Barton Creek would be a nice place to settle down and raise a family. Geoff shook himself. He didn't plan on marriage any time in the future. He still had too much to accomplish, but if and when he did decide, this would be the place. Chicago had much to offer, but everyone was in a hurry and didn't have time to care for each other as they did here.

A flash of blue caught his attention, and he spotted Rebecca entering the newspaper office. She would be the perfect diversion for a few days. A pretty girl could always make time go by much faster. Rob might be jealous, but when the oil business was done, Geoff would no longer try to woo the attentions of Rebecca. Rob wanted to marry the girl, but Geoff hadn't met a woman yet who could entice him to give up his freedom and independence, although Rebecca might come close. He pictured her racing Star Bright with her hair streaming behind her. That young lady was full of surprises.

A stroll down the street brought him to the doctor's office. Two men stood on the porch. He recognized one as Doctor Carter, so the other must be the new doctor. Geoff waved at the men.

"Hello, Mr. Kensington. Come and meet my new associate."

When Geoff stepped to the porch, the doctor said, "This is Doctor White. He and his wife arrived on the train this morning."

Geoff extended his hand. "We heard you were coming to town, but the mayor didn't say when. It's nice to have you. I'm just a visitor here myself, but I can tell you this is a nice place and filled with good people."

The new doctor shook Geoff's hand. "Thank you. My wife and

I look forward to living here. She's in with Mrs. Carter now. We have arranged to have rooms at the hotel until we have a place of our own."

Doctor Carter then proceeded to explain the improvements they planned to make to the building where they stood now that a second doctor had arrived. What had once been Doc Carter's living space would serve as wards for patients who needed to stay overnight. He grinned at Geoff and patted Dr. White's back. "Nobody knows this yet, but I'm planning to retire at the end of the year so the missus and I can enjoy time with each other. We even plan to go back East and visit our families there. Don't say anything, because we want to make the announcement to the whole town in a few weeks after we tell our family here."

Geoff didn't know why the man should be telling him such news, but then maybe he trusted a stranger to keep the secret more than family or friends would. "I won't tell a soul." He tipped his hat. "It's been nice meeting you, Doctor White."

On his walk back to the hotel, he stopped and peered up at Rob's law office windows. He seemed to be a smart lawyer, and Geoff liked the young man. Under other circumstances, he would hire Rob to handle the plan for the oil on Dawson's land, but that would only create a conflict of interest. Still, it would be good to have the lawyer on his side.

Everything depended on becoming a closer friend to Ben Haynes.

Rob relished the roast beef and potatoes Ruby served for their noon meal. This made the second day this week he'd come home for lunch, and today his father joined them.

Caroline sipped on her glass of water then directed her gaze at him. "How are you and Rebecca getting along these days? You seemed quite friendly on Tuesday."

"*Becky* and I are doing just fine. She's upset over what happened at the ranch, but Mr. Lansdowne ran three of her articles in the *Chronicle* this week. That made her quite happy, and I'm sure she's pleased that we closed the cattle deal with Geoff Kensington." If only that concluded the man's business and he'd leave town, Rob would feel much better about Becky.

Caroline laughed and buttered a roll. "Doesn't she get angry with you for calling her by her nickname? Not that it would make any difference to you." She leaned forward. "I've seen her about town with Mr. Kensington a time or two."

He frowned slightly. "Yes, they're friends, but then Becky is friends with most everybody."

His mother patted her lips with her napkin. "I must say that you two could find better companions than those Haynes siblings. Neither one of them pays as much attention to you as you would like for them to." She narrowed her gaze at her daughter. "I still think you should have found someone when you were away at college. I know plenty of young men were around."

Pink flushed Caroline's cheeks. "None of them interested me, Mother. Matt will decide what he wants to do about us before long."

"And what if it is not to marry you?"

"Then I will handle it if or when that happens." She turned to her father. "Do you have any idea when the motor car you ordered will be delivered?"

Rob locked gazes with his father and waited for the reaction that would come with the news he had learned yesterday.

"It's here. I'm going down to Oklahoma City to pick it up tomorrow. I thought we could all go and make a day of it."

Caroline squealed then jumped up to run over and hug her

father. "Oh, how wonderful. I can't wait to ride in it. Just think what the people of Barton Creek will say about a motor car in town, the very first."

Mother straightened her shoulders and held her head high. "Of course it's only fitting that the mayor of the town should have the first one. A man in his position should set the pace. I'm sure others will follow his lead as soon as they see our car."

Rob sat back and listened to them go on about having a new means of transportation. He thought of the Dawson land and the deposit of oil. He didn't know how many people were aware of what was there, but Ben and Sam must make a decision about it soon. With the coming of the automobile, more oil would be needed to make the fuel to run them.

Ben and Sam said they didn't need the money and weren't really interested, but they didn't truly understand the value such a deposit would be to the country in general. Ben said he didn't want to see Barton Creek become another Tulsa with oil rigs marring the landscape and people pouring into the town.

Rob could understand his feelings, but that was progress, and the sooner people could accept the fact, the better off they'd be. It had taken awhile, but now they wondered how they got along without electricity, the telegraph, and even the telephone. Automobiles were becoming more common, as were other inventions, like refrigerated coolers for the home and even electric machines for washing clothes. At a recent town council meeting he had reminded them that if Oklahoma wanted to be a state, she needed to tap into all the natural resources she had available, and that most definitely included oil.

Rebecca closed the freshly printed newspaper and sat looking in satisfaction at her bylines on the front page. Mr. Lansdowne had changed very little in what she had written. Perhaps now he'd consider the story she'd done on the speeches at Guthrie. Of course, the event itself was out of date, but the subject matter would always be relevant to her and should be to women all over the Territory.

The announcement had been made only last Tuesday, but the new doctor's wife was with Aunt Clara when Rebecca had gone to see her at lunch. The young woman, Anna White, had impressed Rebecca with her knowledge of what was going on in the world, especially since she had lived in Colorado prior to coming to Barton Creek. At last she had someone only a little older who understood what the women's suffrage movement was all about. She could hardly wait to spend more time with Anna, and perhaps she'd have some influence with Lucy and Dove, although Rebecca doubted her cousin would ever support women voting.

As if she had read Rebecca's thoughts, Lucy walked through the door with Amanda in her arms. The little girl squirmed and bent toward the floor. Rebecca jumped up and ran over to relieve Lucy.

"Come see Rebecca." The child wrapped her arms around Rebecca's neck. "My, she's growing fast. I believe she's heavier than when I held her last time."

"And she's into everything since she started walking. She doesn't like to be carried at all anymore. That's why I didn't leave her with Dove. The boys are enough for her along with her two."

"What brings you to see me?" Rebecca jostled Amanda on her hip and held the child's hands so she wouldn't grab at the brooch on her shoulder.

"We came into town for supplies, and Charley and Micah wanted to come in and visit with Dove's boys, Danny and Eddie, and their new friend, Billy Dorsett."

Rebecca laughed. "I guess Dove does have her hands full, and when school starts in the fall, Charley, Billy, and Danny will be in the same class. I pity that poor teacher." Five months were all that separated the boys in age, and what one didn't think of, one of the others would.

"It's a good thing Charley knows what will happen to him if he gets into too much trouble at school. But that's not the reason I came to see you. While here, I wanted to let you know the family will be coming to our house for dinner on Saturday evening. I hope you will plan to come and bring Rob or Mr. Kensington if you'd like."

A family dinner aroused Rebecca's curiosity. "What's the occasion for the family to get together?"

"Oh, nothing special. I thought it would be nice to be together on a relaxed evening rather than Sunday afternoon."

Despite her casual demeanor, Rebecca sensed something else behind the dinner, but from past experience, she knew Lucy would say no more than this about Saturday. "All right, I'll be there. Are Aunt Clara and Doc coming? I could ride out with them."

"They'll be there, but wouldn't you rather bring Rob or Geoff?"

"Not really. Being with the family will be enough." Especially since whomever she did bring with her would immediately be the object of family speculation. That was one problem she didn't want or need. She wanted to focus on her career and writing more articles her editor would publish.

Lucy reached for her daughter. "This little girl is ready for a nap. I'm hoping she'll sleep long enough for Dove, Ruth, and I to have a good visit." Amanda yawned and rested her head on her mother's shoulder. "Whatever you decide will be fine as long as you're there. I'm sure Aunt Clara and Doc will be happy to bring you out with them." She turned to leave, shifting the child on her hip.

Rebecca tapped her chin and watched Lucy make her way down the street toward Dove's house. Her mind swirled with questions as to what Lucy had up her sleeve. Something was going on, and this was one dinner she'd make sure she didn't miss.

Chapter 21

When the weekly edition of the *Barton Creek Chronicle* reached the public, Rebecca's joy at seeing her name as a byline on the articles she had written soared to a new level. This had been her dream since her days of writing essays and themes in school. They appeared word for word as she had written them. Even her one obituary and the report on an afternoon social of the Ladies Bible Study Society satisfied her this week.

When she came down for breakfast on Saturday morning, all the boarders around the dining table greeted her with congratulations once again. Catherine Claymore served Rebecca a plate of eggs with biscuits. "We're so proud of you. Those days of winning awards for your essays have come to fruition."

Her beaming smile added to the satisfaction of a job well done, but even amidst the compliments from other boarders, her yearning for more in-depth stories continued. This was but the first step on a long journey ahead.

Mrs. Claymore poured coffee to refill cups of various boarders who chatted about the extremely warm weather, what President Roosevelt was doing in the White House, and thoughts on when Oklahoma would become a state.

Rebecca finished her meal and prepared to leave, but Catherine stopped her. "If Mr. Kensington plans to stay longer in Barton Creek, tell him I will have a vacancy at the end of next week. Mr. Simmons is leaving."

"He's completed his cattle business with my father, so I don't think he'll be around much longer, but I'll tell him." Actually, his presence in town several days after the delivery of the herd to Guthrie surprised her, but it also pleased her, and she wasn't sure why. She certainly harbored no romantic feelings for him, or at least she tried to convince herself she didn't, but he had become a good friend and a pleasant dinner companion.

After changing into her riding attire, Rebecca made her way to the livery, looking forward to a leisurely morning ride, even though she planned to ride out to Lucy's after the noon meal instead of waiting for Aunt Clara and the doctor. Going early would give her time to visit with her cousin, and perhaps she could even help with meal preparations.

Geoff strode out of the hotel and headed toward her. He stopped and tipped his hat. "Good morning. I surmise by your outfit that you are headed for the livery and a ride on Daisy. Mind if I accompany you?"

She smiled up at him and welcomed his company. "Not at all. I wanted to get in a ride before the day heats up, but Daisy is back at the ranch. I'll be riding Star Bright."

He walked beside her, completely at ease in his Levis and boots. Geoff had certainly adapted to the ways of the cowboy in fine fashion, and he looked good doing it. His dark eyes gleamed with excitement as he talked with her.

"I have what I hope is pleasant news for you. I plan to stay in Barton Creek for several more weeks."

His words sent shivers of surprise and delight through her. "Oh, that is wonderful. I figured you'd be leaving soon." Then she remembered Mrs. Claymore's words. "By the way, if you're tired of the hotel, the boarding house will have a room available the end of next week."

Geoff's eyebrows shot up. "Really? I had despaired of ever leaving the hotel. I'll check with her soon as we return."

Jonah had Star Bright saddled for her when they entered the stables. "Saw you coming and knew what you'd want."

"Thank you. Mr. Kensington is riding with me, so I'll wait for him to saddle up."

Geoff headed for his horse and with practiced skill had the horse ready in no time. Rebecca mounted her filly. "Looks like you're turning into a real cowboy, and it suits you."

Red rose in his face, and he dropped his gaze. "I enjoy riding, and these clothes are much more comfortable." He pulled on the reins. "Where are we headed?"

"Um, no place in particular. Star Bright needs the exercise." And Rebecca needed the time with the horse. She had fought the yearning to return to her tomboy ways ever since she'd come home, but sometimes she had to give in to them. Today was one of those times.

Rob turned the corner onto Main Street just in time to see Becky and Geoff ride out of town. He'd hoped to spend some with her today himself, but now it appeared he'd have to wait. He turned toward the telegraph office. He'd sent two wires this week to people he knew in Chicago in order to find out more about the man who had purchased cattle from Haynes and Morris.

A feeling in his gut that wouldn't go away had prompted Rob to follow up on the inquiries he'd made a few weeks ago. Ever suspicious, his lawyer instincts had kicked in and warned him not to trust the man from Chicago, no matter how pleasant he appeared to be. That and the fact that Geoff showed such great interest in Becky had given him the incentive to find out more.

"Good morning, Mr. Weems. Do you have any messages for me?"

The balding man peered from beneath his visor. "Came in a little bit ago, and I planned to bring it over to your house." He picked up a piece of paper from a stack beside him and handed it to Rob. "Hope this doesn't cause a problem. Mr. Kensington seems to be a nice man."

"We'll see." He grasped the paper and headed back outside before reading it. Mr. Weems didn't need to see Rob's reaction to whatever had arrived.

His eyes sped across the brief message. As expected, Geoff had not been completely truthful about his purpose for being in Barton Creek. The man not only worked for a beef packing company in Chicago, but he also represented an oil group.

Now Rob had to make a decision as to what to do with the information. He tapped the paper on his fingertips and walked to his office. Once there, he checked through the files for the information he needed. No time to do anything about it now, though. A glance at his watch reminded him that the train to Oklahoma City would be leaving shortly.

Today, Rob and his family would ride down to pick up their automobile. Excitement rose in his chest at the prospect. Having the first car in town would certainly be a coup, and he couldn't wait to take Becky for a ride in it.

Rob closed his office and headed for the depot. He arrived only moments before the whistle announced the train's arrival from the north. His parents and Caroline were already waiting on the platform.

Several passengers disembarked when the train rolled to a stop. Rob noted all of them were men, and of the five, two of them looked rather staid with their business attire. The others were drovers in cowboy gear, probably looking for work on one of the ranches. Before he could observe which direction the men took, his father herded them toward the train.

For a moment he wished he hadn't agreed to go with them. He should be around when Becky and Geoff returned. He wanted to give the man every opportunity to reveal his true reasons for being in Barton Creek.

His mother beckoned to him when he hesitated at the steps up to the train car. "Come, son. Don't dally. This will be a great adventure, and just think of the envious looks we'll have when we return in our car."

Rob shrugged and boarded the train. For today, Geoff could wait.

Rebecca lifted her face to the sun and breathed deeply. "I love being outdoors and riding." Her eyes opened wide. She had just admitted what she'd tried to keep secret. "You won't tell anyone I said that, will you?"

"And why not? I think it's wonderful that you enjoy such things. I have come to love being outdoors myself."

Her cheeks burned, but not from the heat of the day. "It's only that I want to be seen as an independent young woman with a career and not some schoolgirl who loves to race horses and rope calves."

Laughter rang out as Geoff slapped his thigh. "You rope calves too? That I'd like to see."

"Well, you won't, but I was as good if not better than Matt most times." The memories of those times when she and Matt competed to see who would be the fastest to get a calf down for branding brought a smile to her face and her heart.

"What made you change your mind about that?"

Rebecca thought for a few moments. Love for the old ways of living competed for her knowledge of what women could do in the world if given a chance. If she got stuck on a ranch like Ma or Lucy, she'd never have a part in changing things. Life had so much more to offer than that.

"It's hard to explain, but I want to be a woman who can change things, and I think I have that opportunity through my writing and working on the newspaper."

"Sounds like you have your life mapped out. Write good articles, get them into print, then move up to larger papers and more opportunity to change the world."

Put like that, it didn't sound quite as appealing, but it *was* her dream. Still, Geoff understood her better than Rob or her family ever could. If Rob had his way, she'd be in Barton Creek the rest of her life, taking care of him and a family. Not that marriage and family would be so bad, but they weren't in the plans she had for her life at the moment.

The heat from the sun began to bear down, and rivulets of perspiration ran down her neck. She used her neckerchief to blot them up and noticed Geoff beginning to look pale. She handed him her flask of water. "I think you need a drink. You're not used to this type of heat, are you?"

He grasped the container and gulped down the water. He then wiped his mouth on his sleeve and handed it back to her. "No, I'm not. Chicago gets hot, but not like this, and there I can stay mostly indoors and out of it."

"I think it's time we head back. I plan on going out to Lucy's ranch this afternoon. I was going early, but I think maybe now I'll wait and go with Aunt Clara and Doc."

Before she turned, the wind picked up and stirred up the dust on the road. Grains of dirt and sand bit at her skin, and she shielded her eyes. She'd seen this happen before. Dust storms could come on fast and create havoc without much warning. An orange-brown glow showed on the horizon, and Rebecca reined in Star Bright.

"Geoff, that dark cloud coming this way is a dust cloud. A storm is coming, and we need to get back to town." She pulled her kerchief up over her nose and told Geoff to do the same.

"Do you think we can outrun it?"

"Yes, and we need to warn the people in town so they can get all their doors and windows shut in time."

She kicked her horse into a full gallop. "Run like the wind. We're in a race for our lives." If ever Star Bright had run fast, she had to do it now. Rebecca glanced behind her and saw Geoff keeping close behind.

The wall of dust came closer. From the looks of it, this one wasn't as bad as some in the past, but it would leave a layer of dirt and grime over everything it passed. Depending on the length of the storm, they may be cleaning up from this for days and perhaps even weeks.

Specks of flying dirt hit her face and arms, stinging her even through the fabric of her shirt and kerchief. She pulled the brim of her hat lower to shield her eyes from the swirling dust. She kept her mouth closed and breathed only through her nose protected by the bandanna. Never had she been so thankful that wearing one had become as much a habit as wearing her hat or boots.

She glanced at Geoff. His chest heaved and his head bobbed up and down. She yelled at him and gestured with her hand. "Breathe through your nose into the kerchief."

He nodded and pulled the bandanna tighter. When he appeared to be better, Rebecca slapped the reins on either side of Star Bright, urging her onward. When they reached the edge of town she began shouting. "A dust storm is coming! A dust storm is coming!" People began hurrying back to their homes and businesses. Rebecca jumped off her horse at the livery.

"Jonah, a dust storm is right behind us. Close everything up tight. I'm going to help Mrs. Claymore."

Geoff arrived a moment later and swung off his saddle. "Is there anything I can do to help you, Jonah?"

Rebecca didn't have time to worry about Geoff or Jonah now. They could take care of themselves. She raced down the street as the wind picked up and whirlwinds of dust formed and danced across her path. She could already taste the grit in her mouth. Dinner would be dusty tonight if they had any at all.

When she arrived at the boarding house, Mrs. Claymore had everyone hopping to make sure all the shutters were closed tight. Every little crack and crevice had been filled with bits of rags and cloth. Every other time the wind had kicked dust into a storm, she'd been at home, not in town. Thoughts of her family filled her mind, and she worried about how they would fare this time.

In her own room, she made sure the windows were tight, but even then the tiny grains would sneak in and cover everything in a fine layer. Looked like she'd spend the next few days cleaning up dust and dirt from everything she owned.

She flopped down on her bed. Dust storms, tornados, droughts…all good reasons to get out of this town and go back East.

Chapter 22

*R*ebecca opened the door to her room. Although the winds hadn't lasted long, it had been long enough to coat everything in her room with a layer of dust so thick she could write her name in it. This would take hours to clean up, but there'd be time for that later. She hurried back downstairs to offer her assistance to Mrs. Claymore.

When Rebecca entered the kitchen, Mrs. Claymore stood at the sink pumping water into buckets. She glanced up and said, "Take the broom and sweep what you can from the floor. I'll come behind you with the wet mop and hope we can get it all."

Mrs. Claymore had been in enough dust storms to know that starting with the wet mop first would only make mud and a big mess. Rebecca had made that mistake once when she had tried to clean up her room on the ranch without wiping down the furniture with a dry cloth first.

Gray dust with a tinge of red covered every surface in the kitchen as Rebecca started on the floor. Swirls of dust formed as she swept the linoleum flooring. "What about the food? How much will you have to throw away?"

"The canned foods and things in packages will be all right, and the food in the ice box is unharmed, but everything else will be thrown away. I'll make soup from the canned vegetables for later since we missed lunchtime entirely."

One of the other residents poked her head around the door

opening. "Is there anything I can do to help? The men are upstairs in their rooms and probably won't be down right away. Olivia and I want to help though."

Mrs. Claymore stopped her work and said, "Florence, that's sweet of you. If you two ladies would take some of those rag cloths over there and wipe down the furniture in the parlor and dining rooms, I would be most grateful. I'd like a clean surface to eat on later." She turned back to her work then stopped. "Oh, yes, and please let the men know I will prepare a meal as soon as I can to make up for the one they missed during the storm."

Florence nodded and picked up the cloths. "I've never seen anything like this. I suppose I do need to go over to the school later and check my classroom. I'm sure it'll be filthy. I wonder if we'll even be able to have school on Monday."

Rebecca paused in her sweeping. She'd completely forgotten the dinner tonight at Lucy and Jake's. Surely Lucy wouldn't have it now with the storm. She'd have her hands full with cleaning her house and taking care of her children. Still, curiosity about the reason for the dinner filled Rebecca. She shrugged. Whatever it was, Lucy would tell them later.

Florence left the room, and Rebecca returned to her task. She spent the next hour helping Mrs. Claymore get the kitchen in order. A large box contained food tainted by dust. The two of them emptied the pantry shelves and wiped them down. The closed door to the pantry had kept most of the dirt out, so much of what was stored there had escaped the grime.

When she completed that chore, Becky excused herself and headed for her aunt's home.

Aunt Clara greeted her with a hug. She wore a kerchief around her head as well as one covering her face. She pulled it down to speak. "I'm so glad to see you're all right. We've had several come in with breathing problems, and Doc and the new doctor are treating them now."

Rebecca swallowed a snicker. Doc Carter hated his given name of Flavius, so even Aunt Clara called him "Doc," along with everyone else in town. "I've been helping Mrs. Claymore with cleaning at the boarding house. From the looks of things here, I don't imagine we'll be going out to Lucy's this evening."

"No, dear, as you can see we have our hands full. I just pray none of the children fall ill from this dirt. So far I believe it's only a few adults who've been affected, but we'll probably see children later on."

"I'm glad to hear that, not that I'm glad any are ill, but adults do handle these things better. All our long-time people know what to do in times like this, but I worried about those who never experienced it before. Geoff and I were out riding when we spotted the storm coming, and I know he was having difficulty breathing."

"If he went straight to the hotel, he'll be fine. That place is tight as a drum according to the manager."

Rebecca laughed. "I've heard him bragging about that, but even so, I imagine those rooms got a dusting just like everything else." She hugged her aunt. "Looks like you have everything under control here, so I'm going back to help at the boarding house."

She left and headed back up the street. Mr. Lansdowne hailed her. "Miss Haynes, I must see you a moment."

Her editor ran up then stopped and bent over to catch his breath. After a moment he raised up and said, "I forget how this dust affects one's lungs." He covered his mouth and coughed.

Rebecca patted his back. "Are you sure you don't need to see Doctor Carter?"

He cleared his throat then rubbed his forehead. "I'm fine, but it's the printing press I'm worried about. I covered it best I could with a canvas, but if any dirt got in at all, it'll stick to the surfaces and make a mess."

"Oh, dear, I hadn't thought about that. Do you need my help?"

"Not with the cleaning, but seeing as how you did such a fine job with your stories last week, I am hoping you will take over writing about this storm. See what damage has been done, talk to the people and get their stories, and then say something about dust storms in general. That way, I'll have more time to take care of the press."

Rebecca's heart jumped in her throat at the request. He believed in her writing enough to give her this assignment, and her mind began spinning with ideas. "Of course, Mr. Lansdowne, I'll be happy to do that. I'll get right to work on it."

With a nod of his head and a thank-you, he turned and hurried down to the news office. Rebecca planted her hands on her hips and surveyed the town, trying to decide just where to begin her stories.

On the way back to Barton Creek, Rob and his father spotted the huge cloud of dust racing from the north toward their hometown. His father immediately turned the motor car around and headed back to Oklahoma City to escape the storm. Not that the city wouldn't feel the effects, but it did appear the bulk of the cloud would move more to the west.

His mother fussed all the way back with concern for their home in Barton Creek. His own thoughts centered on what the town would think when they realized their own mayor had not been around when the storm hit. He understood his father's reasoning in keeping his family safe and out of harm's way, but the citizens of Barton Creek might not.

They drove into Oklahoma City to find the streets nearly empty. The people here were preparing just as those in Barton Creek would be doing. His father headed for a nearby hotel.

Rob surveyed the four-story structure. It should keep them away from the biting bits of dust that he felt even now as the wind picked up. "Looks like we'll get the edge of the storm, but I'm worried about what is happening in Barton Creek." More specifically he worried that Becky and Geoff had been out riding instead of safe in town when the storm hit.

"We'll get back there as soon as we can. There's no sense in endangering all our lives." Father spoke to the manager. "Is there a place my family and I can stay for a few hours?"

The manager nodded. "Yes, you can go into the dining room. We'll have coffee and pastries for refreshment, but we can't serve a full meal until later this evening." Even as he spoke, people crowded into the lobby.

Father acknowledged the manager's word and herded his family to the dining room, where they were able to find a table far away from any windows or doors. From the look on his mother's face, she was most unhappy with this development. Rob swallowed a chuckle. She wasn't so much distressed by the storm as she was about how her grand entrance into Barton Creek in a brand-new motor car would not be as effective or grand when they finally arrived.

He leaned toward Caroline. "You've been awfully quiet in all this commotion."

"I've just been thinking about our life in Barton Creek and how dull it is compared to what I've seen here." Her hands brushed at her skirt, and she kept her head lowered.

Rob sensed more to her words than she stated. "Let's walk over to the pastry table and see what they have to offer."

She shrugged but stood and followed him. "I thought perhaps

you didn't want to speak in front of Mother and Father. Now, what's the real problem here?"

The lights from the chandeliers exposed the glistening tears in her eyes. "I'm not really sure. I feel so alone. Mother has her friends with the different societies she belongs to, you have your work, as does Father, but I have nothing to do and no really good friends."

"What about Alice? You and she were once very close."

"We're still friends, but she has Eli now, and they're always off on a trip to Wyoming or Montana. Matthew is too busy with the ranch to pay any attention to me. Seems like everyone who is anywhere near my age is married or busy with their own lives."

Her statements gave him pause to think. Many new people moved into Barton Creek every month, but they were either married couples with young families or older men looking for work. No new young people had made their way to the town in many years. Even in his own situation he realized Becky was the only one his age now. The others they had grown up with had either left Barton Creek or were married and making their own way.

A sigh escaped Caroline's lips and her shoulders drooped. "I love Matt, but he doesn't have time for me with all the responsibilities at the ranch."

"That's true, but they have a good number of cowboys to help them." He hadn't understood Matt's apparent disinterest in courting Caroline, but the young man must have a good reason. A few years ago he'd spent all his time at church and in town with her, but now it seemed they barely acknowledged each other.

Becky and he had a similar situation, but at least she did things with him. Still, her ambitions and dreams didn't include marriage in the near future, and her faith in God was not anywhere near what it had been before she had gone to Wellesley. Now Geoff had entered the picture, and she had more in common with him than she did Rob. The memory of the telegraph from this morning clouded his mind. He must let Becky know the truth, but in so doing he ran the risk of alienating her against him rather than Geoff.

"Do you ever think either of them will show interest in us? What is it about us that pushes Becky and Matt away instead of bringing them closer?" His sister's words brought him back from his reverie, but he had no answer for her.

He wrapped an arm around her shoulder. "We can only pray that they will find their future plans do include us. In the meantime, we must do everything we can to keep our relationships with them alive."

Caroline placed a pastry on a plate and picked up a napkin. "I like the city, and I might consider finding work and moving. Life is much more exciting here."

"Don't even think such thoughts. We need you with us." But even as he said the words, he heard the selfishness they manifested. His voice softened. "I'm sorry, you must do what you think is best for you, and I'll help in any way I can."

Things were changing everywhere, and at the moment, he could think of nothing that would slow progress. He could either accept and embrace the new options, or he could fret and stew for the way things had always been. He followed Caroline back to the table where their parents sat talking. If only things could change, but somehow also stay the same, his life would be much less complicated.

Caroline's statement about the boredom she felt in Barton Creek bothered Rob. Perhaps a change would be good for Caroline. Mother would most certainly object, but unless she involved Caroline in more of the activities of the church committees and the Ladies Guild that oversaw many of the civic activities of the town, Caroline had good reason to want to move. Things would change when Oklahoma became a state and their father ran for a congressional seat from their district. A move to Washington DC would catch the fancy of any young woman and might be just the thing to make Matt sit up and take notice.

As his mother and Caroline talked, his mother's attitude bothered him. She truly believed her children deserved better in life than the Haynes siblings could provide. As far as Mother was concerned, both her children deserved better life companions than a rancher and a suffragette. But for him, his mother couldn't be more wrong. Becky was the girl he wanted to marry, and until she herself told him no, nothing his mother could do or say would convince him otherwise.

Chapter 23

*A*lthough Geoff's chest still ached some, the coughing from last evening had stopped. He now sat at a table for breakfast and listened to other diners as they talked about yesterday's storm. Reports of lost cattle and other livestock as well as damage to property reached his ears.

His plans for riding out to inspect the Dawson plot once more were still uppermost in his mind. At least his cattle deal had been finalized and the herd sent on to Chicago before the dust hit. He signed the tab for his meal and headed out the door toward the livery.

Already a few wagons and buggies headed for the church yard. He didn't understand why they didn't stay at home and clean up their property, but their being here meant he'd have more time for his inspection.

A strange sound reached his ears. He turned to see a motor car coming around the corner. His eyes opened wide. This was the last thing he'd expected to see in Barton Creek.

The driver continued to honk the horn as people scattered to escape the machine. Geoff peered at the vehicle and realized Mayor Frankston and his wife were seated behind the wheel of the automobile. People emptied from the various places along the street to investigate the noise. The mayor grinned and waved at everyone as the car carried him and his wife down Main Street.

Geoff wanted to laugh out loud at the sight, but he kept his amusement to a chuckle. Horses shied away and riders had a diffi-cult time controlling them as the motor car passed by. A common sight in Chicago and even Oklahoma City, the black vehicle trimmed in brass made a grand entrance. Evidently the car had not escaped the grime of the storm yesterday, or its black body would be much shinier than it appeared now.

The idea of more cars in Barton Creek served to add to the importance Geoff now placed on his mission. Surely Ben and Sam could see the impact the cars had on the oil industry. The time for action had come.

Geoff watched the parade of people following the motor car to the church, where they gathered around the mayor and Mrs. Frankston. Now that would make a good story for Rebecca to write up for the *Chronicle*. But the new car would have to wait. He had more important issues to attend to at the moment.

He headed for the livery to find Jonah. The owner met him at the door. He was dressed in his Sunday best and wore a black bowler hat instead of the straw one he usually had on. "Can you saddle your own horse? I'm heading to church for the services today."

"Sure, no trouble, but why are you going to church? You're usually here all day on Sundays."

"After that storm yesterday, I aim to be thanking the good Lord it weren't no worse than it was. I seen plenty in my day, and that coulda been a bad'un."

"I see. Well, you go on and I'll take care of myself." Let the man go and worship his God and be thankful; Geoff had more impor-tant things on his mind.

The road to the Haynes ranch and Dawson land gave evidence of the destruction from yesterday. A yellowish-red dust covered every surface left exposed. Some of the trees had even been stripped of most of their leaves, and broken limbs littered the landscape. How thankful he was now to have been able to get back before it hit full force. Even though his room at the hotel had been secure, dust still managed to get in and coat everything. The hotel management had assured him that they would clean up his room as soon as possible, which would probably be later than sooner.

The manager of the hotel had said this storm wasn't much compared to some they'd had in the past. If that was so, Geoff was glad he hadn't been around for others. He'd take the blizzards of Chicago any day over storms with dust and dirt.

He made the trek to the oil deposit without incident. After a half hour inspection, he determined the deposit to be extensive. Evidence of what lay beneath the surface could be seen in a wide area of the land. Several times he stopped and rubbed dirt between his fingers. The storm had blown away much of the topsoil so that the riches below were more exposed. This might be even bigger than that last find over near Tulsa.

Twice Geoff had the distinct impression that someone followed him or observed him from a distance, but each time he turned to look, he saw nothing but the barren land. He debated about talking with Ben Haynes today or waiting until Monday. Finally he decided to head back to Barton Creek. Although it didn't matter to Geoff, Mr. Haynes didn't seem to be the type to discuss business on Sunday.

When he arrived back at the hotel, he decided to take a good hot bath before eating. He headed through the deserted lobby and climbed the stairs. At the landing he stopped when he spotted the door to his room slightly ajar. Were the cleaning people working on Sunday? He strode over and pushed open the door, but before he knew it someone grabbed him from behind while someone else punched him in the gut.

He bent over double as another blow hit the side of his face. He fought to free himself, but the man held tightly. Geoff's vision blurred as another blow hit his head then another to the stomach.

The next moment he was on the floor. He pushed up once, but a foot held him firm.

"You stay away from that land out yonder. Stay away from Mr. Haynes too. You go back out there, and it might be the last time you go anywhere."

He was yanked up from the floor again and hit several more times. His eyes swelled shut, and the coppery taste of blood filled his mouth. Finally they dropped him and gave him one last kick before leaving.

Geoff lay on the floor, doubled over in pain with his breath coming in gasps. Everything around him swam in a blur of blood and sweat. When he tried to pull himself up by the bedpost, the pain shot through him like an arrow, and he slumped back down to the floor.

His body relaxed and the room faded away.

Rob stepped out onto the porch of his parents' home. A good church service and an excellent Sunday dinner filled him with deep satisfaction. Although a light coating of dust still covered everything even after cleaning, the world looked bright and beautiful. A scripture he had memorized as a young boy came to mind. He would make a joyful noise to the Lord, and he would serve the Lord with gladness and come before God's presence with singing. Yes, God was good and had spared the town from a true disaster.

He set his hat firmly on his head and bounded down the steps. His parents always rested after dinner on Sundays, and Caroline had retired to her room to read. That meant he had free time on his hands. Now might be a good opportunity to confront Geoff with his knowledge of Geoff's employer and his hidden motivations for doing business in Barton Creek.

He stopped when he turned the corner to Main Street. A quiet Sunday afternoon meant few people out and about, especially with the heat from the July sun bearing down. Every other establishment had shuttered doors except for the hotel. Even the saloon sat quiet and empty on this Sunday afternoon.

At the doctor's place, he stopped when he noted several people there. He strolled over to see what the problem was. He recognized the Bailey family and the Harrises too.

"Good afternoon. Are all of you here to see Doctor Carter?"

Mr. Bailey extended his hand. "Good afternoon, Mr. Frankston. We brought two of our young'uns in to see the doc. He says they'll be OK, but he's keeping them for awhile to make sure the dust didn't do damage to their lungs. Neither one could stop coughing this morning."

"Sorry to hear that, but I'm sure Doctor Carter and Doctor White will take good care of them."

A woman stepped onto the boardwalk. Rob's eyes opened wide when he recognized Ruth Dorsett in a dark dress covered by a white apron. She beckoned to Mr. and Mrs. Harris. "You may come in and see your children now."

She smiled at Rob. "Do you need to see the doctor?"

"Uh, no, um, I was just talking with these folks." He peered at her and knit his brow. "I'm surprised to see you here. Are your children all right?"

She laughed and opened the door for Mr. and Mrs. Harris. "I'm helping the doctors. I've been doing it for several weeks now. Doctor Carter remembered I had nurse training and asked me to assist them. I'm glad to help. We've had quite a few people come in with coughs and lung problems since the storm yesterday. The doctor is treating them for a form of dust bronchitis. Dr. White has some new ideas for treatment that he learned in Colorado. Thankfully we have what he needs on hand."

"They are fortunate to have your assistance." Rob tipped his hat and made his way across the street toward the hotel.

Rob's mother had commented this week on what a good seamstress Ruth was. Now she was able to use her nursing skills too. Becky had mentioned that fact once during one of her spiels about women and their right to vote and work in whatever profession they chose, but he hadn't paid that much attention to it.

He needed to start listening to Becky more. Some of her ideas were not as far-fetched as they seemed. Women did have it harder when it came to choices as to how they would spend their lives. If they chose marriage, they had to wait for a man to decide she was the choice. If they wanted to have a career, few choices were available. The few women who had managed to enter a career had a hard time of it.

Maybe it was time to revise his thinking. Becky loved what she did at the paper. From now on he vowed to show more support for her successes and listen to what she had to say. He chuckled at the thought that he might even learn something himself.

He entered the hotel and scanned the empty lobby. Even the hotel was extraordinarily quiet today. Shrugging, he headed up the stairs, hoping he'd find Geoff in his room. He pulled the wire he'd received from his pocket. He held a great deal of interest in what Geoff would have to say about its contents. If he was straightforward and answered truthfully, Rob would be more than interested in what the man knew about the oil deposit on Dawson's land. Perhaps together they could persuade Ben and Sam to reconsider their objections to drilling.

The door stood slightly ajar, so Rob knocked and called Geoff's name. No answer came, and Rob pushed the door open to offer a wider view of the room. At first glance no one seemed to be there, but then Rob heard a groan and shoved the door open all the way.

Geoff lay crumpled in a heap at the end of the bed with blood on his face. Rob rushed to the still form and knelt beside him. "Geoff, Geoff, can you hear me?"

Another groan and Geoff turned his head. All Rob could see was blood and a very swollen eye and cheek. "Don't move, Geoff," he said. "I'm going to get the doctor."

Chapter 24

*E*very inch of Geoff's body hurt. His head pounded like a blacksmith's hammer and anvil. He heard voices but couldn't distinguish who was talking. When he tried to open his eyes, only one would cooperate. He peered up into the faces of Doctor Carter and a very pretty young woman. His one lid blinked and looked again. They were still there, but why were they in his room?

When he tried to speak, his tongue wouldn't work, and only gibberish came from his mouth. The young woman placed a cool hand on his arm. "Lie still and don't say anything. You were badly beaten, and we've brought you to the infirmary to recover."

Beaten? Then the images came back. Two men held him and pummeled him with their fists. They had warned him, but what was it? Oh, yes, stay away from the oil deposits. Somebody had sent him a warning, but who? His brain felt like mush at the moment and his body like a train had run over it. Surely every bone had been broken.

Doctor Carter leaned over him, and a light shone in his eyes. "Looks like you took a good beating, young man. You're lucky that Rob found you when he did."

At the moment lucky was the last thing he felt. He tried to speak again, but he could only grip the doctor's hand with the one hand that didn't hurt.

"Don't try to talk. I'm giving you some laudanum to help with the pain. You need to sleep now. One of us will be here with you through the night in case you wake up again." The doctor stood and nodded to the woman with him.

Through the haze in his one good eye, Geoff realized the woman was Ruth Dorsett. She lifted his head just enough to give him something to drink. He wasn't sure what it was, but he let the bitter liquid slide down his throat. It must be the laudanum the doctor mentioned. He tried to smile, but even that hurt his face.

Ruth placed her hand on his forehead. "I'm taking first watch, so you sleep and let your body began its healing. If you start hurting bad, call out and we'll give you more medicine." She squeezed his hand and smiled. Her voice and cool touch fell over him like pleasant rain.

He closed his eyes as the laudanum took effect and the pain eased. Through the fog in his brain he heard snatches of conversation between the doctor and someone who sounded like Rob. He'd have to thank the young man later. Geoff heard mention of broken ribs, a black eye, cuts on his face, and bruises near his kidneys. He'd like to get his hands on the goons who had done this to him. But that would have to wait. All he wanted at the moment was sleep.

Rob walked to the door with Doctor Carter. "I'm going down to report this to the sheriff. When will Geoff be ready to talk with him?"

"Probably sometime tomorrow morning. He was beaten badly, and the kick to his kidney may have done some damage. We'll have to wait to see on that. Anyway, I plan to keep him sedated through the night to give him a good sleep."

"That's good." Rob glanced around the room. "You're full up tonight, I see. I hope we have no more emergencies tonight."

"The renovations aren't quite complete, but we'll make do. I have all the children in one room on cots. They'll be better by tomorrow evening, and I'll send them home. Right now one parent is with each child, so they're taken care of, and Ruth will stay with Geoff until Dr. White comes to stay during the night in case any of the patients need him. I'll be back in the morning."

"Looks like you have everything under control, so I'll get on down to the sheriff's office."

Once out on the street, Rob headed for the jail. He heard someone call his name and turned to find Becky running toward him. She caught up and panted to catch her breath. "Is it true that Geoff was beaten?"

"Yes, I found him in his room. He's at the clinic now." He hoped this wouldn't draw her closer to Geoff. Rob still had misgivings about the man and his purpose for being in Barton Creek. Until that purpose was clear, Becky didn't need to be so involved with Mr. Kensington.

"Who would do such a thing? Was he hurt badly?"

"I think he'll be laid up a few days. He has cracked ribs, a black eye, and lots of bruises. Doc gave him a sedative, so he's sleeping right now, and Ruth is with him."

"This is terrible! Nothing like this has ever happened before, at least not to someone I know."

"Yes, it is bad, and I'm on my way to report it to the sheriff. Walk with me."

She nodded and followed along beside him. Before they reached the jail, two horses thundered around the corner. Becky gasped beside him, and he recognized the men from Ben Haynes's ranch.

They jumped off their horses and raced into the sheriff's office. Becky picked up her skirt and ran after them, and Rob followed close behind. Something must have happened at the ranch for these men to be in such a hurry.

Becky burst through the door of the building. "Hank, what's wrong? Why are you here?"

The foreman of the Rocking H ranch grabbed Becky's arm. "Miss Haynes, the stables caught on fire and burned while everyone was at church. Monk and I and the rest of the men were out with the herds when we saw the smoke and hightailed it back. We were able to get the livestock out, but couldn't save the building. Your pa and the others are rounding up the horses." He turned to the sheriff. "Ben thinks this was a deliberate fire. He's much too careful about lanterns and things that could burn out in the stables."

Sheriff Claymore shook his head. "I don't understand why anyone would burn a barn full of animals. This on top of the slaughtered cattle this past week makes me wonder what it is about the Haynes that someone doesn't like." He strapped his gun belt around his waist.

Rob had an idea about why the two things happened and couldn't help but wonder if Geoff's beating was but another part of a larger scheme to get the oil. "Sheriff, one more thing happened. Geoff Kensington was badly beaten by someone this afternoon. He's at Doc's and is pretty banged up, so they've sedated him for the night."

Sheriff Claymore let his breath out in a huff and shoved his hat back on his head. "What's happening to this town? I haven't seen the likes of this in all the years I've been here." He turned to Hank. "Let's get out to the ranch and see what's going on out there. I can talk to Mr. Kensington later."

Becky ran out the door, calling over her shoulder, "I'm going with you." Before Hank could stop her, she was outside and running to the livery.

Hank shook his head and motioned to the other cowboy. "Might as well wait a minute for her. She's as stubborn as they come when something happens to her family."

How right he was. Rob remembered times when that stubborn streak had shown itself. Like the one time he'd criticized Matt because he hadn't paid enough attention to Caroline, she defended him and wouldn't speak to Rob for several days, even after he apologized.

Out on the street he saw Becky emerge from the livery on Star Bright. She joined the two cowboys and the sheriff as they took off for the ranch. Rob offered up a prayer for everyone concerned in the fire and the beating.

"Rob Frankston, I need a word with you."

Aunt Clara stood before him pointing her finger at his chest. "I just saw Becky and the sheriff ride out of here like a coon dog after his prey. What's going on?"

He knew better than to keep anything from Clara Carter. She'd have his hide if he didn't tell the truth. He grasped her arms. "There was a fire out at the ranch. Something or someone burned the stables. The sheriff went out to investigate."

Her hands flew to her mouth and smothered her cry. "Oh, no. Was anybody hurt?"

"Not that I know of. Hank said they got the livestock out too. It happened during church. Hank and the rest of the men were out with the cattle when they spotted the smoke. They were able to save the horses and other livestock, but couldn't save the building."

She shook her head then grasped Rob's arm. "Doc told me Geoff Kensington was beaten and is in the clinic. What is going on around here?"

"I don't know, but I'm sure the sheriff will find out and let us know."

"I need to go out to the ranch and help Mellie." She pursed her mouth in the way he'd seen her do many times before, and he braced himself for her request.

"Rob, be a dear and get a wagon to take me out there. I need to leave our buggy here for the doc in case he has to go out on a call."

He sighed, knowing there was no good way to get out of taking her, but it did give him a good excuse to see Becky and be there for her. "Of course, Aunt Clara. I'll go home and get our buggy. I'll pick you up at your house."

She reached up and hugged him. "You're a good boy, Rob Frankston, and my niece is foolish for not seeing that. You love her, so go after her." With that she turned and ran back to her home as fast as her plump little body could take her.

Rob stepped back in surprise and watched her a moment. That had come out of the blue. Of course he loved Becky, but he'd been giving her space to find herself and what she really wanted out of life. Perhaps the time had come to step into that space and let her know his feelings and hopes for her and a future together.

Rebecca stomped around the yard, gazing all the while at the smoldering ruins of the barn. At least Hank and the others had seen the smoke in time to get the horses to safety. If they hadn't been so close to being home, they might have lost everything.

Fury raged inside her at the idea of someone coming onto their property and deliberately setting the fire. Nature may take its course, as it had with the tornado and prairie fire of 1897, but those they couldn't control. She bent to pick up a blackened harness strap that had separated itself from the rest of the debris. She tossed it back onto the smoking heap of rubble the men were piling up.

Pa and the sheriff stood off to one side talking and comparing notes. Ma swept dust and ashes from the porch, and the harsh *swoosh* of the bristles against the wooden planks gave testimony to her anger. Adversity had struck this family many times before, and they had always bounced back. This time would be no different. Her main hope at the moment was for Pa and the sheriff to find clues as to what had happened and who was responsible.

At the sound of buggy wheels, she raised her head to see Rob and Aunt Clara rolling in. Of course Clara wanted to be here for Ma, but why was Rob with her? Then she remembered the patients Doc had in his clinic. Her dear aunt had waylaid Rob and convinced him to bring her out here.

She pulled off her working gloves and went to meet them. "I'm so glad you came."

"I am too." Ma spoke from behind Rebecca.

Rob jumped down and came around to assist Aunt Clara from the buggy. She hugged Ma then Rebecca. "I'm so sorry this happened. Rob tells me it may not have been an accident."

Ma gripped her apron with clenched fists. "No, it doesn't look like it was."

Pa waved from where he was with Sheriff Claymore but didn't join them. Ma motioned to Aunt Clara. "Let's go into the house out of this heat."

Rob stepped to Rebecca's side, and she grinned up at him. "I'm sorry you got roped into bringing her out here, but I know how stubborn she can be once she has her mind set on something."

"Just like someone else I know."

Rebecca jerked her head around. "Just what is that supposed to mean?"

He tweaked a bit of hair. "Just what I said. You have the tenacity of a dog chewing on his favorite bone. When you want something, you go after it."

She planted her fists on her hips and narrowed her eyes. "And what's so wrong with that?"

This time he laughed. "Nothing's wrong with it. It's just that sometimes you...never mind. Let's talk about something else."

He didn't finish his sentence because the teasing would rile her, and he knew it. She pushed her hat off her head and tossed her hair over her shoulder before striding off to join Ma and Aunt Clara.

From the corner of her eye she watched him amble over to where her pa and the sheriff still talked. Her anger mystified her for the moment. Seemed like every time Rob was around, things happened inside her that she didn't want to happen.

She went inside the house, and Ma insisted on pouring her a cool drink. Aunt Clara sat with her at the kitchen table. "Did you see the mayor and his family come into town this morning in a new motor car?" Aunt Clara asked.

Rebecca shook her head. "No, but I heard about it." It had been the main topic of conversation around the boarding house dinner table at noon. Once more the mayor had to be the first to have something new. At least Ma had a new sewing machine before everyone else, but then Mrs. Frankston probably didn't even know how to sew.

"I've seen a lot of changes in my day, but this is the strangest one of all. Imagine riding around in a contraption that loud for any length of time." She settled back into her chair. "Enough of that. I want to hear about you and Rob."

"What? There is no me and Rob." What had brought on this train of thought? Aunt Clara and Rob must have discussed her on the way from town. "Besides, it nobody's business whom I see or allow to court me."

Aunt Clara laughed at that and shook her head. Ma set a plate of cookies on the table and joined them. "What is so funny?"

Rebecca clenched her teeth as anger simmered deep inside. "Seems Aunt Clara and Rob have been discussing me behind my back."

Aunt Clara reached over and patted Rebecca's knee. "No, honey, we didn't discuss you, but anyone with half an eye can see how much he loves you, and you once felt the same way about him."

True, she had cared about him and even dreamed of marrying him, but that was before she realized the other opportunities out in the world. "It's not that way now."

Aunt Clara said nothing but smiled with that knowing look of hers that always told Becky to sit a spell and listen to whatever had to be said. Rebecca sighed and resigned herself to the forthcoming lecture, and knowing Aunt Clara, it wouldn't be limited to Rob Frankston and her relationship with him.

Aunt Clara wasted no time. "Rebecca Susan Haynes, I don't know what they taught you at that school, but I've begun to regret sending you off for your education. Women's suffrage is a good cause, but there's no reason to be consumed by it. Be careful that you don't miss out on something very special in your life while you're out chasing a cause. A young man loves you, and you must consider carefully what you will do in response, or you may regret it the rest of your days."

Aunt Clara's keen eyes seemed to pierce right through Rebecca, and she dropped her head to avoid the gaze. A long, awkward silence filled the room.

"Would you like a cookie, Becky?" her mother asked, handing her the plate.

Rebecca sent her mother a grateful look. "Yes, please."

With a sheepish glance at Aunt Clara, Rebecca took a bite. She knew her aunt was right. She had much to consider in the days ahead—not only her own feelings, but also the feelings of a very old and beloved friend.

Chapter 25

*R*ebecca rode in the buggy with Rob back to Barton Creek with Daisy and Star Bright tied behind. Since the stables were burned, she had no choice but to bring the horses back to town where Jonah could care for them until the barn and stables were rebuilt. Pa, Matt, and the rest of the crew were building a temporary corral for the other animals tonight. The idea of someone burning the building deliberately both angered and frightened her.

Although Aunt Clara decided to spend the night with Ma, Rebecca felt her presence in the buggy as she remembered what Aunt Clara had said. Her aunt's words still rang in her ears, and they did make sense, although Rebecca had not wanted to hear or accept them.

Rob said nothing, as though he sensed her need to think. Too much had happened in the past few days to keep her mind clear and focused on any one topic. Her ride with Geoff had been pleasant until the dust storm. Now he lay injured by unknown hands and her father's stables lay in a burned-out heap of debris.

She glanced over at Rob in the gathering dusk. The firm set of his jaw told of his determination not to say anything until she was ready to talk. What could she say? Her mind and her heart didn't cooperate, each going in its own direction. As the sun lowered and painted the sky in lavender and gold, her spirits dropped in dark despair. Never had she been at such a loss as to what direction she should take from here.

If what Aunt Clara said was true, then a decision about Rob had to be made soon. Either she still cared about him or she didn't. It should be as simple as that, but questions and doubts got in the way. He'd been patient and had admired her work as well as taken her wherever she wanted or needed to go. Maybe that was the problem. He was always there, and she had taken him for granted. Then Geoff came along and paid attention to everything she had to say, but deep down inside, good sense told her he wasn't the man she needed.

She studied gloved hands now clasped in her lap. Did God really have a hand in everything as Aunt Clara believed, or did things just happen because evil existed in the world? Surely God wouldn't allow such things as Geoff's beating, the slaughter of the cattle, and the burning of the stables. If He did, then He wasn't as loving as everyone believed.

Finally she could stand the silence no longer. "Rob, do you truly believe that everything happens for a purpose?"

He turned to look her square in the eye. "Yes, I do. The Bible tells us that in all things God works for the good of those who love Him and have been called for His purposes. Whatever happens, including today, is in His will and purpose for our lives."

"Aunt Clara said that when we look back, we can see where God's hand was at work, but in the midst of trouble, His purpose is obscure and uncertain."

"She's right about that. But think of all the times past when bad things happened and the good that came from them later, and you'll see what she means."

Her thoughts traveled back in time to the tornado that had destroyed their home and Jake having to go back to Texas to face killing a man. God had used both of those for good when Lucy gave over half her inheritance to the town to rebuild and Jake had come home a free man. Even the prairie fire had brought Luke and Dove together, and now they were happily married, and Mrs. Anderson had overcome her hatred for Indians. They had looked at those events as miracles when they occurred, but she thought of them as simply God's way of cleaning up a mess.

"I suppose we have had a few miracles in the past ten years. I remember how worried we all were about Jake, but Lucy had such a calm assurance that everything would work out, and it did. I guess I just don't have that kind of faith." She had seen so much in the past four years away from home that indeed her faith had weakened.

"It's still there, Becky. You just have to pray and let God help you find it again. You have so many new ideas, and you want everything to be right in the world, but it's just not that easy to change the way things are."

Although she grimaced at the use of her nickname, she kept silent and only nodded in agreement. He was right, but at the moment she didn't know what to do about it. Her fight for women's rights and her beliefs couldn't be tossed aside like a worn-out toy or piece of clothing. They were as much a part of her as any of the things she'd learned in school or church.

"Becky, I've been doing some thinking about your ideas, and I've come to the conclusion that you are right in so many ways. Women should have a say in who rules this country. And there are women who need to work for a living, and we should make sure their workplaces treat them fairly. I remember a few girls at the university who showed an interest in law. The others laughed at them so that they never even tried after that. I see now that wasn't right. Women should be able to do whatever they want for a career."

Rebecca's mouth dropped open. This couldn't be the same Rob

she'd argued with about these very things. "Do you really mean what you're saying?"

"Yes, I do." He stopped the buggy and turned to her. "Rebecca Susan Haynes, I've loved you ever since we were thirteen years old and you wore that new dress Lucy brought you at your birthday party. I liked you before that, but at your party, I knew you were the only girl I'd ever really care anything about."

Rebecca's heart jumped in her chest, and a chill descended over her. "I...I don't know what to say. I don't have time in my life to love anyone the way you're talking about. I do care for you. You're one of the best friends I have, but more I can't give you right now." She closed her eyes against the hurt she saw come into his.

"If that's the way you feel, then I'll let you have your freedom to do what you want to do most. If you ever change your mind, I'll be waiting."

She turned her head away to let a tear slip from her eye and down her cheek. Her heart pounded, and she could find no words to give him. Life had become too complicated.

Then her mind cleared. If ever the day came when she decided to marry, Rob would be the one she'd want, but the words to tell him that wouldn't come. She had to get her business with God straightened out first.

Geoff stirred and tried to turn over, but the pain in his side left him gasping for breath. He opened his good eye to see Ruth standing beside him. She looked like an angel with the lamp behind her creating a halo of light around her head.

"You're still here."

"Yes, and I can see that you're in pain again. I have more

laudanum for you." She reached for the vial of medication on the table.

He stretched out his hand to stop her. "No, it isn't that bad yet, and I need to talk."

She sat down beside the bed. "If that's what you want, but let me know if the pain is too great. Dr. White will be here shortly to spend the rest of the night with you."

"All right, but first I want to know about what happened after those men used me for a punching bag. I thought I heard Rob Frankston had found me."

Her smile lit up her face and warmed his heart. "You heard correctly. He said he wanted to see you about something and found you lying in a heap on the floor of your hotel room. Rob ran for the doctor, and then they brought you here. You were in pretty bad shape."

"That I can tell from the pain. Every inch of my body hurts." The very idea of even trying to move or turn over made him grimace.

"Do you need that laudanum now?"

"No, not yet." He noted her calmness and the serenity in her face. Of course with her training, she would be confident in what she needed to do and when. Still, there was something there that he had seen only a few times in others. Her light blonde hair covered her head in a simple style with a bun at her neck. A few tendrils on each side of her face had escaped and caressed her cheeks.

He studied her a moment. She didn't have the beauty of Lucy Starnes or Rebecca, but she was indeed pretty. Her blue eyes held concern for him and his condition, but something else was there too. "How do you remain so calm and efficient? I've never seen you ruffled or angry, even with your children."

Her cheeks flushed with pink. "I don't know. I think maybe it's because the Lord is in control of my life, and I want to do everything to please Him."

Ruth was another one of those religious fanatics. He should've known it was something like that. "What does He care about what you do? I just live my life and try to stay out of trouble." Then he had to chuckle. "Doesn't look like I did a very good job of that."

"No, I guess this time you didn't stay out of trouble. However, God loves us all and is concerned about everything that happens to us. When our hearts are full of His love, we want to do everything to please Him and follow His will."

That part of religion had always puzzled him. "But how do you know what His will is for you? And how can He love everyone when there are so many evil people in the world?"

"That's the beauty and wonder of God's love. Have you read the Bible?"

As much as he hated to admit it, the Bible was one book Geoff preferred to leave alone. His father read it, as did his mother, but his father had been so strict in sticking to the letter of the law he read that Geoff had turned away from any Bible teachings. "I haven't taken time to read the Bible since it holds no interest for me."

Ruth covered his hand with hers. "Oh, Geoff, I'm so sorry to hear that. The Bible is a wonderful book with lessons for all of us." She peered at him a moment then said, "Would you mind if when I come on duty tomorrow, I brought my Bible? I have some passages I want to read to you."

He grimaced at that news. Yes, he would mind, but if it meant Ruth would be there, he'd listen. She had such a peace about her that he felt better just to be in her presence. "I wouldn't mind, but don't neglect your family duties to be here with me."

Again came that beautiful smile. "I will be working with the doctors in the days ahead as they take care of the people here. I've had enough training as a nurse to be able to help them. Mama says she can take care of the shop, and I'll still help out when we're not full of patients here. In a few weeks the twins will be in school, and Mama will watch…Oh, my, I'm rambling. You're not interested in all that."

He didn't care what her words said. The sound of her voice brought him great contentment. If she was to be here every day, then he didn't mind how long he had to be laid up. "I'm glad you have everything worked out so you can use your nursing skills to help the doctors."

"It also helps that my husband was a doctor, so I know all about odd hours and emergencies." She pointed a finger at him. "And you were a major emergency today."

He wanted to laugh at that, but any movement at all hurt, so he just grinned and hoped she'd know how much he appreciated her being here.

She glanced at a watch pinned to her apron. "It's way past time for your medicine. I'm giving it to you now so you'll be able to rest better. You have a long night ahead of you."

Before he could reply, a cry from the other room caught her attention. "One of the children must need something." She held a teaspoon to his mouth, and the bitter liquid slid down his throat.

He made a face at the awful taste, but she only grinned and said, "You'll be asleep in no time. I'm going to check on the children and then come back here. Doctor White is due any moment." She turned and left the room.

In a few minutes the crying stopped, and he heard her singing to the child. He lay back on the pillow, great peace filling his heart. Ruth Dorsett was a woman with many talents, and he looked forward to learning more about her.

One last question crept into his thoughts as he drifted off to sleep. Why had Rob come to see him?

Chapter 26

*R*ebecca sat at her desk typing up the article about the burning of her father's stables. She had already completed several human interest stories about the storm as well as the one about Geoff's beating. When she completed the article, she typed (30) to signify the end and leaned back and stretched. She had been at work yesterday morning getting all the details and information correct for the paper on Friday.

Mr. Lansdowne had spent that same time cleaning the printing press and now was testing it to see if it would be ready for the next printing. Molly had been in and out all morning running errands and providing coffee and doughnuts for her father. The news office had been busier than Rebecca had ever seen it, and it made her feel even more a part of the business now.

Molly set a cup of coffee beside Rebecca. "Have you heard any more about Mr. Kensington? What happened to him was terrible."

"I haven't been to see him today, but he was able to speak with the sheriff some yesterday, and as far as I know, he has no idea who could have done it. Mrs. Claymore said this morning at breakfast that her husband was frustrated because of the lack of clues for the fires and the beating."

Molly plopped down in her chair and picked up a pastry. "It's been a strange week. Just think, only one week ago today we were having fun at the July Fourth celebration, and then all this stuff began happening. It's almost like somebody put a jinx on our town."

Rebecca wouldn't go that far, but somebody had it in for the people of Barton Creek. The one good thing to come out of it all was that the cattle sale went through and Geoff was staying in town. Of course, the beating would have caused that anyway, but it was nice to know that he planned to stay even before that happened.

Molly turned back to filing away some papers, and Mr. Lansdowne continued with the testing. The *clink, clunk* of the press provided a noisy backdrop, and the odor of the ink permeated the room.

Rebecca stood and swallowed the last bit of her coffee. "I'm going out on the streets for a bit, and I may drop in to see Geoff Kensington. Do you want me to do anything else, Mr. Lansdowne?"

He rose from his bent-over position by the press and peered from beneath his visor. "Since you're doing most of the writing this week, see what you can learn about the new doctor and his wife. I understand they are staying with the Carters instead of the hotel."

Her heart did a little skip beat. He trusted her with more work. "That's right. I'll go for a visit now. I'm sure Mrs. White can tell me about their coming here."

Her mind filled with the desire to do a better than usual job with the article and carried her on a cloud of anticipation as she headed for Aunt Clara's. At the front stoop, Rebecca hesitated, remembering the stern lecture Sunday evening. She straightened her shoulders and held her head high. No matter what Aunt Clara thought, Rebecca had a job to do. She knocked on the door, opened it, and called out her aunt's name.

Aunt Clara rushed into the parlor, drying her hands on her

apron. "Dear child, I was just peeling potatoes for dinner. What brings you here?" She reached out and hugged Rebecca.

"Actually, I came to see Mrs. White. The paper wants to do a feature article on them for this Friday's edition. Things have been so hectic that we didn't get it done for last Friday."

"Oh, how nice, I'll call her." She walked to the bottom of the stairs. "Anna, someone's here to see you."

A few moments later Anna White descended the stairs. She wore a brown gored skirt with a cream-colored shirtwaist, and her red hair was styled around a frame to form a pompadour in front. She spotted Rebecca and grinned. "Oh, you're Clara's niece, Rebecca. Don't you work for the paper?"

"Yes, and that's why I'm here. I'd like to talk to you about your husband and you coming to Barton Creek."

Aunt Clara gestured toward the sofa. "You two sit and have a visit. I must finish our dinner preparations." She headed back to the kitchen.

The noon meal would always be dinner for Aunt Clara, and she never failed to have a bountiful table of meat and vegetables, as well as one of her wonderful fruit cobblers. Rebecca sniffed the air. Peach was the fruit of the day. Perhaps she could finagle an invitation if she stayed long enough. But business came first.

"May I call you Anna?"

"Of course. I'm not much older than you, and 'Mrs. White' always makes me feel older."

"Wonderful." Rebecca retrieved a pen from her handbag and flipped her tablet to a clean page. "Now, what made you and Dr. White decide to come to Barton Creek?"

"Dr. White, Roy, wanted to start out a practice with an older, more experienced doctor from whom he might learn as well as inherit the office when the older doctor retired."

Rebecca made a note to ask Aunt Clara if Doc was retiring.

He'd been around a long time, and it wouldn't surprise her if he did. "How did you learn about Doctor Carter?"

"Oh, Roy saw an ad in a medical journal for a practice here. It sounded like what he wanted, so he made inquiry."

Rebecca took an immediate liking to the young woman before her. She had a glow about her that spoke not only of her love for her husband but also her pride in him. Following him to unknown territory took great courage, and she admired that in Anna. "What do you think of Barton Creek so far?"

"Your aunt and uncle have been most kind to us. In fact, everyone has. We were going to stay at the hotel until we could get our own place, but they insisted that we stay here with them." She leaned over in a conspiratorial manner and patted her stomach. "Not many others know it, but we're expecting our first child toward the end of the year."

Rebecca gasped and sat back against the sofa cushions. "Really? My birthday is in December." She peered at Anna. That must be part of the cause for the glow about Anna. "May I put that in the article?"

Anna laughed. "Do you think that would be appropriate?"

Heat rose in Rebecca's cheeks. "You're right. People would be somewhat shocked to see such information in the paper. I'll keep your secret until you're ready to tell."

The next half hour was spent in pleasant conversation. Rebecca itched to ask Anna her opinions regarding suffrage, but she hesitated to do so where Aunt Clara might hear. Her aunt had already expressed her opinion in no uncertain terms, and Rebecca didn't want to cause trouble today.

Aunt Clara entered the room carrying a cloth-covered tray. "I'm taking this over to the office. Ruth is there and she can serve Mr. Kensington while Doc and Roy come back here to eat." She stopped at the screen door and turned to Rebecca. "You're welcome to stay for dinner if you're so inclined. I'll be back in a moment."

"Of course I'll stay. I smell peach cobbler or pie."

Anna jumped up and headed for the dining room. "I'll take care of the table and getting the food on."

Rebecca followed Anna and offered her services. The least she could do for a free meal was help out in the kitchen. Thankfully, she hadn't forgotten all her skills in that area.

Geoff felt a hand on his arm and opened his eyes. Ruth stood by his bed, and he smiled at her. "You're still here."

"Yes, and I have lunch for you. Mrs. Carter sent over some of her roast beef and potatoes and some peach cobbler. Do you feel like eating?"

His stomach rumbled in answer. He hadn't been able to eat much since the attack, and now the aroma of the food Ruth held was too tantalizing to resist. "I believe so." He tried to push himself up, but lacked the strength to rise more than an inch or so.

Almost instantly Ruth's hands were under his head and back to support him and help him sit up. "It'll be a little difficult for you to move freely on your own for a few more days."

"Thank you. That food sure smells good."

She fit a tray with legs on it over his lap then set the food on it. Geoff picked up a fork and stabbed a piece of meat. Ruth's hand covered his.

"Let's say a little blessing for this food. I'm sure it'll taste much better if we do."

He nodded and waited for her to speak the words. He'd learned how important her faith was to her and wanted to honor it.

"Father, we thank You for the food today and the hands that

prepared it. I pray that it will nourish and strengthen Mr. Kensington's body and help him on to full recovery very soon. Amen." She opened her eyes and smiled at him. "Now, eat hearty."

He grinned and shoved the meat into his mouth. The sweet taste of prime beef satisfied his palate. Mrs. Carter had outdone herself, and he looked forward to the peach cobbler for dessert.

Ruth pulled her chair over and opened her Bible.

"Aren't you going to eat? You've been here all morning."

"I'll have my meal later when the doctors get back. Now, what shall I read today? We can continue in John or I can go to another book if you prefer."

She'd read the first two chapters of John yesterday and several of the psalms. Geoff searched his brain to remember parts of the Bible he'd read as a child, but nothing came to mind except the book of John. "Go ahead with John. I enjoy hearing your voice."

Her cheeks turned pink, and she fumbled with the pages. What she had read didn't sound like any of the things his father so often quoted. If Geoff or his sister did anything to anger him, Father would immediately quote a scripture then use a switch or a paddle to let them know not to do whatever it was again.

Ruth's soft voice soothed his pain as she read the words from the apostle John. "This is from the third chapter."

He listened to a story about a man named Nicodemus. When she finished the chapter with the verse, "He that believeth on the Son hath everlasting life; and he that believeth not the Son shall not see life; but the wrath of God abideth on him," his heart constricted in pain, not from his wounds but from the meaning of the words.

His eyes closed tight, but the picture of his father speaking of the wrath of God being on sinners chilled him. "Ruth, do you believe God pours out His wrath on us when we sin?"

She hesitated before answering as if thinking about how she

should answer. Finally she said, "Yes, He does, but not before the sinner has the opportunity to repent of his sins and seek God's loving forgiveness and mercy. Remember verse sixteen? 'For God so loved the world, that he gave his only begotten Son, that whosoever believeth in him should not perish, but have everlasting life.' He offers his love and mercy to those who believe in Him. Jesus went to the cross to pay for all our sins."

Geoff let the words sink into his mind and fill his heart. A God of love and mercy who forgave sin instead of punishing every misdeed was a God he wanted to believe in. His throat tightened and tears threatened, but Ruth would not see him cry.

"Do you believe God wants to forgive your past sins and give you a new life?"

At the moment he wasn't sure, but if it meant peace in his heart, then he should believe. A firm conviction gripped his soul. "Yes, I do want to believe that, but I don't know how."

Ruth moved his tray and grasped his hand. "All you have to do is to believe in Jesus and ask Him into your heart."

"That's it? It's that easy?" Geoff couldn't see how something so simple could actually change a life, but he wanted it. He was tired of the things he had to do to keep his job and make a living. At Ruth's nod, he gripped her hand. "I believe Jesus will forgive me."

"That is all He asks. He will take care of you. Look how He sent Rob Frankston at just the right time to find you and get the doctor. You could have died from your injuries."

A peace settled on Geoff that he had not felt in his lifetime. God had protected him, and now he had a job to do and some confessions to make. "You're right, and I need to see Rob Frankston as soon as possible."

He noted tears in her eyes as she removed the pillow and lowered his head back on the bed. Geoff had never had such tender, loving care, not even from his mother. He'd never forget this day or the pretty young woman who helped him find what had been missing from his life.

"You've done a wonderful thing, Geoff, and when I go out to eat, I'll find Rob and tell him you want to see him. I'm sure he'll come right away. He's really been concerned about you and how you are getting along."

As soon as he explained the real reason for his business in Barton Creek, Geoff planned to wire Mr. Barstow with the news that if the company couldn't promise something better than money to Ben Haynes, then Geoff would resign and take his chances on finding employment in Barton Creek. This town had done much more for him than he had ever dreamed possible when he stepped off that train back in June.

Chapter 27

*R*ob emerged from the building housing his office and bumped into Ruth. He reached out to steady her. "I'm sorry. I should look where I'm going."

"No harm done, and I was coming to see you anyway. Mr. Kensington is awake and wants to see you."

Her face held a glow that spoke of great happiness. "From the smile on your face, he must be getting better."

"Oh, he is, and even better is...no, I'll let him tell you. I must get home to relieve Mama of the baby and check on my children."

Rob tipped his hat, his curiosity rising. "Then I won't detain you and will go now to see your patient." He watched her rush down the street to her mother's dress shop. For someone new to town, Ruth had certainly made herself useful. The two doctors must be happy to have her as their nurse.

He headed toward the infirmary, his eagerness to find out what Geoff had to say hastening his step. Since he must be improving, Rob planned to ask about the information in the wire he had received.

Doctor White greeted him at the door. "Hello, Rob. It's good to see you again, and under much better circumstances. I take it you're here to see Geoff Kensington."

"Yes, I am. It's good to hear that he's doing much better. I really worried about him that first night."

"And well you should. That blow to his kidney could have been much worse than it was, and thankfully he didn't lose too much blood. You can go on upstairs and see him now. He's our only patient for the moment. The children were all released to their parents last night."

That was a relief to hear. Thankfulness for safety from the storm and for his finding Geoff when he did had been at the forefront of his prayers the past two days. "Thank you. I guess Ruth has been a big help to you this week."

"Indeed she has. She's a very talented and efficient young woman. Of course, being a mother herself, she made the children feel more comfortable."

Rob nodded and headed for the stairway. He stopped outside Geoff's room and glanced inside. Geoff sat up reading a book on his lap. His left arm was encased in bandages, and a large bandage covered the cut on his forehead. A lamp sat on a bedside table and provided light. Rob knocked before going in.

Geoff looked up with a wide grin gracing his face. "Rob, come on in. You're just the man I've been waiting to see."

Rob pulled up a chair to sit beside Geoff's bed. Although one eye was still swollen shut and had turned a deep shade of purple and blue, he looked so much better than he had Sunday evening. "You're certainly looking better than the last time I saw you all bloodied up."

Geoff reached out and shook Rob's hand. "And I have you to thank for that, but something much more important has happened."

That is when Rob noticed that the book Geoff had been reading was the Bible. Now that was strange, seeing as how the man rarely attended church or professed any kind of faith. "And what might that be?"

Geoff shook his head and his one good eye sparkled. "Ruth has been reading the Scriptures to me, and it has been most amazing.

I went to church with my family when I was a young boy, but I never heard the beauty of the words like she read to me. She has led me to a faith that I never realized existed."

Rob's mouth dropped open, but he quickly snapped it shut. So that was the reason for Ruth's happiness and Geoff's great improvement. "I say, that's a wonderful thing, my man. Having God in your life will reap great rewards." He reached into his pocket for the wire. "But I have something I need to ask you about concerning your reasons for coming to Barton Creek."

"Let me explain something to you, and then if you have questions, ask away. First, I did come here to buy cattle, as Mr. Barstow's meat packing company in Chicago wants only the finest beef, but he also owns interest in an oil company that is drilling down in Texas. He heard about the oil around Tulsa and then rumors that there was an oil deposit around here. He sent me to not only buy the cattle but also to investigate the rumors and make Mr. Haynes an offer for the land."

Just as Rob suspected, the oil deposits were at the bottom of why Geoff had come. Then alarm raced through him. Everything had to be connected. The slaughter of the cattle, the burning of the Haynes's barn, and even Geoff's beating all must have happened because of the oil.

"I can see your mind is working overtime, just as mine has. The men who attacked me left with a warning for me not to go out to the place where I discovered the oil. Rebecca told me about her father's stables burning, and I started putting it all together just as you have."

Rob still wasn't sure he could trust Geoff, but at least the man seemed to be telling the whole truth for a change. "What about your boss? Would he resort to these tactics if he didn't think you were doing the job?"

"I don't think so. I've known him to do some shady things

before, but never anything like this. All I can think is that someone wants to hurt Ben financially so he'll be forced to sell that land for drilling." He reached for some papers with his good arm. "Since the issue has come to a head, I have a few ideas I want to run by you, and then see about talking to Ben about those oil deposits. From what I've seen, they could be even bigger than that strike near Tulsa."

"I think Ben should do something with that land too. What with motor cars and other gas-powered engines becoming popular, we'll need more oil to run everything." Still, as protective as Ben was about that land, it would take powerful persuasion for him to change his mind.

"Those are my feelings exactly, but I can understand how Ben wants to protect the land for his cattle. Even with all the other inventions coming along, people still need to eat, so he doesn't want to do anything that might keep his beef from being among the best there is. Besides the fact that he seems to just love his land and ranching."

"You've hit the problem square on. I know there are ways to keep both resources going, but too many people only see the money to be made and forget about the environment." He'd seen what had happened to farmland suddenly overrun with oil derricks and pumps, and it wasn't always a pretty sight.

"Yes, and that's what I want to show you." Geoff spread out the papers he had. "See, he's diverted the creek so it bypasses where the oil is. He doesn't use that part as rangeland because he said the grass doesn't grow well. He doesn't want his herd in all that gooey oil either. My idea is to fence off that portion of the land to keep the cattle out, and then drill just a few wells. We could put pipelines in underground to move the oil to another location where it would be put into barrels for shipping cross country."

Rob examined the drawings. What Geoff said made good sense.

If they could make Ben see that his grazing lands would not be disturbed, he might have a better attitude about drilling on the other part. "This looks good. Have you talked to Mr. Barstow about it to see if he agrees? Sorry, dumb question; you've been here and not able to get to the telegraph."

Geoff chuckled and rolled the papers back up. "I'll write it all out, and if you could send it, then we can find out soon what he thinks."

"That I can do." He noted the sudden grimace on Geoff's face and the pain in his eyes. "Looks like you're overdoing it. Why don't I stop back later this evening, and we can take care of that wire. You could use some rest right now."

"Thank you. I do want to get this taken care of as quickly as possible. Just let me write it out now, and then I'll rest easier." He grabbed a pencil and a blank sheet of paper from the table beside his bed and wrote. "At least I still have use of my right hand. Doctor White doesn't want me moving the left one much until my arm does some more healing." Geoff concentrated for a moment then finished the note and handed it to Rob.

He glanced at it, and then his eyes opened wide. "This says you'll quit the company if things can't be worked out."

"Yes, I want to do what's right with these men. I've come to admire them and don't want to see them hurt in any way."

Rob shook his head in amazement. Everything he'd mistrusted in Geoff had been blown aside in less time than it took to tell it. This man could be a very good friend.

But then he thought of Becky. If Geoff stayed here, he might seek her favors, especially since he'd started a new life of faith. That meant Rob would have to work even harder to see that Becky turned to him instead of Geoff.

Of course with her recent success at the paper, she might not be interested in either one of them. Geoff might give up on her, but Rob never would. Aunt Clara had told him to pursue her, but she'd also said if he gave her freedom, then when she came back to him, he'd know it was true love that brought her. He respected Aunt Clara and prayed that both pieces of her advice were right.

He said good-bye and went downstairs. He wanted to get the wire off immediately and then find Becky.

Rebecca left Aunt Clara's house both satisfied and dismayed. The meal prepared had been delicious, and she had enjoyed Anna's company as they talked more about her move to Barton Creek. Then Aunt Clara had delivered her announcement. She and Doc Carter planned to retire at the end of the summer.

When asked if that was the big surprise Lucy had planned for the dinner the night of the dust storm, Aunt Clara said no. The surprise, whatever it was, would have to be revealed by Lucy.

Rebecca's heart filled with sadness at the thought of her aunt and uncle leaving Barton Creek. She had come to love her father's aunt with all her heart. Aunt Clara had great wisdom and strength that had helped the family through more than one crisis, and she had extended that wisdom to many others in town.

Aunt Clara was also one to speak her mind, and Rebecca had been on the receiving end of a few of those remarks more than once. She thought of what her aunt said about Rob on Sunday evening and then Rob's revelation on the way back to town.

Her heart felt torn in two because she did care about Rob, but she had to consider the dreams she had for her career and her future. As if on cue, Rob walked out of the clinic at the same time she arrived to visit with Geoff.

She bit her lip. To say Rob was handsome would be an understatement. If he were in Oklahoma City, young women would be clamoring for his attention.

He spotted her and waved. "Hello, Becky. I was planning to find you, and here you are."

Her heart quickened at his smile, which had always charmed her. "Oh, and what did you have to tell me?" She stopped in front of him and peered up into his dark brown eyes, which contained excitement that must mean something important had happened. "Did you find out who beat Geoff or who burned our stables?"

"No, nothing like that, but it's still remarkable. Geoff is much better and is resting. We had a nice, long visit." He extended his arm. "Come walk with me down to the telegraph office, and I'll tell you about it."

As much as she'd like to, she'd been away from the news office too long. "I'm sorry, Mr. Lansdowne expects me back. I'll walk with you there, but I have a story I need to finish."

"Good enough."

As he told her about Geoff's real reason for being in town and the plans for the oil deposits, Rebecca's thoughts whirled like winds in a storm picking up bits and pieces. Her mind couldn't wrap around what he told her. To think that Geoff had been after the oil the whole time didn't sit well with her at all.

"I can't believe he'd be so sneaky. He was lying to us all along. All he's interested in is the oil. How can you trust him and believe he'll do what he says?"

"I have a message for Mr. Barstow in Chicago. That's what I'm taking to the telegrapher's place now. If he won't agree with Geoff, then Geoff says he's quitting his job."

"Quitting his job? If that happens, what in the world is he going to do?" If he stayed in Barton Creek, he'd have to find work, and that may be difficult. Of course, she didn't know what skills he had other than making people believe one thing when he was actually doing another.

"We discussed some alternatives, but he believes Mr. Barstow will go along because he wants the oil so badly." He paused and grinned like a cat licking cream. "The best part is that Ruth has been reading the Bible to Geoff, and he has taken Jesus into his heart."

Rebecca's mouth fell open and she shook her head. "What are you saying? How can that be? He doesn't even go to church." This was more than she could comprehend. How had a smart man like Geoff fallen for the idea that he needed God to get along in the world? Hadn't they both been getting along quite well without Him?

"You'll have to talk to him to find out about that. And he also plans to be in church as soon as the doctors release him from the clinic."

They had reached the news office, and Rebecca stopped. She placed her hands on her hips and looked squarely into Rob's eyes. "I don't know what's going on in this town, but some pretty strange things have been happening, and this one really makes me wonder if everyone is going out of their minds. Go on with your wire. I have a story to write."

She strode through the door and into the office. Molly looked up and asked, "Goodness, something has you riled up. You look like you could bite a few nails in half."

"Everything around here is going haywire. I can't explain now. I have to think and get a story written." What with Aunt Clara's announcement, the news about Geoff, and all the other things that had happened in just a week's time, Rebecca wasn't sure if she'd ever be able to explain any of it no matter how many articles she wrote.

Once again life took turns that only served to complicate matters even more than they already were. One moment she wanted to leave the town for bigger and better opportunities, and the next she wanted to stay and fix all the problems that seemed to keep coming. Deep inside, though, she knew Rob Frankston was at the root of all her indecision. What in the world was she going to do about him?

Chapter 28

*R*uth strode to Geoff's bedside. "How are we doing this
afternoon?" She lifted his hand to take his pulse.

He'd be surprised if she didn't find it racing because his heart
beat faster when she entered the room. Her presence brought a
sense of calm and peace he'd never felt around another women.
That she had shared her love of God with him made her even
more special. Only two things kept him from thinking about her
in his future.

The first was the fact she already had a family and had enjoyed
the love of the man who had given her those children. He wasn't
sure if he was ready for such a family or that Ruth would even
consider him as anything other than a friend. The second involved
the uncertainty of his own future in Barton Creek. If he lost the
job with Barstow, he'd be a poor candidate for a husband, much
less a father to three children.

After she checked his temperature and wrote it on his chart, she
helped him to sit up in a chair. The movement didn't hurt as much
today as it had yesterday evening when he tried it. At this rate he
could be ready to leave in a few days. He'd have to remember to
see if Mrs. Claymore would still have a room available.

When she leaned close to assist him, the clean, fresh scent of
her hair filled his nose. Lavender must be what she used, as it
reminded him of his mother.

Ruth smiled and placed a pillow behind his back. "There, that should help until I can put clean linens on your bed. Nice, crisp sheets always lift the spirits. That's why we feel it's important to change them daily."

"Isn't that a lot of trouble for whoever does the laundry?" He'd hate to be the one to wash and dry those things every day, but of course they probably had more than one set.

"Not really. The laundry in town does them for us. They have those new machines that wash everything much more quickly, and they give the doctors a big discount on the price too."

She tucked in the ends then folded them into perfect square corners. It reminded him of how his mother always made the beds at home. Ma had called them "military" corners. Whatever they were, the bed looked much neater. He shook his head. So many things reminded him of her in the past few days when he hadn't thought about her for a long time. He didn't really want to remember those younger days at home.

"That's nice of them. I've taken a few things of my own there, and they do a right good job with my shirts and pants." Also his undergarments were in better shape than if he had done them, but he wouldn't mention that to her.

In what seemed a very few minutes, Ruth had completed changing the sheets and had arranged the white cotton bedspread at the foot of the bed. "Would you like to stay up for awhile longer? It'll do you good and help you regain your strength more quickly."

"Yes, I'd like that. Are there no other patients here?" He had heard activity downstairs, but the second floor had been rather quiet.

"You're the only one in bed at the moment. No others have come in with serious enough injuries or illnesses to be detained." She turned to the door. "If you don't need anything else, I'm going back downstairs to assist the doctors with afternoon patients. Be sure to call out if you need help or anything else."

When she was gone, he missed her bright smile and the clean, fresh scent she carried with her. He picked up the Bible she left for him and began to read. He'd never realized how many interesting stories could be found in this book. He noted one named Ruth and decided to read it to see if the biblical Ruth and his nurse Ruth were anything alike.

He had read only the first chapter when Rebecca popped in. His eyes opened wide when he saw her. Since a visit Tuesday evening and his telling her about his salvation, she hadn't been back. "Well, hello, Miss Haynes. It's nice to see you again."

"I just wanted to see how you're getting along. I'll bring a newspaper by tomorrow so you can read the stories I wrote about all that happened."

"I was afraid you weren't coming back after the way you left the other evening."

"Well, I was just so surprised when Rob told me about it that I had to come see for myself. I couldn't believe that you actually decided religion had some value after all."

He wanted to laugh but realized she seriously doubted that religion or faith would do anyone any good. "It's made me a new man, Rebecca. I've never had such peace and assurance that what I'm doing is right and what the Lord wants me to do."

"I felt that way when I was younger, but with all I've seen and all that's happened to my family, I'm not sure faith has much to do with anything anymore." She settled into another chair. "Let's don't talk about religion. It's too boring. I want to know more about what you want to do with my father's land."

That he could tell her, and perhaps she'd be instrumental in swaying her father's mind once he heard from Barstow one way or the other. He showed her the drawings and plans he'd shown to Rob. She studied them with interest but made no comment. She probably didn't understand what she saw like Rob had.

"What it all means is that your father can benefit from the profits of the oil strike, have his rangeland, send Dawson his cut, and still be giving the country what it needs to keep industry thriving. It'll make Oklahoma even more appealing as a state."

"If you think you can really keep Pa's land from being completely ruined, then I'm all for him drilling for oil. If we impede progress, we impede the well-being of our entire nation. I want to be proud of Oklahoma, and this will make that pride well deserved."

Another ally in their camp, and he hadn't resorted to devious means to acquire it. He enjoyed doing business this way much more than Barstow's plots and schemes. "We haven't heard back from Mr. Barstow yet. As soon as we do, I'll know which actions to take."

He'd already told the sheriff about the warning those fellas who beat him up had given, and he was willing to stake his life on the connection of that with the slaughter and burning at Ben's place. Only time and good work on the part of the sheriff would reveal whether or not they were all part of one big scheme to get Ben to sell or drill. It couldn't be a sale because of the Dawson contract, so he prayed he and Rob could get to Ben with their plan before anything else happened.

Mellie sat beside Ben on the seat of their largest wagon. They were headed into town so Ben could purchase supplies he needed for rebuilding the stables. Lumber had arrived at the depot, and he planned to haul it back to the ranch. Jonah offered to help by using his freight wagon to load up and deliver more wood.

Of course that held no real interest for Mellie; she was more concerned with seeing Aunt Clara. If anyone knew what was really going on in Barton Creek, that lady would. Mrs. Frankston may pride herself on knowing the right people and always being in the right place, but Aunt Clara always knew more about the people and what was going on in their lives than anyone else in town, and without gossip. If what she had to say wasn't plain fact, it didn't get said.

Ben pulled the wagon to a halt at the Carter house. He came around to help her down, and at the same time Clara burst through the screen door of her house.

She hurried out to them. "Land sakes, Mellie and Ben. I didn't expect to see you two today. You must have come in for that lumber down at the station. Knew it had to be yours so you could rebuild your barns. How'd you get it so fast?"

True to form, the little lady had all the information and facts, but always wanted more. Ben chuckled beside her. "Aunt Clara, that's the beauty of having wire service. I knew of a lumber mill down in Texas, wired them for what I need, and they sent it up to us by train."

"Well, I declare. Things are getting done a lot faster these days, and it's getting too fast for my blood. I prefer slow and easy." Then she laughed and wrapped an arm around Mellie's waist. "Come on in and sit a spell. Ben can go get the lumber while we catch up on our news."

That's exactly what Mellie wanted. "I'll be here when you're ready to leave, Ben. Take as long as you want."

She walked beside the older woman into the house. A young woman stood when they entered the parlor. Mellie nodded in greeting. "Mrs. White, Anna isn't it? I remember you from church last week. We're delighted to have another doctor in town to lighten Doc's load."

"Thank you, Mrs. Haynes. If you'll excuse me, I'll go upstairs with my needlework and give you two ladies time to visit with each other."

After she left, Aunt Clara pulled Mellie over to the sofa. "Now come and tell me how things are at the ranch."

"They're as well as can be expected. Ben and the boys made a makeshift shelter for the animals to keep them out of the sun during the hottest part of the day. Of course they're usually out in the fields, but since those other cattle were slaughtered, he's keeping the livestock closer to home, leastways the horses and our two cows. The hens haven't produced as well since the fire until this morning." She removed her hat and patted her hair to search for stray tendrils. "But that's of no real interest. Tell me what's happening in town. We heard about Geoff, but has anything else been going on?"

Aunt Clara settled back against the cushions as if to get ready for a nice long talk. "For one thing, Ruth Dorsett has been nursing Geoff Kensington and reading the Bible to him. From what I understand, he's a believer now."

"That is good news. I hope that will have some influence on Becky. She gets all bristly every time I mention church or religion to her." She'd welcome whatever influence anyone could have over her wayward daughter at this point.

"She's been to see him a few times, but I don't know what they discussed. She was here for lunch the other day, and she interviewed Anna White for the paper."

"How nice. I like that young couple. They will be a great asset for Barton Creek." She pursed her lips and nodded toward the stairway. "It appears to me she may be in the family way too, but I haven't heard anything about that."

Clara shook her head. "You could always spot a woman going to have a child before anyone else. Even Lucy was surprised when you said something to her before she told anyone about their first one."

Mellie shrugged her shoulders and grinned. "It's just a knack I have. So, it's true about Anna."

"Yes, but they haven't announced it yet." She set her lips in a firm line for a moment then said, "I'm going to tell you something that we'll tell everyone else this Sunday. Doc is going to retire at the end of the year and let Doctor White take over the practice."

Mellie's mouth dropped open. That was the last bit of news she expected to hear today. She figured Doc would keep going until someone had to carry him out of the clinic. "I can't believe it. What are you going to do? He's been in medicine so long."

"We're going back East first and visit with family we haven't seen in many years."

"What about your house? Are you going to just close it up and leave it sit?"

Aunt Clara laughed and shook her head. "No, no, dear Mellie. Anna and Roy are going to live here while we travel."

"What a splendid arrangement." Then she clasped her chest. "Is that the surprise Lucy had for us at the dinner we had to cancel?"

"No, it isn't. I'm pretty sure I know what that is, but I won't say because it's Lucy's news. I'm afraid she thinks not everyone in the family would approve."

That only served to whet Mellie's curiosity even more. But experience told her she'd not get another clue from Aunt Clara. Whatever Lucy had to tell would come when she was ready to reveal it. It couldn't be another baby since everyone would certainly approve of that. Mellie's mind went off in several different directions in speculation, but Clara's hand on her arm brought Mellie back to the moment.

"I know you're curious, and so am I. If it's what I surmise from the few talks we've had in recent weeks, then all of us will have to support her and Jake, and before you jump to conclusions, they are not planning to leave Barton Creek."

Mellie let her breath out in relief. "That did cross my mind. I suppose I can wait, but when is she going to tell us? Maybe our next family dinner. I'll have to get everyone together Saturday evening."

"That will be good. I think she's anxious for everyone to know. But on another note, I'm worried about Matt and Caroline. Every time she's around him, she looks as if she's in pain. She loves him so much, but he seems to be blind to that fact. Much like Becky is to Rob's love for her. Becky and Rob are still young and working out their lives, but Matt is drawing close to being twenty-five, as is Caroline, and it's time for those two to either get together or find someone else."

Mellie felt the same, but she didn't know what to say to her son about Caroline. Certainly he couldn't find a prettier or finer girl anywhere. The only drawback she could see for the two young people was Mrs. Frankston. That woman had done so much to alienate members of her family that the damage might be too great even for love to overcome. Still, deep in her heart, Mellie believed that love could conquer whatever obstacles were put in its path. She had only to look at Dove and Luke to know that was true.

"Aunt Clara, the time has come to quit waiting and start acting. I don't mean we are to meddle, but we can do everything in our power to get those young people together. And I'm starting with Becky. No matter what she may say, family and home mean more to her than a career off somewhere else. She just doesn't realize it yet." She closed her eyes and envisioned her daughter. Such a stubborn one, but with her talents and her love of life, she'd make Rob a wonderful wife. Now all that remained was to make sure Becky found that out before it was too late.

She stood up. "I'm asking Becky to invite Rob to dinner Saturday night. And you make sure she does just that, and don't ask them to ride with you and Doc, understood?"

Aunt Clara chuckled. "You'll have no arguments from me!"

Chapter 29

*D*octor Carter and Doctor White had both agreed that Geoff was well enough to leave the clinic. Ruth helped him pack up his belongings that Rob had brought from the hotel. "I'm so thankful that Mrs. Claymore has room for you," Ruth said. "You will be much more comfortable there than at that hotel."

Geoff grinned and finished buttoning his shirt. "It feels good to have on my own clothes again." He still favored his broken ribs and the arm with the deep cut on it. His bruises were now only greenish spots that no longer hurt, and the cut on his head was healing nicely. "I understand she's a mighty fine cook too."

"That she is. The two older ladies who live there will probably be looking after you too. One is Miss Florence Hilton, a schoolteacher, and the other is Widow Jarvis. I've met them both at church, and they are very nice."

"That reminds me, I'll be able to attend church this Sunday. I imagine quite a few people will be surprised to see me." So much had changed in the week he'd been under Ruth's influence. Her charm and grace as well as her loving Christian spirit had made such a difference in his life.

"Mrs. Dorsett, er, Ruth, could I be so bold as to ask if you will allow me to escort you to church this Sunday?"

Ruth's eyes opened wide, but she smiled and said, "Yes, you may, and I would be delighted to attend church with you. Billy and Sally can sit with Ma and Pa, and Emma will be in our new nursery, so you won't be bothered by them."

At the moment the idea of sitting in church with Ruth and her baby girl and the twins had a most pleasing attraction, but it would be better to get to know Ruth before taking on the children. "That will be fine. I can walk down to your place."

"Oh, no, you don't need to walk that far. I'll stop at the boarding house, and we can walk the rest of the way together."

"Thank you, that will be ideal." That sounded much better since even the thought of walking very far at the moment taxed his strength. His body would probably remind him frequently of his injuries in the days ahead until he'd completely healed.

Geoff glanced around the room he'd occupied the last week. It held three other beds just like his, with side tables and small chests for personal belongings. No one else had come in to occupy the other beds, so he'd had plenty of personal attention during the week. He'd miss Ruth's reading the Bible and her tender care.

She handed him a package. "I bought this for you in hopes that you'd take to reading it yourself."

He tore off the brown paper and held a black leather Bible in his hands. "Oh my, this is nice." Geoff smiled up at her. "You didn't need to do this, but I'm very pleased you did. And I do promise to read it." And that was a promise he planned to keep.

At that moment Rob popped his head around the doorframe. "All ready to go? I've come to escort you to your new quarters. I brought the buggy so you wouldn't have to walk."

Geoff stood then grabbed his side. "Oh, that still hurts some. But say, your pa wouldn't let you drive the motor car?"

"Not on your life. That's his baby for the time being. He said I could afford to get my own at what I was making as his partner."

"The buggy will have to do then."

Ruth headed for the door. "I'll go down and check on any medications the doctor wants to send home with you. Since the drug store opened last spring, Doctor Carter doesn't have to keep as much on hand as he did, so you may have to pick them up from the pharmacist."

"That'll be fine." He waited until she was out of earshot then turned to Rob. "Still haven't heard anything from Mr. Barstow? I thought sure he'd wire back by now."

"Nothing so far. I even checked before coming to get you."

"That's really strange, but we can't let that hold us back. Now that I'm regaining my strength, we can plan how to speak with Ben and Sam and help them see what a boon it would be for Barton Creek to have use of their oil." The sooner he could get that business taken care of, the sooner his conscience would ease about the whole business. He prayed they'd be understanding and would listen to the plans.

Rob nodded. "Since they don't like to discuss business on Sunday, I'll make arrangements for us to meet with them early next week."

"All right, I'll wait until you tell me when." Geoff's respect for the young lawyer had grown considerably in the days since the accident. He hoped they could now be good friends, for he sensed a loyalty in Rob that was very rare in the business circles in which Geoff had been involved.

"Miss Haynes, step into my office a moment, please."

Mr. Lansdowne's voice gave no clue as to whether he was pleased or displeased with her work. He was the most difficult man to understand, and she never knew what he was thinking. She entered his office and waited for whatever he had to offer.

"Have a seat, Miss Haynes." He nodded to the chair by his desk.

She spotted a copy of today's edition of the paper in his hands. Perhaps he didn't like what she had written, but if that was the case, he wouldn't have printed it. She sucked in her breath.

He peered at her over his glasses as he so often did. His bushy eyebrows raised and his forehead creased. She braced herself for a scolding.

"I must say I am quite pleased with the way you've handled the assignments I've given you. The piece about Doctor and Mrs. White is an excellent human interest story as well as quite informative."

Her breath came out in a swoosh. "Thank you, Mr. Lansdowne. Anna White made the story easy to write."

"Now, I can see you have a talent for writing, and since you enjoy it so much, I'm going to give you more. I'm planning to increase our editions to three a week for now and to a daily by the first of the year. Our circulation numbers are going up, and we've had a large number of merchants asking for ads in recent days."

Rebecca's heart hammered in her chest. Expanding the paper and giving her more writing assignments fulfilled the desires she'd had upon returning home. "You won't be sorry, Mr. Lansdowne. I'll do my very best." Her only worry was that she might not be able to keep up, especially with Molly going off to school at the end of the summer.

As if reading her mind, he continued, "I've taken out a few ads in other papers for more help. We need someone to handle the advertising and circulation. You and I should be able to handle the news items, but we do need help with subscriptions and artwork for the ads that I hope will continue to increase. Molly is talented in the art department, but she needs more training. Anyway, I'm making you assistant editor."

Rebecca gasped and sank back in her chair. Assistant editor

meant more responsibilities and her name on the paper as well. What a wonderful surprise, and to think she'd been worried that he wasn't pleased with her work. "Thank you, Mr. Lansdowne."

She turned to leave when he stopped her. "I'm not through yet."

"Oh, I'm sorry."

He placed his fingertips together and tilted his head. "I've been thinking about the story you wrote about that suffragette meeting over in Guthrie. You are an intelligent young woman who looks at facts and evaluates them. Most women aren't like that, because they are not educated to think that way."

Rebecca's heart pounded. Was he going to support the women's suffrage movement?

"I'm not against women having the vote, and if more of them were informed as to who is running for an office and what their platform contains, they could make an intelligent decision."

He tapped his fingers together. "Miss Haynes, I'd like for you to set up a column in which you begin to inform women about suffrage and what it can mean for them. Teach them how to evaluate candidates and know what each stands for. Do you think you could do that?"

What a question. Of course she could do that. At the moment she wanted to jump over his desk and hug him, but that might not sit well with him. Instead, she clasped her hands and bobbed her head. "Oh, yes, sir. I would enjoy doing that. So much information is available that I'll have no trouble at all filling a column."

He made a growling sound then waved his hand. "Very good. Now get back out and see what other things you can find to do." He bowed his head over some work on his desk.

She contained her excitement until she had closed the door behind her. Then she did a jig hop and step and pumped her fist.

Molly stood by the railing with a wide grin on her face. "Papa told you about expanding."

"Yes, he did, and he named me assistant editor, and—" Rebecca paused for effect—"He wants me to write a column about women's suffrage." She still had trouble wrapping her mind around that little fact.

Molly squealed and hugged Rebecca. "I knew it. I knew it. Papa is as smart as I thought he was." She stood back with her eyes sparkling with happiness. "I told him I wanted to go to school and learn more about drawing and art so I can come back here and help him. I've grown to love being around the paper, and fixing up ads for merchants here is much more fun than still-life pictures."

Rebecca wanted to sing, shout, and dance at her good fortune. Her dreams were on the road to becoming reality. She had to share with someone, and she knew just who that would be.

At the noon hour she walked out of the news office and headed for Rob's office. She could hardly wait to share her news with him, but a closed sign hung on the door. He must be having lunch somewhere.

Geoff thought he might be released today, and if that was true, Rob might be there so he could help move Geoff's things over to the boarding house. Mrs. Claymore and the other ladies were already talking about how they would take care of him when he arrived. She had to chuckle at their excitement. After all, it wasn't often that a handsome young man needed their nursing care. Not that Geoff would need nursing, but a little tenderness from those sweet women would help his spirits.

He'd be excited about her good fortune too, but she would wait and tell Rob first. She also wanted to ask them both about any further developments with her father concerning the oil on the Dawson property. Neither one of them had said much since Rob first explained what they wanted to do. It made some sense to her, but she'd let them figure it out.

At that thought, Rebecca stopped short. What had she just said to herself? If she intended to make a success of her new position, then she needed to understand everything. No matter how complicated the explanations might be, she determined at that moment to learn everything she could about the oil business and write an intelligent article about it.

When she arrived at the clinic, she found Ruth talking with Doctor Carter. "Good morning, you two. Is our patient ready to go home yet?"

Ruth's cheeks turned pink. "Yes, he is. Rob is up with him now getting the last of his things together. Rob brought the buggy so Geoff wouldn't have to walk."

"Rob is here, good." Now she could share with both of them. A noise behind them caused her to turn around. Rob and Geoff descended the stairway. Geoff's face still looked rather pale, and pain was evident in his eyes. Ruth rushed over to him and lifted one of his arms to lie on her shoulders and support him.

"I'm so sorry you had to come down the steps. Do you need to sit and rest a minute before going outside?"

Ruth's eyes and touch held such tenderness that Rebecca looked harder at the couple. Geoff had definitely taken a liking to the pretty young woman who had cared for him all week, and from the look in her eyes, Ruth returned the feeling.

Then another truth dawned on her. She was delighted for them! She held no jealousy toward the couple, and she could sincerely hope their relationship became more serious.

She smiled and walked over to the trio as they crossed the room. "It's good to see you up and about," she exclaimed. "I came to help you get to the boarding house, but I see you have some good helpers."

Geoff glanced from Rob to Ruth with a smile. "That I do, but I appreciate your concern. Besides, I can use all the help available."

Rob and Ruth helped Geoff out to the buggy and Rebecca

followed them. They stepped out into the bright sunshine of the July afternoon. As hot as it was, people scurried about taking care of errands and tasks on Main Street. She marveled once again at all the changes in her hometown while she'd been gone. At the rate it was growing and with Mr. Lansdowne's announcement today, her world was certainly expanding and looking brighter every day.

At the boarding house, Mrs. Claymore and Widow Jarvis helped Rob get Geoff settled in his downstairs bedroom. Florence Hilton had a tray with hot tea and fresh-baked cookies ready for him. Rebecca stifled a giggle. Those three ladies would have Geoff spoiled rotten with all their attention.

Rob stood in the doorway and smiled. "I see that you're in good hands with these ladies, Geoff, so Rebecca and I will take our leave. I'll let you know as soon as there are any developments on our business."

She knew what that business was and wanted to know more. She followed him out the door and down the steps of the boarding house.

Before she could ask anything, Rob stopped at the end of the walkway to the house. "OK, I saw how excited you were back there in the doc's office, and I don't think it had anything to do with Geoff Kensington. Want to tell me about it?"

"Oh, yes, it's the most wonderful news. Mr. Lansdowne is expanding the paper and he named me as his assistant. He's even going to hire more people to help in getting the paper out."

"That is wonderful. I'm really proud of you. The stories in today's edition were outstanding. You have a real talent as a writer."

Coming from him the words meant more than she had ever imagined they would. He truly was happy for her success.

He linked her arm with his. "By the way, your mother stopped by this morning and invited me out to the ranch tomorrow evening for dinner. She asked if I would take you. Is that all right?"

Rebecca shot him a glance. She was a bit suspicious of her mother's motivations, but she said simply, "That would be fine."

He wrinkled his brow a moment. "Do you think perhaps we could mention the plan Geoff and I have to your pa? He'll be in a good mood with your news, so he might listen to us."

"Oh, yes, I meant to ask you about that. Geoff seems pretty certain that he can drill in a way that won't ruin the land for the cattle." That was the only way Pa would have anything to do with any ideas Rob or Geoff might have.

"I think so. Geoff's really knowledgeable about drilling and such, and I've come to trust his judgment this past week. I think we can become really good friends."

"You'd make good business partners too. Now I'm really excited for tomorrow night. We have so much going on. Maybe we'll finally get to hear Lucy's news too." She paused, then added, "I'm glad you're coming."

Rob's face filled with delight, and she realized that she meant every word. Let her family think whatever they wanted about her relationship with Rob. He was her best friend, and who knew, someday he might become something more.

He patted her arm. "Now let's go have some lunch at Dinah's. I'm sure you have much more to tell me."

"Yes, I do," she said.

As they entered Dinah's for lunch, she sighed in pure contentment. She'd never been happier than she was at this moment, and she had done it all on her own. Nothing and no one could spoil the joy of personal success.

Chapter 30

*A*fter breakfast on Saturday, Geoff enjoyed time on the porch talking with Rebecca. She brought him up to date on her position at the paper. "Congratulations on the promotion. I knew you would make an impression on him eventually."

"I'm truly excited and will do my best for him. I do hope he's able to find additional employees soon. Putting out the extra editions will require more of us. Mr. Lansdowne says now that he has access to his own telegraph, he can get news from the AP wire service. It will greatly enhance the ability of newspapers to publish news much more quickly so it's not old by the time we get it."

Geoff listened with amusement. When Rebecca talked about the newspaper and writing, her eyes lit up, and she couldn't stop moving her hands or talking. No wonder Rob was in love with her. Such animation was rarely seen in women he knew. Must be living on a ranch that contributed to her openness and outgoing personality.

"Just think of the famous men and writers who once worked for newspapers. Mark Twain, Bret Harte, Stephen Crane, and even Charles Dickens all had a newspaper connection. It's all just so fascinating, and I'm right in the middle of it here in Barton Creek."

Geoff didn't reply. He'd rather just sit and let her go on with her enthusiasm. He wished it would rub off on her father in regard to the future of oil.

A flash of blue from the street caught their attention. Rebecca jumped up from her chair and ran down to meet Ruth, who had the twins in tow.

Rebecca grabbed Sally's hand and walked with her back to the porch. Ruth and Billy followed. "Look who has come to visit us, Mr. Kensington. Sally, do you remember Mr. Kensington from the train when we came here?" The train whistle blew at that moment as if to bring the memory to mind.

The little girl smiled but stood close to Rebecca. Billy, however, ran up the steps and skidded to a stop by Geoff's chair. "Hi. I remember you. I'm Billy."

"Yes, and I remember you. You're also a friend of Danny Anderson and Charley Haynes, I believe."

The boy's eyes opened wide. "How did you know that? We're going to school this year. I'm in first grade."

Geoff laughed and then glanced up at Ruth. His breath caught in his throat at her serene beauty. He longed to stand, but with his injuries, he still had trouble moving.

"Good morning, Ruth. It's nice to see you."

"I thought the children would enjoy a walk. With no patients at the clinic right now, I have time off."

Rebecca said, "Billy and Sally, come with me. I think Mrs. Claymore has some fresh-baked cookies." She winked at Geoff and led the children inside.

Ruth sat in the wicker chair beside his on the porch. "The children love Rebecca. She really has a way with them."

He was nodding his agreement when someone hailed him from the street. Geoff gasped and stared at the two men. Rob he expected, but when he recognized the other man, his mouth fell open. What was Mr. Barstow doing in Barton Creek?

Rob grinned and accompanied the man to the porch. "Look who just came in on the morning train. I happened to be down by the wire office and came out as he was inquiring about finding you, so I introduced myself and brought him here."

Geoff's facial expression attested to his own surprise just as Rob's had when he first met the man. He was as anxious as Geoff to learn why the man had chosen to come to Barton Creek rather than wiring his answer.

Mr. Barstow removed his bowler hat and stepped up onto the porch. "I'm glad to see that you are recovering from your unfortunate incident." He bowed toward Ruth. "And who is this lovely young lady, Mr. Kensington?"

Geoff's face filled with red as he introduced her. "This is Mrs. Ruth Dorsett. She helped nurse me back to health this past week. She stopped by for a visit."

The look that passed between them told Rob all he needed to know about the two. Geoff was as smitten as a schoolboy with his first crush, and by all indications, she returned the feelings. What a blessing Ruth had been to Geoff, and Rob couldn't be happier for them to find each other.

Ruth moved toward the door. "If you gentlemen will excuse me, I will check on my children. They must be full of cookies by now. It was nice to meet you, Mr. Barstow."

Rob appreciated her sensitivity to the reason for their visit. Geoff would be just as anxious to learn the reason for Barstow's visit as Rob himself was.

After Rob and Barstow settled into their seats, the man lost no time in getting down to the crux of the matter. "I received your wire and found it to be most interesting. I ran your ideas by a few of our men, and they seem to think what you suggest will be very workable. I decided to come see the land for myself as well as to check up on you and your condition."

Rob's insides tingled with excitement. If Mr. Barstow approved their ideas and was willing to help preserve the rangeland, then Ben and Sam surely would go along with the idea. He listened while Geoff told his boss about the beating, the slaughter of cattle, and the burning of Ben Haynes's stables. When he laid out the whole picture, Mr. Barstow couldn't help but see how it was all related.

When Geoff finished, Mr. Barstow stroked his chin. "I think I may know who's behind your beating and the other events. Let me do some checking, and then I may have information for your sheriff. Too bad you didn't get a good look at those men you saw out on the range and in your room, but I can almost guarantee they were the same."

Rob had drawn the same conclusion, but hearing it from someone else like that caused his anger to simmer. He'd be patient while Barstow investigated, but they needed an answer soon before anything else happened.

Mr. Barstow asked Geoff, "When do you think we might go out and talk with Mr. Haynes?"

Geoff looked to Rob for the answer. "I'll be seeing Mr. Haynes tonight at a family dinner. I don't think it would be a good time to talk business, but I will tell him that we want to meet with him to discuss the oil deposits. He won't do business on Sunday, but I'm hoping he'll be willing to meet with us on Monday."

"That sounds like a plan to me. Now if you'll excuse me, I need to check into the hotel and send a few wires. I'll be back to visit with you later, Geoff." He turned to leave, but then glanced back at Geoff with a frown. "You weren't really going to quit, were you?" Then he laughed. "No need to answer that. I think I know what you'll be doing here for awhile."

When the man turned the corner to head back to the hotel, Rob grabbed Geoff's hand. "Looks like he's willing to work with us. Now all we have to do is pray Ben Haynes and Sam Morris have the same inclinations." They shook hands, and Rob realized he had as good a friend in Geoff as he could ever want.

Rebecca and Rob drew near the ranch in his buggy. He'd insisted on this rather than riding their own horses. After all that had transpired in the past few hours, she was more willing to do so in order to have a better chance to talk. She had met Mr. Barstow and liked the man right away. That he agreed with Geoff and Rob and their plans added to her admiration. Now if only Pa and Sam Morris agreed, everything would be all set.

Aunt Clara and Doc arrived just ahead of them. Rob hitched his team to the post and then helped her down from the rig. The hot, muggy weather had already plastered her shirtwaist to her back, and despite the parasol she carried for protection, her face felt uncomfortably warm. At least the house should be somewhat cooler.

When the four of them entered the room, she spotted an unfamiliar face sitting next to Lucy. Rebecca searched her brain but couldn't come up with an identity for the woman. Perhaps she was a friend of Aunt Clara's, but then she didn't appear that old even though gray streaked her dark hair, and her attire spoke of someone who knew fashion. By the look on Ma's face, something was wrong. Rebecca went over and hugged her mother.

Ma hugged her back and whispered, "Have a seat. Lucy has something to tell us."

Rebecca bit her lip and stepped away from her mother to take a seat in one of the chairs. Rob, Aunt Clara, and Doc did the same.

The tight smile on her aunt's face led Rebecca to believe the older woman wasn't looking forward to the announcement.

Lucy grasped the woman's hand. "I know you're curious about who this is. I had planned to tell you last week before the dust storm but couldn't. She came in on the morning train, and Jake went in to pick her up." She swallowed hard, patted the woman's hand, and said, "This is Hilda Bishop, my uncle Rudolph's wife."

So this was Lucy's surprise. The gasps that went around the room were almost like a small explosion. Ma bit her lip and looked ready to cry, and Pa's mouth was set in such a grim line that Rebecca feared he might say something in anger. Rebecca didn't understand herself. Lucy's uncle Rudolph had sent a man to try and kill her before she could get her inheritance, and now his wife sat in Ma's parlor.

Lucy gazed at each one of the family around her. "I know you are shocked that I would invite Aunt Hilda to come here, but Uncle Rudolph died in prison, and she had no place to turn. She had nothing to do with his schemes, and I remembered how kind she always was when visiting us."

Ma finally found her tongue. "But what is she going to do out here? She doesn't know any more about living on a ranch than you did when you first came."

"I know that, but she can learn just like I did. She's going to help me with the boys and Amanda, so that I can better take care of my other responsibilities. Amanda has already taken to her and doesn't mind Aunt Hilda holding her or feeding her." She gazed again at each one as though searching their hearts. "I pray that as the good Christian family we are that we will accept Aunt Hilda and not hold anything Rudolph did against her. I pray you show her the same love you showed me when I first came."

Aunt Clara was the first to break the silence after Lucy's speech. "Well, I, for one, have been the recipient of the Hayneses'

Chapter 31

*B*ecky had told Rob to wait until they could see that Pa's frame of mind was positive before approaching him about the oil deposits. After Lucy's surprise announcement earlier, she wanted to be sure the shock had worn off and that all family feelings were friendly. As usual, Aunt Clara was the one to set the tone, and everyone had followed her lead.

The atmosphere had definitely improved to the point that Rob grabbed Becky's hand and pulled her aside. "I think your pa's in a better mood now that he's had dinner. We should talk to him now about Geoff's plan and then make plans to head back to Barton Creek. I don't like to travel those roads after dark even with my carriage lamps."

"I agree. I'll approach him in a few minutes and ask if he can step into his office." With the hubbub surrounding Lucy's aunt, Rebecca had as yet not told them her news about her promotion at the paper.

With all of them gathered in the parlor after supper, she decided now would be as good a time as any to reveal what she would be doing from now on. She stood and clapped for attention. "I have some important news to tell you about myself." Everyone's eyes focused on her; even Charley and Micah sat still.

"Mr. Lansdowne told me that he is going to expand the paper to three times a week soon and then to a daily paper by the first of the year. It all depends on how many more reporters and clerks we can hire to handle the added responsibilities."

Words of approval spread through the group. Pa spoke up. "You mentioned 'we.' Isn't that Mr. Lansdowne's responsibility as the editor?"

"Yes, Pa, but he promoted me to assistant editor, so I will be interviewing prospects as well. In addition he has given me my own column to inform the ladies of Barton Creek regarding important issues concerning them so that when we are allowed to vote, we can all make intelligent decisions."

A general buzz of conversation began with several talking at once. Finally Ma held up her hands. "Let Becky finish. We are very proud of your accomplishments thus far, so tell us more."

Everyone became quiet again, and Rebecca continued. "He thinks I have great writing ability, and so I will be writing more news articles with him handling the editorials. I'm truly excited and honored by Mr. Lansdowne's confidence and trust in me."

Pa came over and hugged her. "I'm proud of my Becky. You had a dream and you went after it. God has been so good to all of us. I hope you see this as His way showing you His blessing."

"Thank you, Pa. Your support encourages me so." Maybe he was right about God. She hadn't prayed for awhile, but thanks seemed to be in order for all the good He was bringing into her life.

Then she remembered what else she wanted. "Pa, Rob and I need to talk to you privately." At his smile, she realized he misunderstood. "This is business, and it's very important. Can you come with us to your office?"

Rob had joined her and now stood beside her. Pa looked from one to the other then said, "All right. I'll listen to what you have to say."

He turned to the rest of the family. "If you'll excuse us for awhile, we have some business to discuss." He headed for his office, and Becky followed with Rob.

From the smiles and whispers Becky knew they thought it had to do with her and Rob and their relationship. Let them think that. They'd know the truth soon enough.

Once in her father's office, she let Rob do the talking. His voice held such confidence as he spoke that her admiration for him grew to new heights. When he'd completed his presentation, Pa sat back in his chair, supporting his chin in one hand, his elbow resting on the arm of his chair.

Rebecca fidgeted with her skirt, the ruffles at her neck, and her hair while waiting for his reply. Rob stood still with his hands clasped behind his back. She envied his calm presence of mind, but she couldn't keep from moving about the room.

Finally Pa leaned forward. "If Mr. Barstow can guarantee this is what he'll do, then I think we can work something out. What time do you want us to meet on Monday?"

Becky squealed and Rob let out his breath in relief. "I have set a ten o'clock time on my calendar. I'll let Geoff and Mr. Barstow know the time when we return."

Pa stood and stretched forth his hand. "You are a smart young man, and I appreciate the candor in presenting Geoff's ideas. I'll send Matt over to tell Sam, and we'll be there on Monday." He and Rob shook hands, then Pa clapped Rob on the shoulder. "Good doing business with you, son."

When they reentered the parlor, every eye turned toward them in expectancy of news Rebecca couldn't give them. She smiled and walked toward the hat tree for her parasol and hat. "Rob and I need to head back to town. Our business is done, and we have things to do in Barton Creek, but we'll see you in church in the morning."

Ma planted her hands on her hips. "Is that all?"

Rebecca kissed Ma's cheek. "Yes, that's all for now. Geoff had a business proposition for Pa, and since he couldn't come, Rob and I presented it. He'll tell you more about it later."

She and Rob climbed into the buggy. After settling onto the seat, she grabbed Rob's arm and slipped her hand under it. "That went rather well, don't you think?"

"Yes, I would say your father is ready to talk business with Mr. Barstow. It'll really be a boon for all of this area. More jobs, more people, more business for those already here will mean a lot of changes."

"And we're right in the middle of it all. Progress is what makes our nation great, and soon Oklahoma will officially be a part of it." She laid her head on his shoulder. "I am so happy I could burst." Her heart was so full of joy at everything that had happened over the past week. Even Geoff's beating had worked out for good. The verse that Rob had mentioned danced across her mind. Something about all things working together for good for those who loved God and were doing His work. Could it really be true?

"Rob, do you believe the Bible is really true?" she asked.

He looked in her at surprise at the sudden change of topic. "Yes, I do," he declared. "It's God's Word to His people. It gives us promises, instruction, and everything we need to find salvation and live."

He believed it, and so did Ma, Pa, Aunt Clara, Lucy, Ruth, and even Geoff. How could she have gotten things so mixed up? "But why do such terrible things happen?"

Rob thought a moment before answering. "I say God gives man a choice of what he should do. Evil men who don't believe in God make bad choices and do evil things. That's what happened to Geoff, the cattle, and your pa's barn. Evil men struck out against others to get their own ways. And then sometimes God uses storms, fires, blizzards, floods, earthquakes, and all sorts of natural disasters to bring us closer to Him."

She considered his answer. It did make sense, more sense than some of the things she'd been spouting about God. "Geoff's beating certainly brought him closer to God. Do you think God will forgive me for saying all the things I have against Him this past year?"

"Of course He will. All you have to do is ask." He stopped the buggy and grasped her shoulders. "Rebecca Susan Haynes, God loves you with all His heart, and so do I. I love you just the way you are, so full of life and excitement."

He stared at her a moment then pulled her to him. The next thing she knew his lips were pressed against hers. At first she didn't move, but then something stirred inside her and she wrapped her arms around his back. This was nothing like that kiss stolen behind the barn on her sixteenth birthday. That had been the kiss of a young boy, but this was the kiss of a man in love, and she found herself enjoying every moment of it simply because it felt so right.

Suddenly he pulled back. "I'm sorry. I shouldn't have done that, but I couldn't help it."

She lifted her fingers to his cheek. "Don't be sorry; I'm not. I care a great deal about you, Rob, but I don't know what I want at the moment. Please be patient with me."

He caressed the back of her head. "I will, and like I said before, I'll be waiting when you do know." The he picked up the reins and headed back to town.

Rebecca said nothing the rest of the way into Barton Creek. Her fingers touched her lips where his had been, and she could still taste the kiss. *God, help me to make the right decision. Show me what I should do. I haven't talked to You much in the past year or so, but I need Your help now.*

A calm assurance filled her. God was in charge now, and He would guide her in the right direction. Rob's kiss had stirred feelings she didn't know she had or at least had kept buried. Whatever else happened, she couldn't keep Rob waiting forever.

When Rob arrived home after seeing Becky to the boarding house, his father sat in his study reading. He gestured to Rob. "Come in and have a seat. We haven't had much chance to talk lately."

Rob entered and sat across from his father. "I've had a rather interesting evening."

"How so?" Father reached over and picked up his pipe.

"For one thing, Lucy's aunt from Boston arrived and is staying with her. Seems her uncle died in prison and his wife had no other family to turn to. I suppose since Lucy was once in the same situation, she felt the need to help the woman."

His father nodded and puffed on his pipe. "I still say Lucy Starnes is the most loving and generous woman in this town, so it doesn't surprise me, but that can't be all."

No, not by a long shot it wasn't all, but at the moment he wasn't sure how much more he wanted to share. He decided to steer away from the business with Mr. Haynes. "Father, what brought you and Mother together, and how did you know you were in love with her?"

His father remained silent for a moment and let the smoke from his pipe swirl above his head. "I met your mother when I first went to St. Louis as a young lawyer. Her father was as protective of her as I've been with Caroline, but he gave permission for me to call on her."

Rob tried to imagine his mother as a young woman but had difficulty doing so. Her reputation for harsh treatment and words to those she felt beneath her did not speak of such a person. "What was she like then?"

"Pretty, full of life, fun to be around, generous in spirit, and she listened to me and my ideas." He sighed. "I think I've done her a great disservice bringing her and the two of you out here to the Territory. I've always been one to love adventure and came even though she really didn't want to. Those first years were hard on her, and she didn't enjoy her life like she had in St. Louis."

Rob tried to remember those early days, but he'd been so young all that came to mind was the fun of being around horses and having so much room to roam and play. He had a vague memory of a young woman who took him and Caroline to many places in the city and had fun with them. That had all changed when they came West.

"She was very excited when I was elected the first mayor of Barton Creek. It once again gave her a place of honor and leadership. I'm sorry to see that it's gone to her head, and now she can't see the good in anybody except those she feels are on her level." He shook his head and leaned forward in his chair. "Does this have anything to do with Rebecca?"

Heat rose in Rob's cheeks. "Yes, it does. I love her, but at the moment she doesn't return that love. I kissed her this evening, and once I started, I didn't want to stop, but I did. I had to."

Father again sat silent for a few moments. Finally he said, "Son, Rebecca reminds me of your mother when she was young, with her love of life. If you love her, don't ever do anything that will quench her spirit. Let her be who she is. If she loves you, she will come to you with all her heart, holding nothing back, and she will love you the rest of your life."

The words made sense, and he saw his parents' relationship in a new light. Mother had sacrificed a lot to support Father's dreams. Perhaps the move to Oklahoma had changed her. Rob decided at that moment he would be more thoughtful and caring toward his mother and pray for the Lord to soften her spirit.

He also vowed to follow his father's advice and let Becky be herself. She'd turned one corner tonight to being the Becky he'd always known. Now if she could dig deep and find her love for him again, he'd have both the old and new wrapped up in one beautiful woman.

Chapter 32

*R*ebecca's thoughts spun like a tornado in her mind all
night long. In the heat of the July night, the sheets stuck
to her body as she tried to get comfortable and rid her mind of
questions. Rob loved her, and she cared so much about him, but
she was on her way in her career. Pa was about to enter into a
business partnership that would bring prosperity not only to the
family but also to Barton Creek. Geoff and Ruth had found something together that could bring them happiness for a lifetime.
Aunt Clara and Doc planned to retire and travel.

All these things were good, but as they brought changes to
Barton Creek, so would they bring changes in her life. At the
moment she couldn't comprehend what all this would truly mean
in her own daily life. If she could only know what God wanted
from her, then her mind might rest and give her peace.

A thought suddenly dawned on her. For so long she'd said God
was just a crutch that people used in times of trouble. But here
she was, swimming in blessings, and whom did she turn to? God!
How ironic that God had not used trouble to get her attention.
She hadn't been beaten or lost a loved one or suffered any kind of
personal harm. Instead, God had put two big blessings in her path
and now was asking her to choose.

So what should she do? The only person she could talk to was
Lucy. She trusted Ma and knew she'd have wise words, but Lucy
would understand the turmoil washing over Rebecca's soul like

the banks of the creek after a heavy rain. Tomorrow Lucy would be in town for church with her family. They would all be at Aunt Clara's for dinner afterward. That would be the perfect time to take her cousin aside and ask for much needed advice.

With that decision Rebecca rested easier and finally fell asleep.

Knocking on her door awakened her the next morning. "Rebecca, it's time to be up," Mrs. Claymore called. "You don't want to be late for church."

Rebecca bolted upright. No, she didn't want to be late today. The service would mean so much more this morning. "I'm up, Mrs. Claymore. I'll be down shortly." She scrambled from the bed and gathered up the clothing she planned to wear.

Half an hour later she bounded down the steps and into the dining room. All heads turned to her when she sat down to eat. Most of the others were already finished. Miss Hilton and Widow Jarvis shook their heads and pursed their lips, and the men went back to their eating, except for Geoff, whose eyes danced with amusement.

"Sorry I'm late. I overslept." She reached for the plate of eggs and helped herself.

No one said anything more to her but resumed the conversations they were in when she had sat down. Geoff leaned over and whispered, "A late night with Rob?"

Rebecca's cheeks filled with heat with the memory of Rob's kiss. "No, we didn't come in late, but you were already retired, so I didn't want to disturb you." She picked up a biscuit and buttered it. "Pa agreed to meet you and Mr. Barstow tomorrow. Rob will tell you all about it today."

Geoff's face reflected his excitement. "I plan to attend church with Ruth today, so I'll see Rob there. Your pa was really agreeable to the plan?"

"Yes, and he said he'd talk to Sam Morris. So it looks like you will have a deal."

Geoff's loud yes brought glares from the ladies and stares from the men. He nodded at them and offered his apology with a huge grin. "Sorry, but Rebecca has just given me good news about a business proposition."

After breakfast, Rebecca finished her preparations for church. When she came back downstairs she saw Geoff leave with Ruth and the twins. Billy held Geoff's hand and gazed up at him with adoring eyes. Geoff reached out for Ruth's hand, and she held Sally's on her other side. Rebecca's heart filled with warmth at the beautiful sight they made.

She smiled and lifted her face to the sky. God would give her the answers she needed today. She was sure of it.

During the service Rebecca squirmed with anticipation of talking with Lucy. She wasn't sure exactly what to tell her cousin, but something would come at the right time.

Again the kiss from last night burned on her lips. She cut her gaze to where Rob sat with his family at the same time he looked at her. She moved her hand in a little wave then jerked it back down and stared at the front. Her toes tapped on the floor.

Ma grabbed Rebecca's leg and whispered, "Be still."

Rebecca nodded but couldn't help smiling. So many times Ma had done that very same thing when Rebecca was a child and couldn't keep her feet still.

Geoff went forward and joined the church at the end of the service. Her soul filled with joy as the pastor introduced the new Christian to the congregation. Ruth's face shone with love, and even her parents beamed their approval.

A crowd gathered around him after the benediction, but Rebecca knew she'd see him later, so she hurried to accompany her parents to Aunt Clara's. The house filled with family and laughter, and her aunt asked Doctor White and his wife to stay. Congratulations were sounded all around the table when the couple announced they would have a baby arriving that winter.

The happiness around the table and in the members of the family gave Rebecca much joy and satisfaction. These people loved her no matter what she did or who she tried to be. God did too. That's what Rob had told her last night, but the reality had not sunk in as it did now.

As soon as the dishes were cleared, Rebecca approached Lucy. "Could you spare a few minutes and talk with me?"

Lucy glanced over to the sink where Aunt Clara, Ma, Aunt Hilda, and Anna White laughed and washed dishes. "I think they have things under control here. Let's go into the dining room. I think the men have taken over the parlor. Matt is outside with the boys and Amanda is sleeping, so we shouldn't be disturbed."

Once they sat down, Rebecca clasped her hands and breathed deeply. "Last night on our way back to town, Rob kissed me, and I liked it." She leaned her arms on the table and blinked. "I care about him, always have, but I don't know what to do. With my new promotion and responsibilities at the paper I'm finally doing what I dreamed of all the years at school. I don't want to give it up, but I want a relationship with Rob too. I'm just not sure I want marriage and a family."

Lucy reached over and grasped Rebecca's hands. "Love is one of the most complicated things in life. It isn't really an emotion, although our emotions become so involved. It's our actions and what we want for the other person. You know what you want for yourself, but what do you want for Rob?"

Rebecca blinked at the unexpected question. "I...I want him to be happy and have what he wants. But he wants me to love him and...oh dear, now I'm even more confused."

"Think about this. What if Rob were no longer available? What would your life be without him? Would you be better off without him in your life? If he found happiness somewhere else, could you let him go?"

A life without Rob in it might not be life at all, but Rebecca had no right to hold him back if he found someone else. "I'd have to let him go, as much as it would hurt. He deserves to be happy." A new thought dawned on her. That's what he was doing with her. He was letting her go her own way because he wanted her to be happy.

"You'll have to decide if your life would be better with him or without him. Pray about it, and let God lead you to the right decision. I loved Jake, and we had no idea what the outcome in Texas would be, but we both trusted our futures to God, and He worked it all for good and brought us back together."

Lucy had given her much to think about, and it all came back to what would be best for both of them. "I will pray about Rob and what I should do. I just wish God would tap me on the shoulder and say, 'This is what to do.' Then I would do it."

Lucy laughed and hugged Rebecca. "Yes, life would be much easier if His answers were always that plain." She sat back. "I hear Amanda. We can talk more about this later if you like."

Rebecca shook her head and stood. "No, I think I'm OK now." But her heart and soul were still torn with indecision.

Rob sat across from Caroline in the parlor. "Would you like to go for a spin in the motor car? Father gave me permission in case we wanted to drive around town."

His sister fanned her face. "Oh, no, it's too hot and the car too noisy. I'd rather stay here where it's cooler."

He slumped back in his chair. He had asked Becky to have

dinner with his family, but she had plans to be with her family at Aunt Clara's after church. It was probably just as well. After what his father told him, Rob decided to make more of an effort to spend time with his mother, and Becky may have only agitated her.

"You don't look very happy, little brother. Could it be Becky Haynes causing that sadness I see in your eyes?"

"Yes and no. I was thinking about what Father told me about Mother last night. Do you remember what she was like before we came here?"

"Yes, Mother was quite different when we lived in St. Louis. Moving out West took her away from the life she knew. Here she wasn't important until Father was elected mayor, and then she could resume her role of being a lady of influence."

"That's about what Father said, and it helped me understand more about the way she is now and why." He leaned forward with his hands between his knees. "Mother doesn't approve of Becky, but I love her and want to marry her."

"Have you told Becky that?"

"I have, and she says she cares for me, but her dreams are about to come true at the paper with her promotion and all the things she'll be doing now."

"At least you have some idea about her feelings. I have no clue as to what Matt thinks."

"I've been praying for Becky, and all I want is for her to be happy in whatever she does, with or without me." That's what he wanted, but without Becky, his life would not be as happy and fulfilling.

Geoff had found Ruth, and her sweet spirit would be the perfect match for his brains and business acumen. She'd keep him from doing anything foolish. Luke had braved his mother's refusal to accept Dove because he loved her. Then God had worked a miracle there, and Mrs. Anderson embraced Dove with love and approval in the end. He didn't need a miracle like that, but he did need guidance, and that could come only from God.

Later that night as he lay in bed with a prayer on his lips, God's answer came as clearly as if he'd heard Him speak. Peace like a river, the peace Isaiah spoke of and the peace that Jesus promised, fell upon him, and he knew what his next steps would be.

Chapter 33

*R*ob greeted Mr. Haynes and Sam Morris when they entered his office Monday morning. Geoff followed right behind them with Mr. Barstow. This morning Geoff had chosen to wear a business suit, which did seem more appropriate than the cowboy attire he'd taken to in recent weeks.

"Have a seat, gentlemen, and we can get this started. Now here is the contract drawn up. I made copies for each of you. I believe you will find they outline everything we spoke about on Saturday evening, Mr. Haynes, and also what Geoff and I discussed with you, Mr. Barstow."

The men read in silence for a few minutes. Ben Haynes was the first to speak. "Now, are you certain that you can assure us that the fences and equipment you bring in will be only on the Dawson land? It won't affect any of our land or our cattle?" He gestured toward Sam Morris to include him.

"That's right, and Geoff and I will be here to oversee the construction. Then Geoff will remain here as the company representative and will be in charge of all operations here."

After fifteen more minutes of discussion and assurances, the men nodded in agreement and made ready to sign the papers that would allow drilling on the property west of Ben Haynes's ranch.

Mr. Barstow signed his name with a flourish then sat back in his chair. "I have a bit more good news to share with you. I made a few inquiries, and just as I suspected, a certain rival of mine wants this property. He's the one who sent men here to beat Mr. Kensington, burn your barn, Mr. Haynes, and kill your cattle. I've informed the sheriff, and arrests should be coming shortly."

Rob's mouth dropped open, and he saw the same amazement in the faces of the other men. Ben Haynes reached over and shook Mr. Barstow's hand. "Now that's the best news I've heard in awhile. We plan to go forward with our charges against them, and I hope you will too, Geoff."

At the young man's nod, Ben Haynes stood. "Well, I can only say this has been a most productive morning." He shook Geoff's hand. "I'm glad we were able to do business with you, both with the cattle and with the oil."

Mr. Barstow grinned and slapped Geoff on the back. "I'm happy with the work he's done here, and we will probably be buying more cattle from you men. What you sent was prime grade and just what our packinghouse wants. But I'll get back with you on that."

Mr. Morris and Mr. Haynes shook hands with Barstow again and excused themselves to go back to their duties at their ranches.

Geoff remained behind when the other men left. His excitement led him to pound his fist into the palm of his hand. "Rob, my boy, we did it. This is going to bring some great changes to your town. Or our town. I plan to stick around for quite awhile."

"And I don't suppose Ruth Dorsett has anything to do with it, does she?"

"You better know she does." He shot Rob a glance. "Now you'd better get busy before Rebecca Haynes slips from your grasp. You two were made for each other."

Rob laughed. "And I've figured out just how to make her want to spend her life with me."

"I wish you luck, my friend." He reached for his hat and headed out of the office.

With God's help, no luck would be needed. Rob gathered up the papers on his desk as satisfaction with a well-done job settled in. He loved being a lawyer, and someday it might take him down his father's path to politics. For the time being, however, he was content to be drawing up wills, contracts, and agreements for the people of Barton Creek. If the oil strike was as big as Barstow believed, he'd have even more people to serve. He might even need an assistant or at least a clerk to help him with his clients.

The morning was still early, but he was anxious to see Becky. The time left until noon would be more like a day than a little over an hour. He'd taken the kiss on Saturday night that he planned for July the Fourth, and with most pleasing results. If all went as well today, perhaps another one would come his way.

He opened a folder to work, but Becky's face kept intruding into his thoughts. The feel of her lips on his had been even better than he had imagined. The fact that she had returned it gave him even more pleasure. Somehow today he had to convince her that he loved her enough to give her everything she wanted.

Becky yanked out the sheet of paper in the typewriter. This was the third time she'd ruined a page with mistakes. Her nerves clashed together like out-of-tune keys on a piano. She glanced at the watch on her bodice. Pa, Mr. Morris, Geoff, and Mr. Barstow should be about finished with their business and the contracts signed.

How she itched to be there herself, but they had no need for her presence, and besides, Pa wouldn't have allowed it. Pa was still too old-fashioned to think women knew anything about business. What if Matt had been a girl? Where would Pa be now without someone to take over the ranch for him? But he did have Matt, so things wouldn't change.

She tried again to concentrate on the story at hand. She'd already written up her article on the oil agreement and what it would mean to Barton Creek. A giggle escaped her lips. She'd like to see Mr. Frankston's face when he learned what a coup his son had handled and that oil was coming to Barton Creek.

The words Lucy had given yesterday still rolled around in Rebecca's mind, but after much prayer and restless sleeping last night, the answer had come in the wee hours of the morning. Now that her decision was made, she wanted to see Rob and tell him.

Someone tapped her shoulder. She jumped and grasped the lace of her blouse over her heart. "My goodness, Molly, you scared me silly."

"I'm sorry, but you were in such deep concentration you didn't hear me call your name."

"Oh, no, I didn't. I apologize. What can I do for you?"

"I have the ads ready for Anderson's Emporium and Peterson's Bakery. I'm going to take them to get approval for this week's edition." She held out the drawings for Rebecca to see.

"These are wonderful, Molly. Your father will be very pleased." Molly really had talent, and the fact that her father finally recognized the fact and that she was interested in a career in art and journalism excited Rebecca. "I think Mr. Anderson and Mr. Peterson will like them too."

Molly beamed and carefully placed the ads in a portfolio and headed out on her errand. Rebecca glanced up at the clock. Another half hour before she'd see Rob. She turned back to her typewriter and the story at hand.

"Rebecca, are you ready?"

She jumped and almost fell off her chair. "Rob, I didn't hear you come in."

"The door is open, so the bell didn't ring. You really need to do something about that. Anybody could walk in here off the streets and rob the place or worse."

Rebecca had to laugh at that. "Who would want to come here to rob us? We don't keep any money on the premises."

"Better to be safe than sorry, I always say." Then he grinned at her in that crooked way he'd done so often in their school days. It still made her heart glad even after all these years.

She turned and pulled a sheet of paper from her machine and stacked it with others on the desk. "I'm all done, and I want to know all about the meeting."

He waited while she put two huge pins into her hat to secure it then held open the gate for her. "It went very well. Mr. Barstow said he told Sheriff Claymore he had an idea about who was behind all the bad things that have happened, and he's out searching for the men now."

That was good news. She wished the men would have to pay for the damages, but at least if they got caught they'd be put in jail. "I hope he does that soon. I hate to think what else they might do."

He let her exit the door and then joined her on the boardwalk. "Another good thing is that Mr. Barstow has put Geoff in charge of the operations here, so he'll be around for awhile."

"I think that would have happened with or without the job. He and Ruth are becoming very close. He had dinner with her and her family yesterday, and I think Mrs. Weems likes Geoff very much, leastways that's how it appeared in church yesterday."

"I'm not surprised. Once you get to know him, Geoff is really a nice fellow."

He was, but the contracts and what she wanted to tell Rob were more important at the moment. She caught a glimpse of their reflection in the window of the bakery. Rob in his suit and she in her red skirt and cream-colored blouse made a handsome pair and confirmed the decision she had made early this morning.

As they stepped down to cross the street, Rob held her elbow. His hand was as a branding iron even through the fabric of her sleeve and sent sharp blades of heat through her arm, yet the feeling was more pleasant than painful.

"I think your father and Mr. Morris will be quite pleased with the way things work out with the oil drilling. At least I hope they will."

"If the oil company upholds its end of the deal, then there will be no problems." Pa would be most cooperative if the men kept their end of the contract.

Rob stopped in front of Dinah's. "I'm not really hungry yet. Would you mind walking over to the park with me?"

Her heart flip-flopped in her chest. That would give her the opportunity to tell him what she had decided. "That sounds like a very nice idea. I'm not very hungry myself."

Neither said anything as they headed for the park. Rebecca's mind rolled through the words she had chosen to make sure they said exactly what she wanted to say.

They found a bench under a few shade trees and sat down. Rob took her hand in his. "I've been thinking about us and our future, and I want you to know how proud I am of all that you have accomplished in the short time you've been home. I'm constantly amazed at the things you know and how well you handle that knowledge." His cheeks turned a bright red.

Rebecca's heart began to pound. He was going to let her go. He wanted her to have a career. She squeezed his hand. "Thank you, Rob, but none of that means anything if you're not a part of it."

His eyes opened wide. "What are you saying?" He held up his hand. "No, wait, don't tell me. Let me finish. I want you to be the best reporter and editor Mr. Lansdowne has ever had. I've spent all these weeks looking for the old Becky, but she was right here in front of me in a bright new wrapping. You have too much to give the world for me to hold you back from your dream, but I also want you to be my wife. If you stay here in Barton Creek, that will be perfect, but if you have opportunity somewhere else, then we'll both go. I can be a lawyer anywhere."

This time Rebecca's heart pounded so hard she feared it might stop altogether. Here he was offering her the world she had dreamed of as well as himself. A sob tightened her throat, but she had to tell him. "Oh, Rob, I decided that no job was important enough for me if you weren't a part of my life. We belong together, and I'd rather be your wife than a reporter any day."

"You mean that, I can see it in your eyes." His fingers caressed her cheek. "A very wise woman told me that if I let go of my own dream for someone I loved, that dream would come back to me even better than before."

Then a huge grin split his face. "However, I don't intend to let you forsake your dream. Think of all the good you can do here in Barton Creek. We need someone who can tell other women about the things you believe and help them make wise decisions when the time comes."

This was more than Rebecca could ever have hoped for. "You mean writing my column explaining the women's suffrage movement and the importance of voting for those who will shape our future?"

"Yes, and whatever else Mr. Lansdowne has for you to do."

Rebecca lifted her face to the sky. She had been obedient in following what she thought God wanted her to do, and then He'd given her the desires of her heart "I love you, Robert Andrew Frankston." Then a giggle bubbled from her throat.

Rob leaned back. "What's so funny?"

"I just remembered something. I ran down that hill at the Wellesley Hoop Race so I could be the first and prove their old tradition was bogus, and I won." She giggled again. "But I guess I just proved it right. I will be the first girl in our class to get married." She attempted to lay her head on his shoulder, but her hat got in the way.

He laughed then pulled out the pins and laid the hat aside. She whispered in his ear, "And I don't mind your calling me Becky. That's who I am." She didn't care who was around or what people might say about such a public display. She was ready for another kiss.

Just before his lips touched hers he said, "Welcome home, Becky. I've been waiting for you."

Look for
OTHER BOOKS IN THE
Winds Across the Prairie series
—— *by Martha Rogers* ——

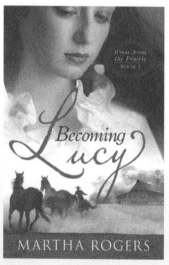

978-1-59979-912-4

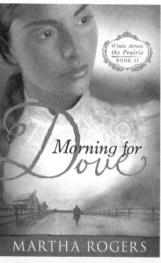

978-1-59979-984-1

In 1896, after her parents' death, heiress Lucinda Bishop flees to Oklahoma to live with her aunt and uncle. But life takes an unexpected turn when she meets ranch hand Jake Starnes, a drifter who is running from his past. As their friendship grows, can she learn the power of true love and forgiveness?

When Luke Stanton falls in love with Dove Morris, he is aware of her Native American heritage. What he is not prepared for is the prejudice suddenly exhibited by his family. Can he convince his parents that love knows no boundaries of race or culture when it comes from God?

Caroline's Choice
Chapter 1

Barton Creek, September 1907

Caroline Frankston's hands clinched into fists, her breath coming in short spurts. Through the parlor window, she watched life go on in a normal, orderly fashion, but here in this room, her world lay fragmented like shards of broken glass. Each piece cut into her soul, causing pain that she no longer wanted to bear. The bleeding had to stop.

"If I don't leave this town, I'll never get married." Caroline Frankston spun around to face her mother. "Barton Creek has no men who will ever be interested in me, so I plan to move to Oklahoma City and start a new life there."

Her mother's blue eyes flashed with anger. "You'll do no such thing. You have responsibilities here."

Caroline's jaw tightened. Her mother's demands only caused more determination. "What responsibilities? Going to luncheons and meetings with you and sitting around listening to you decide what people should do?"

The firm set of Mother's mouth warned Caroline to be careful with her next words. Now was the time to stand firm and not back down. "I know you want what's best for me, and right now a move seems to be it."

Mother stood silent, a vein in her neck throbbing in response to the tension in her jaw. A mixture of anger and disbelief sparked from her eyes. She stood tall with her back ramrod straight, meaning she wouldn't back down.

Without waiting for her mother's response, Caroline headed for the door, but not without one last comment. "I'm sorry, Mother. I'll be twenty-seven soon, and if I don't do something now, I never will. I don't want to be stuck here as an old maid with time on her hands and no purpose in life."

She darted from the room and up the stairs before her mother could react and spew forth a torrent of words to thwart the seeds of a plan now planted in Caroline's mind. Father had left a newspaper from Oklahoma City on the dining table at breakfast, and she had brought it up to the bedroom to look through the classified ads. With her fine arts degree, Caroline had few choices for a career. The suffragettes were right with their talk about the limitations set on women in the workforce. However, a degree in literature and languages should be useful for something.

Time had come for a visit with her sister-in-law to seek her advice. She pinned a stylish blue hat on her upswept hair. Although she did love the hat, it had been chosen by her mother, as had most of the clothes in Caroline's wardrobe. In Oklahoma City she could set her own standards and not be dictated to by her mother.

Some of her mother's ideas and beliefs about fashions and social protocol left Caroline with the feeling that no one could measure up to what the mayor's wife expected, not even her own daughter. Being the daughter of the mayor had its advantages, but now they hindered and kept her from pursuing other avenues of interest.

Envy for her brother's freedom gnawed at her insides. Being

male, he could pick and choose what he wanted to do, and he'd proved it with his law office and his marriage to Becky last year.

The thought of her sister-in-law brought a smile to Caroline's heart. She'd joined Becky in the suffrage movement, and a few other women had begun to show interest in the affairs of Oklahoma. Becky even wrote a column for women in the *Barton Creek Chronicle* each week to inform them of the opportunities and advantages of voting for their government leaders. Caroline would miss the gatherings here, but surely such a group existed in Oklahoma City.

She glanced around the room that had been hers since her family's arrival in Barton Creek over fifteen years ago. She'd miss it, but the idea of being on her own filled her with excitement. She raced down the stairs and headed for the front door to avoid another confrontation with her mother. When her voice called out from the parlor, Caroline pretended not to hear and closed the door behind her.

She walked toward town, her feet disturbing the fallen leaves and making them swirl about her feet. Late September should bring cooler air to match the changing of the colors in the trees, but not this year. Caroline wished she'd worn a lighter weight shirtwaist and a less heavy skirt, but Mother had insisted on storing all summer clothes away for the fall season. At the next corner she turned onto Main Street, thankful she lived such a short distance from town.

A few more motor cars dotted the streets, which were now completely bricked. As mayor, her father planned to replace the boardwalks where people now strolled in front of business establishments with real sidewalks. She walked past the post office, the new jail building, and several other stores and shops before reaching the newspaper offices.

The odor of printer's ink greeted her nose as Caroline stepped through the doorway of the Barton Creek newspaper building. The bell over the door jangled and caused everyone but Becky to look up to see who had come in. The staff on the paper had certainly grown since Mr. Lansdowne made the paper available seven days a week. Becky sat at her desk behind the railing separating the office space from the entryway, staring at whatever was in the typewriter before her.

One of the young men jumped up from his chair. "How can I help you, Miss Frankston?"

Caroline smiled and nodded toward Becky. "I'm here to see Mrs. Frankston."

Becky glanced up then. "Oh, my, I was so engrossed in my story that I didn't hear the bell." She strode over to the gate in the railing. "What brings you here today?"

"I wanted to talk with you if you have time, but I can see you're busy, so I'll come back later."

Becky pushed through the gate. "No, no, it's fine. I think I'm in need of a break about now." She turned to the young woman across the room. "Amy, would you tell Mr. Lansdowne I'm taking a break and will be back shortly? I'll stop at the bakery and bring back pastries. He'll like that."

"Of course, Rebecca. Have a nice visit." The young clerk returned to the business on her desk.

Caroline admired Becky's attire. She wore the plainest of skirts and shirtwaists but made them come alive with fashion even though the signs of her coming motherhood were evident. Caroline would have been called a Plain Jane if she wore the same. Something about her sister-in-law gave life to whatever she touched or wore, one trait Caroline sorely envied.

Becky linked arms with Caroline. "Now, let's head to Peterson's for tea and cookies."

When they stepped out onto the boardwalk, Becky breathed deeply. "Isn't it a beautiful day? Although it's too warm for me, I love this time of year."

"I like it too." Although at the moment all Caroline could sense was the stench of horse droppings and the fine layer of dust and dirt over everything. She glanced at the woman beside her. "So, you're still going by Rebecca at the office?"

"Yes. That's my byline on all my articles, so they all call me Rebecca."

Caroline laughed. "But you'll always be Becky to the rest of us."

Becky returned the laugh, but hers had a musical quality that had earned the friendship of most of the people here in her hometown. "I don't mind it at all now. Rob convinced me I could be both, and he was right." She glanced up toward the windows of her husband's law offices.

At least Becky and Rob had rediscovered the love they'd had for each other as youths, and now they were as happy as any married couple Caroline had seen. Mother hadn't been too happy with her son marrying a Haynes, and even now that Ben Haynes headed one of the wealthiest families in the area, her attitude hadn't changed, especially since Becky chose to continue her job at the newspaper after learning a child was on the way. To Mother, Becky was just a girl who wanted to be somebody in a man's world and would always be a cowgirl.

When they had entered the bakery and ordered their tea and pastry, Caroline chose a table away from the window so they would have more privacy.

"So, what is it that you want to talk with me about?" Becky unwrapped her pastry and pinched off a small piece.

Caroline stirred her tea and grinned. "I'm moving to Oklahoma City. My roommate from college has invited me to come live with her."

Becky dropped her pastry, spreading crumbs in its wake. She grabbed a napkin and wiped the bits off the table. "You're doing what? Leaving Barton Creek? But what does your family say?"

"Mother is completely against it, and by now she's probably let Father know, and I don't know what he'll say. It really doesn't matter, because my mind is made up."

"But what about Matt? Have you told him?"

Caroline dipped her head and concentrated on stirring her tea. "You know how much I care about Matt, but it appears that he's lost interest in me. He's barely spoken to me since we were together at the July Fourth celebration. I don't know what else to do."

Becky leaned forward. "I can't tell you much since I don't see him very often anymore. He's been quiet and withdrawn the Sundays we go out to the ranch for a family dinner. When we were younger, we enjoyed doing lots of things together, but that's changed since I came home last year."

They sat in silence for a moment. Caroline's heart ached with the image of Matt sitting astride his great stallion and riding across the range. She bit her lip and leaned toward Becky. "I...I can't bear the thought of being a spinster, and there's no one here in Barton Creek except Matt I would consider as a husband. More opportunities to meet young men are available in the city. Many of my college friends stayed in the city, and I've been writing to several of them, and with Madeline's invitation, the time is right. Although my heart belongs to Matt at the moment, I can't wait for him forever."

Becky blinked and shook her head. "My brother is one stubborn man, but I don't understand why he hasn't been more willing to call on you. I remember how you two were always together for every social event that came along before you went off to school. I guess I always thought you'd be his wife when he finally made up his mind to marry."

"That's just it. I did too, but six years is a long time to wait for someone to make up his mind." And they had been the six longest years of her life. Now the time had come to get on with her life before it passed her by completely.

FREE NEWSLETTERS
TO HELP EMPOWER YOUR LIFE

Why subscribe today?

☐ **DELIVERED DIRECTLY TO YOU.** All you have to do is open your inbox and read.

☐ **EXCLUSIVE CONTENT.** We cover the news overlooked by the mainstream press.

☐ **STAY CURRENT.** Find the latest court rulings, revivals, and cultural trends.

☐ **UPDATE OTHERS.** Easy to forward to friends and family with the click of your mouse.

CHOOSE THE E-NEWSLETTER THAT INTERESTS YOU MOST:

- Christian news
- Daily devotionals
- Spiritual empowerment
- And much, much more

SIGN UP AT: **http://freenewsletters.charismamag.com**

8178